A PLACE IN ENGLAND

For some time now Melvyn Bragg has been
hailed as one of Britain's most talented young
novelists—and A PLACE IN ENGLAND goes
some way towards proving the point. Set in the
years before and during World War II, it is an
invigorating and exciting story of one man's
attempt to pull himself up by the bootlaces from
the degradation of working for others and into a
position of some independence. That
independence, however, is something hard
won and bitterly kept; and the struggle for its
achievement makes Joseph Talentire (whose
father, John, was the hero of THE HIRED MAN)
one of the most interesting characters to
appear in a modern British novel.

'Melvyn Bragg's latest novel places him
solidly in the main tradition of English fiction,
with an honourable ancestry through such
disparate figures as Wells and Hardy, Dickens
and Jane Austen to Henry Fielding'
Tribune

A Place in England

Melvyn Bragg

CORONET BOOKS
Hodder Paperbacks Ltd., London

First published in Great Britain by Secker
and Warburg Limited 1970

Coronet edition 1975

Printed and bound in Great Britain for
Coronet Books,
Hodder Paperbacks Ltd,
St. Paul's House, Warwick Lane,
London, EC4P 4AH
by Hazell Watson & Viney Ltd,
Aylesbury, Bucks

ISBN 0 340 19853 2

To William and Violet Ismay

Contents

Part One

The Big House

Chapter One

Joseph's eyes opened with a blink of fright. Only the first bird in the garden: a thrush. The nightmare slid out of his mind.

He swung his bare feet onto the floor and went to the attic window. On the ledge, in the lid of the cocoa tin, was a butt; a third of the cigarette. Lighting up, he smoked with careful pleasure; short, thrifty puffs.

Still the thrush whistled alone and the young man grew impatient of looking at the tones of grey: lawn, lake, mist and clouds, as heavy and dense as the fells he would see the following morning.

His bag was already packed, even though he had another day and night to endure before his holiday began. He had thought of nothing else for weeks. The bag was pushed well under the bed. It would not do for an intruder to see this eagerness. There were times when his eighteen years needed protection. The cigarette was drawn to its last millimetre, held to the hot skin of his lips by the tips of his nails. He squashed it between unhardened thumb and forefinger.

First the dawn light touched the bark of the silver birch trees, then the mist above the lake, the water itself – all the birds now singing – until he saw clearly this plump Midlands parkland, so gentle and secure. He both liked it and loathed it and could not fathom the contradiction.

To give himself something to do, he made his bed, dressed and splashed his face with cold water: no need to shave. Then, as a treat, he took out a whole cigarette and decided to smoke it through. The huge house was still silent; he would not be called for an hour.

She hid the cake awkwardly in her uniform. It bulged above

her belt and she kept touching it as if pointing out her guilt.

But for her brother she would do anything. She repeated this to herself; the members of her family were her rosary.

Though she had been at the house for five years, May still sneaked through it. Huddled her neck into her lumpy shoulders, screwed up her eyes behind the putty-framed glasses – hesitated before every corner. The maids were in a different wing of the house and she had to come down and cross the main gallery: and though she had polished every inch of it, the place frightened her at this half-lit quiet hour. Yet she knew that if she did not see Joseph now, there would be no chance for the rest of the day.

The moment she entered his bedroom she envied him the place of his own. Never in her life had she had that. It took a physical act of swallowing to repress the envy.

'Here then,' she said, taking out the large segment of apple cake, 'get this inside you.'

Joseph was lying on the bed. He had found an old newspaper and now pretended to be absorbed in it. Having scarcely acknowledged his sister's entrance, embarrassed by the openness of her emotion, he played the lord and without lifting his eyes from the page, held out his hand.

May raised the cake as she walked towards him – she always needed to be reassured that he liked her; teasing made her furious. Joseph looked up just as she was about to slam the juicy segment onto his palm.

'Thanks, May.'

She lowered it gently : his eyes had been kind.

'You had a narrow escape, lad,' she was pleased to say.

Tenderly she watched him raise it to his mouth – still standing sentry over him – and sighed with pleasure as he smiled.

'Oh, May. One of your best. Just – grand – really.' And his tongue cleaned his lips of juice.

'I thought it was maybe a bit heavy.'

'No – light as a leaf, May. Nobody can make pastry like you.'

'Hm! Them apples were nothing special – are they sugared enough?'

'Perfect.' Then because he knew that she would be more

pleased by a small, even unjustified criticism than by any praise, he added : 'Maybe they are just a *little* bit sharp.'

'Don't be so stupid,' she replied, 'they're too sweet if they're anything.'

'They're not too sweet.'

'Give us a taste.' She nibbled at the bitten cake. 'Hm! That pastry *is* a bit heavy.'

She sat on the wooden chair and, as always, folded her arms, jerked back her head, and reflected.

'My Christ, lad, thou even gits a chair.'

'It was here when I came, May.'

'There was damn all when *I* came. An' there'll be damn all when I go.'

'Now, May – it isn't my fault that you share a room.'

'*Share!* Is that what you call it? Oh – *you* don't know Lily hoighty-toighty Peters, my lad – she'd make her own mother feel a lodger.'

'You're older than she is, May, you were there first – you should stick up for yourself.'

'Aha! But my face doesn't fit, see. I mean – I won't say it.'

'Why not?'

'It's your last day.'

'I'll be back, May.'

'Oh – eat your cake and shut up!'

While he obeyed her she wrestled, visibly, with her temper. She loved her brother so much she could have hurt him for not recognizing it. In every action of his she saw their Mother whom she had worshipped : Joseph had held her hand as she had died; an incomparable privilege.

'It's good then, is it?' she shouted, suddenly.

He pointed to a full mouth and shook his head; her relief at this most gentle mockery was great and she rushed out of the chair and bounced onto him, he wriggling further down the bed as she called up half-invented memories of childhood to protract the game.

'Now then,' she warned, as Joseph escaped from under her and advanced, aping threats, 'We've stopped.'

Later she said, 'Trust you to get an afternoon off the day before your holiday!'

'It's just the way it goes, May.'

'Hm! *And* you have good weather.'

'It could rain tomorrow.'

'Anyway, you'll have a better holiday than me.' She paused, then with an attempt at malice which injured her more than it could ever have harmed anyone else, she added, 'Our dear stepmother saw to it that I had a bad time.'

'Now May – that's just your imagination.'

'Imagination be buggered – she made us sleep three in a bed!'

'What's wrong with *that*?'

'She could've offered me the sofa. She'll offer it to you – just watch.'

'Now May . . .'

'You're too young,' she retorted – and for the ten thousandth time went on to say 'You can't remember what your own mother was like.' Then her broad face puckered, became anxious. 'That isn't meant as a criticism, Joseph. Don't think that.'

'He had to marry somebody, May.'

'Why?'

'Well – somebody had to look after us all. We were split up long enough as it was.'

Again he gave her the cue she desired – could do no less – so plain was her longing.

'I could have looked after you, all of you, *I* could.'

'I know May. I know.'

'Just because our father never liked me – no he didn't, now – don't shake your head – after that time when he went to bits – *you* won't remember.' The mystery gave her some comfort for however hard Joseph had pressed her to tell him about the time their father had 'gone to bits' – she had refused.

'Well speak as you find,' said Joseph, firmly, 'she's always been good to me.'

'Oh – I'm not saying anything against her.' May hesitated, and found that the sentence she had spoken misrepresented her position. She made it plain and added, 'Except that he should never have married her.'

'You can't say who he should have married.'

'No.'

With another sudden change, May became sad and defenceless. As he glanced at her – overlapping that wooden chair, thick-bodied, fat even, padded with clothes – he was caught, as always, by the sweetness of her expression at these unaware times.

Near thirty now and made to be a wife and mother, May had never been asked.

'Anyway,' said Joseph, aggressively, 'I'll be glad to get that bloody Garrett out of my hair for a bit.'

Garrett was the butler, Joseph's immediate boss.

'What's wrong with Garrett?' May demanded, knowing full well, but needing to question as he so often questioned her.

'If you can't see that, you're blind.'

'Oh – am I?' she answered, coolly. 'Well if you'd open *your* eyes for a minute, you'd see how well off you are in this place. My Christ!' her control never lasted long, 'you haven't been here ten minutes and you've a room of your own. Look at me! I'm no further than second cook and my prospects is nothing. I would leave this place if it wasn't for you.'

'I know, May : but Garrett's such a slimy character.'

'Ignore him. You're doing very nicely.' She approved of his success. 'He's Nobody.'

As Joseph still looked dissatisfied with her, she added: 'It's better than farm-work.'

'I know, May. It was good of you to tell us about this place. I only got it because of you. I know that.'

'I didn't say it to get your thanks, Joseph.'

'I know you didn't.'

Looks soothed with words.

'Never let it be thought that anybody's doing you a favour by letting you work here, my lad. You do them a favour.' She was solemn.

'It's only Garrett that gets on my nerves,' her brother replied.

May was to be trusted – especially with a secret. 'I keep thinking I'll end up like him, May.'

She breathed very deeply – glad to her heart's core that he should have such confidence in her, tears already primed for the bed that night where she would weep at the recollection.

'Never in this world,' she answered, most tenderly. 'He'll never be anything but a bloody butler.'

'Me neither if I stop here.'

'Oh – you'll go some day.' Decisively said, then put aside. 'Some day. But for the moment – think yourself lucky; there's thousands with no work at all.'

'I know I'm lucky,' he groaned in exasperation. 'You're always telling me I'm lucky.'

'Am I?' she said, accused. 'Just ignore him, Joseph. No wonder he gets mad with you – you're really cheeky with him sometimes. You should be polite – even if he is an old – I won't swear on your day off. Ignore him – just like I ignore cook.'

He had not the heart to point out that a score of times a day she was bruised for all to see by the sadistic little rap of that Irishwoman's bog-bitter tongue.

'But how *can* I ignore him? I hate him.'

'That's nothing,' she said, disdainfully.

They sat for a few moments in silence and in May's mind began the inevitable fantasy of what she would do to Mr Garrett who upset her brother so much.

'It's after six,' said Joseph, taking the pocket-watch from the old chest of drawers.

'My Christ, he has a watch as well,' May muttered.

'You bought it for me.'

'I know.' She sighed and left his room on tip-toe; as if she had been on an immoral visit.

It was the hour when the butler retired to his pantry. Throughout the house a sigh of relief came from the servants, a gentle hallelujah sounding down the corridors. Mr Garrett was charmed by the murmur: each whisper but a comma in the long sentence of his authority.

Feet pointing like the hands of a clock at ten to two, he

lorded it across the hall, savouring the juices which seeped into his mouth in anticipation of the glass of port and lump of Stilton. And there was young Tallentire standing by the pantry door as requested : Oh – the pleasure of settling a small score!

The unlocking of the door, like Garrett's accent, manner and vocabulary, was immensely mannered and Joseph was almost unbearably irritated at the way in which the butler hauled up the keys from a pocket which reached from stomach almost to knees : they were pulled up so slowly, as if they were to unlock treasure, and then regarded and assessed individually, as if Garrett were on too high a level to make such simple distinctions and did not comprehend such base tools.

Inside, the butler sat on his stool and the pneumatic murmur was used to disguise a discreet belch : he had caught sight of the Stilton. Joseph leaned against the door, legs crossed, arms folded – well aware that this would annoy the old toad.

A trick that Garrett had learned from their employer – Colonel Sewell – was to wait, allow a pause. He noted Joseph's attitude and it confirmed his secret decision, nevertheless, he would go through with the charade. Joseph was concentrating his gaze on the thick black elastic suspender which gripped the butler's waxy calf like a tourniquet.

'First things first,' Garrett began, in the manner of Colonel Sewell – even letting his voice die away at the end of a phrase – 'It isn't your business to tell young William' (the hall boy) 'what to do. When you were him – not so very long ago – you listened to me – so does he.'

'He likes cleaning the silver.'

'That's not the point.'

'What is then?'

'He does nothing without my say-so – see?' The officer gave way to the boss.

'What else d'you want me for?'

'I haven't finished with William yet.' He paused. 'You won't rush *me*, Tallentire.'

Joseph shrugged and Garrett interpreted silence as surrender and began to enjoy himself. A glance behind the tins of polish reassured him as to the proximity of the stolen port and he eased himself in his seat, tugged at the knees of his trousers.

'Remember what happened to the fella who was footman before you.' The boss gave way to the tyrant. 'He thought he could tell me what was what.'

The footman, dismissed for stealing port though denying all knowledge of it, had been a friend of Joseph's and he blushed to remember how impotent he had been to prove his friend's innocence.

'That's right,' said Garrett, approving the rush of blood into the cheeks, 'stick out your neck too far and – chop! – off goes your head. Not that *you* stand accused of the sort of thing *he* went in for ...'

'I *never* believed he did it,' scarlet, over-dramatic, Joseph forced his sentence over the butler's bullying tone.

'It was proved.'

'Not to my satisfaction.'

'Your satisfaction, Tallentire, is neither here nor there.' He began to imagine the cheese yielding to his teeth.

'Is that all then?'

'One more thing,' the tyrant gave way to the philosopher: he could afford it now. 'You're too free with the Family.' The Family which he himself served without question; or answer. 'If you want to keep your place – keep it, savvy? You might *think* they're friendly but they're just playing you along. Step out of line and one day – chop!' Neither gesture nor change of expression accompanied the word which fell from the bland face as smoothly as a guillotine from the blue sky. The warning was lost on him, Garrett noted. Chop.

As Joseph went for the bicycle – there were two old bone-shakers in the shed and the servants were allowed to borrow them in exchange for maintaining them – he heard the splash of oars from the lake. Lady Sewell was teaching William how to row: it was an accomplishment with which she endowed all her hall boys. Joseph waited to see them when they came from behind the island and remembered his own lessons.

Near the farm where his father was now hired there was a small tarn and Joseph had pinched or borrowed a rowing boat many a night to go fishing. Yet he had been grateful to Lady Sewell for taking the trouble and too confused by her invitation to admit this competence. She had assumed he could not row and planted him down in the stern, herself taking the oars in a well-demonstrated grip – and off they had gone. She rowed skilfully – which added to his confusion, for though he could row well enough, he was not as graceful as she was. Indeed as she stroked the long blades through the still water he wondered if he *did* know how to row; properly. So he had kept his mouth shut and followed her instructions. These were so numerous and precise – particularly with regard to the wrist movements – that his embarrassment had flushed away all his confidence.

He had been learner enough that day – even pleased when told he had 'no done *at all* badly for a first outing'.

It was a matter for smiling when someone else got the same treatment. 'Shallower, William. Shallower!' The light voice carried across the water and as the boat came into sight he went towards the bicycle shed, the uncomfortable suspicion following Garrett's interview dislodged by his own, stronger recollections.

What he liked to do on his afternoon off was to find a quiet place, settle there and let what might come into his mind. He was rather ashamed of this, thinking that he ought to turn the fortune of the free hours to better advantage. And he had once gone to the nearby town – to the swimming baths, to the park, to the shops – as if he had to amass points for some score that was being kept somewhere. But always he had found himself day-dreaming and the drifting time had spread as the dutiful activities became more perfunctory. Now his method was to race down the drive as if some urgent appointment waited for him; continue that farce through the hamlet and beyond for about a quarter of a mile; then turn off down a lane, make for the river, find a favourite spot and lie down.

The way he kept in touch with what was around him was by concentrating on one object and playing with it all afternoon. Sometimes tree branches; or when it was dull or cold he would huddle against a tree trunk, wrap himself round his knees and look across broken clouds; then he could look up and measure the gap between the clouds and the sky, seeing them now as parted in the blue, now suspended from it, now bringing the sky near, now emphasizing its distance. And in the silence he called up his fantasies; allowing them a furtive liberty in that solitary place.

The fantasies would be of perfect lives: of rescue, adventure and victory in war, sport and love. Scenes barely related to any part of his experience in their content; coming mainly from comics, Hollywood, women's magazines and the football pages of the Sundays: but fed by the impetus that is given when light appears after long darkness. The darkness was also his early life which he remembered only in images; a crack in the wall, a gap between two houses, the wheel at the pit-head, a cliff of slag sheer against the sea. His mother had died when he was seven – he had been holding her hand, yet he had sunk all recollection of that. And his boyhood with his father as wilful as the Old Testament God, their means limited by utter dependence on an oppressive, broken-backed rural economy. But somewhere in there were moments when he had felt things could change – an awareness, a light, a recognition – when he had felt himself open to chance in a way his father was not, perhaps never had been. It was that which had enabled him to accommodate himself to being sent to the Sewells as Hall Boy. The notion of being a servant had been transformed into the idea of being a servant in disguise.

But when he thought about the work he did he squirmed. Despite being in no different a position from his father who was a hired farm labourer, the fact of working inside the house stripped off that essential appearance of independence which outdoor work gave his father. Besides, 'work' was too good a word for this cleaning of shoes, laying of tables and serving of food: yet it would be unthinkable to complain; it was too easy.

This afternoon he was too restless fully to enjoy the peace. The return home brought up so many questions. Had he been educated 'properly', he would say to himself, he would be able to identify the questions and answer them. As it was, they came as a harvest of sensations which he could not gather in. Occasionally he thought that he might 'really' take up reading and get to know a few things : he had unobtrusively borrowed books from Sewell's library. It had not really worked. Once or twice he had found a story he liked; but the books of knowledge annoyed him by their density and his boredom. He fell back on intuition, cultivating an awareness of what the people around him were feeling; so that his most refined exercise was to measure exactly the 'state', almost the 'atmosphere', of others. With May, for example, this morning he had got everything right – including that pretence of ignoring her when she first came in : had he not been preoccupied she would have assumed that he had expected her to arrive (which he did) and this would have led her to conclude that she was being taken for granted, which would have distressed her a little.

As he knew, and he got up, stiffly, gave up the attempt to lull himself into day-dreams – abandoned the football matches, deserted the South Sea Islands, withdrew from the Film Stars – he knew now that Garrett intended to fire him and there was nothing he could do to prevent it.

Lady Sewell looked so unhappy that Joseph felt sorry for her, although his sympathy could understandably have been reserved for himself.

'You see, Joseph, it's one of those times when we all have to make sacrifices.'

The carpet was so deep you could have slept on it; the distance between Joseph and Lady Sewell was more than the length of every house the young man's father had ever inhabited; the velvet curtain would have been considered 'far too good to use' by his step-mother – and folded away in a drawer for ever. The Sewells liked to think they were not rich, but that water-colour which Joseph had always liked would have sold for his year's wage.

'I'd hoped to postpone it – but just this afternoon Garrett said that it would be better to tell you before you went on your holiday. He said that – as it happened – you'd mentioned that you might be looking out for another place : nearer your family.'

'I never said that,' he answered. But she never attended to objections.

'No? He said you'd *implied* it.'

'I didn't say anything about it. I don't want another place.'

'Joseph: I'm terribly sorry – and you've always been so cheerful and helpful – quite the most – *vigorous* footman we *ever* had – but' and now, her duty clear, she was firm, 'someone *has* to go – we *must* cut down. The whole country has to pull in its belt with all these men out of work – it's dreadful. And I *do* agree with Garrett in this – it's much better to tell you *before* you go away – I consider that was most thoughtful of him.'

'Do you want me ...' He stopped. Then, rather sharply, he said, 'You won't want me back after this holiday then?'

'Well. It probably *would* be easier – for all of us, *especially* for you – if you *used* your holiday time to look for something. Colonel Sewell and I have talked it over *most* carefully – believe me, Joseph, *most* carefully – and we decided that we could do without a parlour-maid, an under-gardener and the footman – yourself.' She smiled. 'I must tell you that my husband made the observation that if anyone *had* to go it might as well be someone with your initiative as you would be much more likely to land on your feet than the others. Garrett's been with us for years of course; William is too young and Evans, as you might have heard, has an Unfortunate Past.'

All this was said in a 'public-speaking' tone of voice which seemed to seek applause and in fact Joseph only just held himself back from saying 'thank you'.

'Now then,' she said, briskly, 'I will give you the highest references and wish you the best of luck.' She held out a long arm and most clumsily Joseph touched her hand which grasped his fingers and squeezed them. 'The Colonel will see you in the morning. And Evans will drive you to the station of course as usual. Good-bye, Joseph.'

He nodded, said nothing and went out.

He had no cigarettes.

Garrett's quarters were away from the house, and by the time Joseph reached them he had lost his enthusiasm for a row. Besides, the curtains were drawn and the glow from the window was so cosy that the young man would have felt more like an intruder than an antagonist. And when he considered it, he wanted no more of Garrett.

As he walked around the lake for the eighth time, he heard the chimes from the village church – ten. It was a warm night, he would stay out. Instead of the cigarette, a piece of grass had to make do between his teeth. He remembered that his father had once had to smoke cleat leaves.

His mood surprised him, for he was not distressed or upset but rather excited, as if his dismissal was a pleasant and un-expected present. He was happy to be leaving the place. From the way in which Lady Sewell had said 'the Colonel will see you in the morning,' he guessed that the old man would have one or two families for him to write to. At this moment he hoped not; he would like to be out of service altogether.

He had enjoyed it well enough, he told himself; *and* been good at it. That needed to be emphasized at this particular time. He had taken as accurate her complimentary remarks about his work: if there was a conceit in him it was this; that he could do any job he set himself to – as well, at least as well, as any man. And he repeated that to himself in the dark, blushing at the boast.

But now he was out of work. In the letters from home he had heard about the thousands unemployed, particularly in West Cumberland, and felt even more lucky and even more isolated than he usually did. One of them now, he was glad of it.

It was May who kept him out of the house, circling the lake as if unhappy. He did not know how he could cope with her; for she would be waiting for him in his room and he was moved that she would be so dismayed by his leaving. She would cry and, imagining her tears, his own began to press into his eyes. Somehow she would feel that she was being let down and he would feel as if he were leaving her deliberately. And it made him angry, finally, though he would never have confessed it: why should he have to face her when he wanted to savour all this alone?

What to give her? That was the difficulty. The only thing of any value he had which would serve was the chain he had bought for the watch she had given him. He would gladly have made a present of both watch *and* chain but that would have offended her. The chain – and a letter – saying how grateful he was to her – he would leave them on the hall-table where the morning's post was laid out. The watch-chain would please her.

At eleven he left the lake; reluctantly, but he was afraid that May might panic and raise an alarm. Walking towards the black house his feet were springy on the turf, and he felt more alert than he had done for months. At the house he turned to look a last time at the lake, shivering under the half-moon. 'Shallower, Joseph,' she had said. 'Much, much shallower.'

Part Two

Waiting

Chapter Two

The train stopped at Carlisle, from there he took another train to Thurston and from Thurston he walked the few miles to the village. There *was* a bus, twice a day, but he was unsure of its time of departure and preferred to be on his way.

His case was not heavy though it contained all he possessed. He went under the railway bridge and set off up Station Hill; like most of the smaller railway stations, Thurston's was on the edge of the town and once he had climbed Station Hill, he was in the country. It was a cloudy day but brisk, and he walked quickly, his mackintosh flapping below his knees, the light wind freshening his face.

A few horses and carts passed him by and a black Austin Seven, racketing along the middle of the road – he nodded to them all and turned off into a lane which would take him through the fields to the village. Always as he walked his eyes went over to the fells which began about six miles away, and the outline of the hills made him feel cheerful. He whistled and kicked his way through the grass, feeling certainty as well as relief at having lost that job. The walk shook off the stiffness of the journey, the land was bare, leaves turning yellow and brown in hedges and trees, he had his pockets full of presents and everyone would be as pleased to see him as he to see them. He skirted the village itself for fear that he would meet someone who would pass him the gossip he wanted to listen to in his own home.

This cottage was the biggest that John, his father, had ever had. During those first few years following the death of his first wife John had never stayed at one place for longer than a term. The birth of children, the protestations of his second wife, the bother of being re-hired and moving and re-settling –

none of this had stopped his wandering. But now he had settled.

The place stood two or three hundred yards away from the village, over the railway bridge (the station had been closed down the previous year) in the lane which led to the small mere. A large, most plain building, it had been erected as the house for a farm never completed. It had no running water, no gas, an outside lavatory and forever rising damp.

Although Joseph had scaled that scraggy beech tree in the yard to hide from the schoolmaster after he had led half the school away to follow the otter hunt; set off to school, work and play from the place, climbed onto its roof, jumped from a window, scrubbed its steps and cleared the gutters, it was not the house he thought of as he looked at it but his father.

Whenever he came back to Cumberland he remembered his father so intensely that the images came at him like hail, settling finally to freeze him in admiration – he thought of his working in the mines and living through the pit-accident which should have killed him; the envy of his time spent with Joseph's 'real' mother; and the awe of his strength which would never leave him. Since his childhood, Joseph had been his father's subject : hauled from house to house by him as the man's restlessness had taken its course, worked from the age of eight, disciplined with hand and belt from the age of sense and allowed only flight as an expression of protest. Then, if he could keep running for long enough, his father's temper would break into laughter and they would be more friendly than at any other time, the boy tacking across the field slowly, his wariness diminishing the more he grew sure of his father's affection, even a hand on his shoulder.

Most times he did exactly as he was told. As once when John had taken a foal away from its mare. He'd given the mare to Joseph to hold, warning him that she might be 'frisky'. As John began to take away the foal – pulling it into his arms and easing it from under its mother – the mare had begun to throw her head, squeal, buck and try to snap at the small boy who was frightened almost out of his wits but not quite, for still, as he was jerked up and down, his feet clearing the ground, there was the awareness to hear John shout – 'HOLD! Hold on!' And he did.

For two or three years of his boyhood he had always sidled past his father, his right arm crooked in front of his face, ready to parry the expected blow. Yet the ferocity of some of the beatings did not kill his love. And now as he waited behind the dyke, he shut his eyes and immediately was soaked in scenes in which the man spun all around him. Nights when John would get out the concertina and they would clear the stone-flagged kitchen, send out the younger children as runners to announce that 'there's gonna be a dance at oor house – to-neet!' The girls would be frantic to make sandwiches and raid the loft for cooking apples that would be baked and stuffed as a treat. Between the women's preparations and their bossing, Joseph would weave himself as his father's representative; setting this right, finding that, as handy and finicky as his stepmother – the laughter and the interest warming the kitchen until it seemed to have a score of lamps and not just the two. And when people came! Oh, when the place was full! The Lancers, Three Drops of Brandy, Quadrilles they did! Everybody shouting with that ring of honest happiness he had never heard since – to do with relief from work and poverty and worry and frustration, burning all in one flame of communal pleasure: and conducting it all, playing there, his blue eyes slits of fun, his father.

Joseph saw Mary in the yard. She was running over the yard, her small wooden clogs banging on the flattened earth, the hen she was after tippling drunkenly as it raced away. His eyes prickled with tears seeing her: it was always so when he came home, though never when he left. And this was another reason for his careful approach. He liked to get the tears over before he met anyone.

He had come by the field on the other side of the lane. Only upstairs windows looked over it and so he was safe. He could see into the yard by standing on the small bank on which the thinning hedge was set. He had caught the early train in the knowledge that it would enable him to reach home just before the children came back from school – and he waited for them, still watching Mary the smallest.

He ducked when his step-mother came out to make sure that the little girl was safe, and, a few minutes later, almost gave his position away to run out and comfort her when she began to cry; but the crying stopped, as inexplicably as it had begun. A meagre trail of smoke came from one of the chimney pots : he heard the open-engined report of a rare tractor a few fields away, herons from the mere, a few crows – but most of all the sound of his breath pushing against the silence.

The school-bell had gone – and soon he saw them coming across the field. None of them his full brothers or sisters : of those, Sarah and Alice were married and away, Harry had been killed at the very end of the Great War and May of course was in service. Yet Joseph could not have loved them more. Frank was first, running ahead; he was to leave school at Christmas. Now he was racing to get on and finished with the jobs their father would have laid down for him to do. Donald, four or five years younger, was trotting well behind him but obviously drawn along by his elder brother; he would inherit the jobs soon enough. Finally, Anne and Robert who had just started school, climbing the stile with immense care, trailing to the cottage with such diminutive weariness of carriage as made a small caricature of the homeward plod of labourers coming from the fields. He watched them all into the house, then picked up his suitcase and went across there himself. Tea was on the table and so he could have a place from the instant of his arrival.

For his step-mother there was a package of scented soap, for his father (who would come in two or three hours later) twenty Gold Flake; wonderfully complicated knives for Frank and Donald, games in cardboard boxes for Anne and Robert, and for Mary a doll which shut its eyes and sighed when you laid it down. As he handed out the presents (total cost, over two pounds : four months of hard saving) he fought against the pleasure in giving which threatened to take over all his feelings : not to enjoy the distribution of the presents would have been impossible but there always came a point where he felt that he was showing-off, in some way flaunting his virtue and his luck in front of the others. So he switched the conversation immediately and refused even to look at the gifts – all still spread over the table – afraid that the merest glance would be the occasion for another attack of gratitude.

'And what's Frank going to do?' he asked. Both his step-mother, Frank and himself accepted that the subject could be discussed as if he were out of the room.

'Your father wants him to go into farm-work.'

'That's no surprise.'

'I would like him to stay on at school,' said Avril. She nodded to Joseph as if to show that she shared his memory of a similar wish being expressed on *his* account. 'But that's impossible,' she continued briskly. 'He didn't pass for the grammar school, like you, and the only place he could go would be Workington. Your uncle Seth said that he could lodge in with him – but,' she paused, 'well; we need the money. There's no shame in it,' she added. 'You see your father had to take a cut when he was made groom. But I made him take it. He was working too hard just labouring: he will drive himself, your father, and some-times he'd faint. We didn't write to bother you. It was that thing in the pit, you know: it's more serious than he'll allow. The doctor said he could live to be a hundred if he stopped knocking himself out with work – but if he kept on ...' she hesitated. 'I made an apple cake,' she said, smiling, 'just for your tea – and I've left it in the scullery – Donald – go and bring it – and don't *pick* at it.'

'Where would he be hired?' John asked.

'Mr Dawson told your father he could take another boy on. He could still live here, then.'

Joseph felt a rush of jealousy. *He* had not been so cared for. Though he had passed for the grammar school he had not been allowed to go. At fourteen he had been hired to the best bidder. But he forced the feeling away – long ago he had accepted that while she was always fair to him (though not to his sisters) his step-mother could not but favour those children she had borne herself. She had been good to him though, he knew that, and he had no difficulty in calling her 'mother'.

'And what do you want yourself?' Joseph asked of Frank.

'Aa divvn't know.' Frank blushed and twisted violently in this undesired limelight.

'He's interested in motor cars,' said his mother.

'Aa would like t' be a mechanic,' Frank rushed out, hopelessly proclaiming his ambition. 'Aa would like to work in a garidge.'

'Your father went to see Harry Stamper – but he can't take anybody else on,' said Avril, 'and there's nobody else he knows that has a garage.'

'What about George Moore in Thurston?'

'Your father doesn't know *him*,' said Avril, with such emphasis as implied that George Moore was beyond all knowing.

'Our Alice courted Edward. *I* can always ask him.'

'Can thou?' interjected Frank. 'Can thou just go up and axe him like that?'

'*Any*body can ask him,' said Joseph, moderatingly.

'Not me,' said Frank. 'Aa couldn't axe nobody nothing, nivver.' And he stuffed some bread into his mouth to stifle all further confessions.

As Joseph had once done, so Frank was approaching his fourteenth birthday as a ravine which, if leapt badly, could result in the near-fatal accident of 'getting a wrong start'. In a few days following that birthday, he would have a man's work laid on him. From about the age of six, he had been training for it, doing more and more work around the house and garden, helping his father, spending his holidays on the farm, the summer evenings haytiming, his autumn weekends potato picking. It was as if the severity with which the children were brought up and the insistence that was put on their working, far from being a harsh expression of affection, was the most considerate way in which such parents could arm their children for what would follow. And the boy was watched for his work, his ability at it, his constancy and interest, watched and talked of as someone about to go out to battle so that the men would say, 'He's about ready for work now', 'He's shooting up a bit, he'll be all right now', 'He wants nothing at home, now, let him get to work,' and, most commonly of all: 'Can he work yet?'

Avril, like many of the mothers, accepted this until those

few months before the actual transfer took place. Then she tugged against it, counted the savings she had, regretted all sorts of missed opportunities, resented the lack of other opportunities, vowed that he would be the last to go in such a way, turned this way and that to rescue him, failed and watched him go – over the top.

After tea the children scattered. Remembering May, Joseph refused the offer of the sofa and went up to the room he would share with two of his brothers. There were some books on the window sill – five volumes of the 'Today and Tomorrow' series which he had won over a number of years as school prizes: in all of them a great future was promised, with everything in every way daily getting better and better. He had not liked them much and now used them as a prop for his feet, to keep his shoes off the bedding, as he lay back and smoked a butt.

Had he not carried in him the news of his lost job, he would have basked around the fields in the plenty of his homecoming. But now he wanted to be alone before the revelation. Already he felt that he had cheated them all by holding it back: it must be said before night.

As he lay there he was washed by a misery which seemed to rise from nowhere. He had long heard May and his step-mother talk of his father's 'moods' – and experienced the effects of the foul ones directly. Somehow he had never thought that he too would be enslaved by them. John had had such a hard life compared with his own, and even when his father had once told him that he had been unable to rid himself of this possessing blankness since a young man, he had found reasons for it which did not apply to himself. Yet here, with his family around him, a soft bed, a cigarette, nothing to do, he was swept over, drowned in a despair which was neither pity for himself nor a lament for others but a meaningless thing, opaque to any analysis he could bring to bear on it, an irresistible closing up of the pores of his mind, his body and his senses which submerged him and left him powerless.

The sound of his father's voice pulled him out of it. He had lain there for two hours. He went down the stairs hesitantly, always over-wrought at seeing his father after a long absence –

and as usual covering this beneath an appearance of cocky cheerfulness.

He opened the kitchen door and for a second looked full at the older man before going across to shake his hand. Now fifty-one, John Tallentire was as lean and stiff-backed as ever he had been. His clothes hung baggily on him, the thick wide trousers dropping over the boots, the buttoned waistcoat, collarless shirt and scarf, jacket with full pockets swinging against the thighs like weights balancing his precise walk, cap shoved back from his brow. His face had been cut up in the pit accident and the left cheek was divided in two by a scar, but the scar was deep in the skin and the effect was to bunch the upper cheek, making it rosier, merry under the blue eyes. There was another long scar just below the hairline on his forehead – hidden by cap or hair – and a dry pucker of skin at the right corner of his mouth twisted his lips when he smiled – but again the harm was masked by its consequences, for that twist made his slightest smile irresistible and you could not but smile back at him. The real damage had been done to the base of his skull and his back which was crossed with thin blue welts as if he had been lashed with a cat of nine tails tipped with coal. When he saw Joseph he nodded and held up the new packet of Gold Flake which his thick fingers were fumbling with – and offered his son a cigarette as soon as they had shaken hands.

'Good to see thee lad,' said John. 'Ay. Good to see thee.'

'Good to see thee an' all,' Joseph replied.

'He's grown, mother!' John shouted, though Avril was but two paces away. 'Ay,' he repeated more gently to Joseph. 'Thou's just about filled out, Aa would say.'

'He might shoot up some more,' said Avril, loyal to Joseph's possibilities.

'Nay,' John contradicted her. 'Come on, back to back, lad. Back to back. See thou keeps thee 'eels on't carpet. Theer.'

'Take your cap off, dad,' said Avril.

'A cap's no advantage. Squint a bit on my side woman.'

'I'll get the poker.'

She laid it across their two heads.

'Exactly the same,' she said.

34

'What did I say?' said John. 'He's filled out and finished.'

'He might be taller than you yet.'

'Nivver!'

'Well,' Avril smiled as she looked from one to the other: they were very much alike. 'He's a real Tallentire, anyway.'

John laughed and took his son's shoulder to lead him into the garden. 'A real Tallentire.' To Joseph the remark gave a thrill: no-one but Avril ever said it and she did it to please his father, John thought. Yet the idea of being a 'real Tallentire' appealed to his romantic imagination: not that it was an appeal which had much of a hearing. The only other Tallentires he knew were his uncles Seth and Isaac and his aunt Sarah; little consistency there. Joseph's real pleasure was that the remark contained the implication that he was like his father: which suited him well.

After watching Frank working in the garden, with Donald at his brother's heels like an acolyte – John crooked his finger mysteriously and led his son to a hut he had put up halfway down the next field.

'Pigs,' he said grandly. 'Two. What dis te think o' that?'

They watched the pigs scour the bare ground and Joseph, like his father, regarded the fat, roinking beasts with great pride.

Then, as he had hoped, his father began to tell him of the Shows he had been to that summer with the horses. He talked of each horse individually, of its moods and temper, how he dressed it, how calmed it, how led it, how managed it, the cups they had won, those they had missed, the journeys in the horse-box, 'me snuggled in a bale of straw, Joseph, and oot at yon end like a scarecrow. I always took me best suit to lead them in. Some said it was daft – wearing a good suit like that. But what the hell – I've hed her since I got married and she does no service anywheer's else. And mother can still git her squared up for a funeral or whativver. Your mother was just the same as me for that. If thou's got summat to wear – wear it, she would say. And I parcel it up again as soon as I'm through.'

The fact that these shows put hours on his day, doubling some of them for very little extra – and then only if the horses won – was nothing compared with the pleasure John took in them.

Joseph could see the horses in his imagination, tall, powerful silk-maned greys with polished hooves and finely combed hair draping them like tassels, thick gleaming coats and plaited tails, flowers sometimes in the manes and straw in the tails – beautiful horses that could pull a plough a long day and trot as delicately as ponies. He knew, too, John's care for them – could see the older man working to make them shine, working hard as he always did as if in endless combat with himself not only to see that every job was well done but also to prove to his constant though invisible foe that application alone, though a minor quality, could also draw towards perfection.

While this talk went on, Joseph's pleasure was increasingly spoiled by the knowledge that he would have to tell that he was out of work. After a time it again appeared to him to be cheating not to tell, as if it meant he was getting all his father's confidences on false pretences.

He blurted it out.

John paused a while.

'Thou wasn't fired for badness?' he asked severely.

'No.'

'Thou did *nowt* wrong?'

'No. This butler wasn't fair though.'

'Why not?'

Joseph told him. Again John paused, then: 'Ay – bugger that sort of a man.'

The two men walked slowly up the field.

'But thou's gonna find it gay tricky up here,' said Joseph thoughtfully, 'there's more men out of work now than I've *ivver* seen. We've had poor work, lad, and we've had slave-work. But that was better than no work.'

'Was it?' The two words came without forethought.

'What do you mean – was it?'

'I mean,' said Joseph, unafraid of his father now, however much he admired and loved him, 'I mean sometimes it might be better not to work at all than to work like a slave.'

'Thou's *got* to work, lad.'

'Mebbe so. But . . .'

'No buts.' John did not want a contest with his son. He knew how easily he lost his temper and did not want to crush the younger man in any way. 'Thou's lucky to hev a week's holiday to start lookin',' he said. 'There's many a man widdout that.'

In bed that night Joseph found it difficult to sleep. He tossed about and then forced himself to lie still – he was in the same bed as his two younger brothers and did not want to wake them. All his fantasies were of jobs. Work had to be found and this night's sleep stood in the way of the search. Yet somehow, he whispered it to himself uncomprehendingly, it was not *so* important, this Work.

His movements disturbed Frank. Awake, the boy felt his elder brother close to him and wanted in some way to express the gratitude he had for Joseph's interest in his ambition. He thought hard for something intimately appropriate : to thank him again directly, in the dark, would be too weak. At last it came to him.

'Joseph,' he whispered, 'Joseph ?'

'Yes ?'

'Has thou ivver stripped a gear-box ?'

'No.' He paused. 'Nivver.'

'I have,' Frank replied, happily – and turned to sleep.

The first thing to be done was to get Frank fixed up. That he was no relation at all to Joseph but a 'brother' by marriage (the one child that Avril, a widow, had brought with her) had always made it the more important to Joseph that he should be scrupulously cared for. He wasted no time, set off for Thurston the following morning and went to George Moore's garage.

He found Edward, George Moore's son, under a tractor – and immediately told him of what he wanted. Edward told him where his father could be found and Joseph went up to see him.

The garage was built on two levels – the bottom level opening on to Station Road, the top level backing on to New Street. Between the two was a wooden ramp and on the top level a shop for crystal sets, the new wirelesses and toys. Joseph found Mr Moore in the shop.

'Interested, is he ?' said Mr Moore, the matter being explained.

'Well now. Interested.' He spoke slowly and paused often between words, sometimes between syllables.

'Yes. He's done a lot of messin' about with engines a'ready.'

'Messin' aboot eh?' said Mr Moore, ruminatively. 'Now then. Messin' aboot.'

'You know what I mean.'

'Oh aye. I know. Aye. Now when did he want to come?'

'New Year.'

'New Year eh?' said Mr Moore, meditatively. 'That's reet. It *was* t' New Year thou said.'

Which reassured him, it seemed, as to Joseph's basic honesty.

'Well,' said Mr Moore, after a silence. 'It's bad to git work these days.'

'It is.'

'Yes.' He paused. 'It is.'

'But a boy's wages are less than half a man's,' said Joseph relentlessly.

'They are.'

'And he's not frightened of work.'

'No?'

'No. Me father'll vouch for that.'

'Thou knows, Aa've heard tell of thee father – but Aa've niv-ver met him. Is he a big fella, raither blond, wid a tash?'

'No. He's shortish, black haired – works at Dawson's.'

'Now yon's a particular customer.' To make it clear that he was referring to Dawson in his personal not business aspect, he added, 'He brings some work here.'

'Well Dawson can vouch for him. He's worked at Dawson's.'

'That'd be farm-work?'

'Ay.'

'Not the same thing,' said Mr Moore, tutting slightly as he shook his head. 'Garidge work and farm-work's different basics a' togither. Direct oppisytes, Aa would say.'

'But he's worked on Dawson's tractor.'

'On that John Brown he has?'

'Yes.'

'Aa wondered where that hed got 'til,' said Mr Moore, rather annoyed. 'So this laddo's been tinkerin' wid it, hes he?'

'Ay,' Joseph smiled, 'thou'd better git him in here – then Dawson 'ud be forced to bring it to thee.'

'He would, ay. That's correct. He would. Aye. Tinkerin' eh?' He paused. 'She's a bloody awkward machine, yon John Brown, it's aa te buggery inside, thou knows.'

'Frank keeps it going.'

'Frank, eh? That's his name then; Frank.'

'Ay.'

'Well then,' said Mr Moore – and if he had been cautious before, a new word must be invented to describe the wariness, the ambiguity, the care, the non-commitment, the seizure in the tone which informed his next words: 'Send him along,' he said, 'Aa'll hev a look at him. Then – we'll be like Mr Asquith – we'll "wait and see".'

Down the ramp Joseph had the following exchange with Edward.

Joseph: 'Do you need another lad?'

Edward: 'Thou can say that again.'

Joseph: 'Sure?'

Edward: 'Certain. We're cluttered up. And he won't pay a man.'

Joseph: 'Thanks.'

On the whole he was pleased with the morning's work. There was nothing promised, and he would not be satisfied until Frank had actually landed the job – but as he biked home for his dinner, he felt that he had made a start.

He would have liked to work in the garage himself – and a 'lad's' wages would amount to much the same as he had received as a footman. He had not allowed himself to think of it until now: but it was not only too late, it was impossible. Frank had to be given a decent start.

Chapter Three

Over the next two months he spent six days a week – all hours – looking for work. On Sunday he met others like himself and they played football from light until dark, breaking only for a few sandwiches and cold tea. Some of the men who had given up all hope used to play all week. The energy which went into the game and the pleasure which came out of it made the forlorn apathy over unemployment seem uncanny at times; and though it was a very rare man who would admit to enjoying this necessary idleness, many discovered leisure for the first time in their lives, and privately relished it.

Though this was in some direct sense true and was felt more by younger, single men, the frontal fact was unemployment and the consequences were ugly and often desperate. In those weeks, Joseph saw it everywhere and was frightened by it. For all over the country, at that time in the early 1930's, there were workless men moving ceaselessly; largely ignorant of the system which had brought them to that state, largely ignored by those who ran that system; good men, mostly, who turned anger on themselves rather than seeking to inflict its results on others, who tried to nurse discontent with good humour and kept going because of those who depended on them: women and children first: the man to take all the punishment necessary.

Fear settled on him slowly, like drizzle, soaking, soaking, gradually penetrating the confidence until it touched on the quick of his self-esteem and there lodged fast. In the Sewells' house he had not realized how it was – not at all: and to his shame, he longed to be back there, at times, snug in his attic room, footman's uniform neatly over the chair. Shame because when he was at the factory gates or the pit-head with all the others, waiting to be told there were no vacancies, then there was no doubt that he was himself without any equivocation : even, after the luxuries of the big house, there was something welcome in the knowledge that there was no further to go; this queue for the dole, this shuffle and saving of single pennies, this pinched stomach, these melancholy streets and overcrowded rooms, barefoot children and old men grimacing at the cold – at some times these were firm as a board beneath him.

But whatever the compensations – and their nature as benefits appeared only passingly, not to be truly accounted until later, in reflection – whatever the incidental happiness from seeing his step-brothers and sisters – especially little Mary, through delicacy and a certain poise become the darling of the family – when Joseph got up and when he went to bed he thought of his failure and slowly began to think it really *was* his. Began to fear that he was not man enough to get and hold a job; and as much of his own sense of himself was defined by his work, he would feel the cramps in his stomach and know it was not just the longing for more food. Though he did not believe in labour as his life's purpose – as his father did – yet he was unable to find anything which even began to take its place.

They waited for work, those men, thirty per cent and more of the adult male population; some fought, some begged, some hunted, some crawled, but most waited, circling the system with caution; as if the sea in which they had all once swam had thrown up a monster which lay there, beached, not known to be dead or alive – which might destroy them all.

Two months : eight weeks : he counted the days.

It was Colonel Sewell who got him work. Someone quite near Thurston wanted an 'all-purpose chap' (so the Colonel wrote) 'someone like yourself – willing for anything and pretty capable. Go along and see him immediately.'

The house was no more than twenty miles from Thurston : he was employed on the spot and told that he would be charged only one pound for the uniform left behind by the previous footman : it would be taken from his first month's wages. Oh, and after Easter they might need him no longer – and did he mind sleeping in a cupboard next to the cellar. And smoking was not allowed. Did he smoke? Do him good to stop.

Joseph had met Mr Lenty in his first week at the house – when he had taken the shoes down to be mended – and since then had seen him regularly. Lenty's shop was in a side street of the nearby town and he sat in the window, watching the world, talking incessantly, and mending shoes. He was full fat, the long leather apron truly like a hide on that bovine frame; 'Sitting', he explained, 'sitting makes you swell. The skin closes on you, Joseph, the muscles sleep, the limbs stiffen, the sweat is retained. Any man who retains his own sweat is swollen by it, Joseph. But who can sole and heel walking about a room? No man. Never retain your own sweat!' His face was red as was his neck, his hands and all the hairless surface of his head.

'Hair,' he said, 'was given to man for warmth, Joseph. And now we live indoors and do not need it. Soon everyone will be bald. And the appendix will finally disappear if not in my lifetime, then in yours. Teeth and toes will most certainly follow and I would not be surprised if our nose and our ears were reduced to holes in the head. I won't live to see that.' A man who prided himself not so much on his knowledge nor on any innate powers of reasoning but on his affection for words – 'for running them together, Joseph, and scattering them abroad, for knitting them into patterns and stitching them into shapes: I don't seek out the strange words, Joseph, those that check a sentence and trip the ignorance of men – those are scholar's words – and I leave them to that distinguished body to enjoy in exclusivity. Mine are the everyday, a few Sunday words mashed in like gravy to the potatoes but no Bank-Holiday expressions – if you follow my line. I like to prattle, Joseph, to prate and patter and for every tack I drive through leather I must drive a word in with it.

'A collection of books has been my salvation, Joseph, and education. Had my grandfather on my mother's side not bought that job lot at a church auction – an act of charity, Joseph, and there are none better – had he not paid two shillings and sixpence for Lot 121 – I still have the ticket – I would have been dumb. Speechless. Silent.'

And there they stood – job lot 121 – on the window sill beside him, battered calf-bound volumes, about two dozen – Dickens, Thackeray, the Poems of Hogg, some of Carlyle's Essays – incessantly revised and reviewed by Lenty. Joseph had borrowed and read some of them.

Lenty had always talked so, his wife said – and she put the blame on his left leg. This was much shorter than his right leg and the debility had confined him to bed for most of his youth, 'and there was nothing for him to do but talk and read books,' she said, hopelessly. 'His father had a small public house and they brought him downstairs when he was eleven and made a bed for him in one of the snugs. That was where the talking men went. He caught it then and now he can't get rid of it.'

Lenty had one child, a daughter, Mair. 'My own mother was Welsh,' he said, 'and Mair is Welsh for Mary. In England they put a "y" on the end, having removed the "i", in France they put an "ie", in Spain they juggle it about with your Maria, as in Italy : I am told by Mr Kirkby, the schoolmaster, that the name occurs in every language known to man, Joseph. He takes it as proof of the Garden of Eden. I questioned that on the grounds that in Eden the lady was called Eve. He then proved that he was using a symbol.' Joseph had had a brief flirtation with Mair as much from the overspill of his affection for Lenty as from any real affection for the girl. It had come to nothing and they enjoyed a pleasant acquaintanceship. She, he knew, was 'walking out' with a junior gardener from another House. Joseph came on his free afternoons.

Lenty expected Joseph to make himself useful. Before long, the boy would find himself with a last, ripping off worn soles and heels, tapping the small nails into boots, even cutting out the leather. This did not bother Joseph much. He did not like to be idle when someone else was working : it was a privilege which he could not bear easily. Moreover he enjoyed the work – the smell of leather was as rich as the smell of bread; he liked to carve a sole from a sheet of the stuff and fill his mouth with the bright tacks. He had watched his father mending shoes often enough to be able to pick up the tricks quite easily – and at first, Lenty had taken some trouble to instruct him. Such a master-like position had soon bored the older man, and the moment he had seen that Joseph was passably capable he had allowed him to get on with it.

Lenty was no great craftsman : he had no song about leather and delivered no speeches in praise of the well-made shoe. At times he made a complete mess of it and it was not unusual to see him ripping off a new sole to start again. 'I was not called, Joseph,' he said. 'I heard no voices, felt no divine impulse, in short had no vocation. Yet – strange – I had all the time in the world to think one up. Lying in that snug as a boy I would con-sider my vocation : even after the elimination of the athletic pursuits (due to the leg) there was still considerable choice. The callings of man are as various as his desires, Joseph – and there were many courses open. But however much I made my mind as a clean slate – no hand inscribed thereon the letters of my future. So when one Tommy Black said he needed an apprentice at a sitting-down trade – I took it. Or rather my good father – bless him – did. I was tired of the snug by then. Wider fields, Joseph, even in mice there is a search for wider fields – hence the field-mouse.'

The one room served as workshop and selling shop. When-ever he entered it, Joseph felt cheerful, for besides the sight of Lenty framed by his window like a beaming goblin, and the smell of the leather, there was the effect of that brown suffused jumble – lengths of freshly tanned leather hung on the walls like tapestries, strips of it on the floor, the work-bench littered with it, the peeling cream wallpaper melting (through dirt) to its colour, the heavy books a leather line on the window-sill, boxes of nails, tacks, rubber heels, caps, clips, corkers, toe-plates, laces, eyes, polishes and ointments on the bench which was semi-circular, Mr Lenty sitting in it as if an arc had been carved out of a rude dining table to comfort his stomach – and everywhere shoes, sandals, boots, slippers, clogs, all shapes, sizes and colours, new, finished, gleaming, battered – it was as if the clouds had opened one day and showered footwear on Lenty. This had on Joseph the effect that all such jumbles had – especially those conglomerations which had consistency, which served one end, as this did the shoe: delight.

'Ah, Joseph,' said Mr Lenty with relief and great pleasure. 'Ah, Joseph!' He paused and wiped his mouth on his sleeve. He spat, just a very little, as he spoke, since his upper teeth had been lately reduced to four molars and two rather fangish canines: it was not dangerous to sit near him – but it was as well to keep at least a yard away. 'I was beginning to despair of company this dreary day when the rattle of your back mud-guard alerted me to the remembrance that this was your after-noon off. Those cobbles are like an alarm. I have asked many customers if they could think of a link between cobbles and cobbler but it stumps them all. Where was I? Yes. I cannot re-member the last afternoon I had off – which is to say I can though I prefer to forget it. The left one, yes. Good.

'I had not taken an afternoon off since my daughter's con-firmation when I went to hear the bishop speak – very poor it was, not enough quotations for a bishop. Mr Kirkby gives me more quotations when he brings his slippers in. That being five years past, I thought – use *that* strip, Joseph, I know it has a hacked look but you must do what you can; it is a very hacked shoe – that I deserved another such but waited, Joseph, for a few months, to let things take their course. The *small* hammer: very well, use the large one.

'Then one day Mrs Lenty said that *she* proposed to take an afternoon off: I was astounded.' (Here he held his hammer above his head and paused: the quality of the silence was re-markable: then he brought it down firmly just to one side of the nail, bending it badly, and resumed.) 'Mrs Lenty *never* takes an afternoon off, never, never takes an afternoon off, not to see the bishop or I dare say prince, king, Pope or emperor, Joseph: *you* know Mrs Lenty. Well then, I said nothing – for a moment – and then, without jumping in to question her decision with the impetus of a nanny-goat, admitted to her that I too, was think-ing in the general direction of taking an afternoon off. It was her turn to pause, Joseph, pass the number 5 nails. She, too, good woman, said nothing of an enquiring kind and it was my turn to suggest that we take the *same* afternoon off – to which she assented in a state of great relief – and only *then* did I slip in, most casually, my question. I moved like the slow-worm,' said Mr Lenty, 'and said – Did she have anywhere to go? "Yes," she replied, "a funeral." Did I? No, I said, a walk would be good enough for me.

'The day came, Joseph, make a good job of that, I've just remembered who it's for – I know my talking loses me customers, Joseph, but those are the sort you can do without. Anyway, I have about two thousand pounds in two building societies, besides what Mrs Lenty has in the post office and the cash-box and the large blue jug – I could sit back and live on that, Joseph, if I could get time off. But I can never *finish*. There have been occasions when I was down to a few shoes – no more than four pairs, I remember, once: and I said to Mrs Lenty – "those done, up go the shutters." Up they never went, Joseph, because that cheeky hall-boy arrived the very next morning – the one from Pinkleys' – with twelve pairs to be soled and heeled: twelve! I've been no nearer than ten since that day. Sometimes I think I don't *want* to retire because there surely must be other ways to break free of this vice, to turn this downward spiral into an upward course leading to rest and peaceful free pastures – but I can't see it. And what you can't see you can't want, Joseph – being yet another of Mr Kirkby's quotations, though he called that one "hidden".

'The day came and I prepared myself. Mair had painted a card with the words SHOP SHUT THIS THURSDAY AFTERNOON. FIRST TIME IN FIVE YEARS. MANY APOLOGIES. BEST WISHES. G. P. LENTY, ESQ. – there it is, I keep it by me for a calamity – copper-plate lettering, very distinguished – and I hoped all morning that the usual pattern would be observed. That is, a few first thing in the morning, a few at dinner-time, and a few late on – hardly a soul along the afternoon, Joseph, and despite all sorts of guesses at it I've never been able to really work that out – it's a normal enough town in all other respects – and after dinner, with Mrs Lenty gone about her business, I closed that front door which, as you know, is open every day on the calendar from nine until nine except when it's raining but even then I keep it on the latch.

'Then – good boy, sandpaper the edges of this for me, would you? Yes, a good job you made of that – then I made my pre-parations.' (Here Mr Lenty having disembarrassed himself of the material of his trade by passing it to Joseph, also set down the tools and his two small white hands rested on those bumps beneath the leather apron which were probably his knees.) 'I changed,' he said, lifting the hands from the bumps and patting himself from navel to neck as if testing his resilience, 'from skin to skin. Washed completely. Did not stint. And out of the front door.

'I decided to go to the main street which I had not seen in weekday daylight for five years, and set off. At the Co-op, before I had turned the corner, I met Mrs Charles – would I put irons on her husband's boots and by the evening please as he was walking to a mass-meeting? Back I came – changed, throughout, once more – irons, you know, are a dirty job and those boots were old, very – it took me almost an hour. Still time. Again' (he lifted his hands to the ceiling) 'skin to skin. This time I turned left and decided to make for the park which I have not seen day or night for twelve years at least but I know the keeper – a customer – and hear that his stocks are beautiful. *In* the park then, sitting down, watching the children, very summery, waiting for the keeper, always a good talk in him, when Eric Hetherington comes up. All white because of his cricket flannels. His cricket boots *had* to be re-studded for a friendly with Cockermouth that evening. I looked at them. There was no doubt about it. They *had* to be re-studded.

'I was no more than ten minutes in that park.

'He stood there (where you sit) – talking – all the time I did the cricket boots. I had not changed, but with that talk and the white polish which flaked off all over me I found myself at 4.30 p.m. dirty, exhausted and, in short, defeated. I changed back for the last time and have never had an afternoon off since. Nor a morning. Now then, what was it I started to tell you?'

He was interrupted by Mrs Lenty who came in to announce tea. The men went through to the kitchen for it. An apple cake – which Mrs Lenty had soon discovered to be Joseph's favourite and stuck by as his relentless treat ever since – stood in the middle of the cloth, newly baked, the light brown crust ready to melt on the palate. Bread, scones, jam and fancies stood as at the four points of a compass and the crockery spliced the principal bearings.

At tea Mr Lenty ate well and said nothing.

'This is what I started to say,' said Mr Lenty when they returned to the shop, unfolding a piece of paper before him as if preparing to read out a sermon. 'That is, this is what I meant to start to say when driven off course by an undercurrent of reminiscence, as I remember, just as I am always threatened by what might be called Trade Winds (the customers, Joseph, you see – think hard!) and, to keep the thing at sea, I ask you to regard this piece of paper as a chart, an explorer's map, a map of the mind but no less interesting for that.'

He handed over the piece of paper. On it were the numbers 1 to 20, written out as numerals several times, and beside each numeral, there was the word of the number recorded, as Joseph thought, in several different dialects. 'The sheep-score,' said Mr Lenty. 'Brought to me by my friend Mr Kirkby the schoolmaster after I had mentioned to him your reciting the way the shepherds count here in Cumberland. I was invigorated by that performance and also by the reminder of that particular lump of information,' he went on, battering the heel off a boot, 'and as you know I'm not a man for information – generally. Facts are facts people say, and so they are, but in my experience too many of them clutter up the throat – throttle you, hard things, no give in them. But that stuck – most likely, Joseph – that's right, the large nails in the cocoa tins – because of the way they sounded. Say them again.'

Any embarrassment which Joseph might once have felt at responding to such abrupt demands had long gone. There is a certain fear underlying embarrassment and it was impossible to be afraid of Mr Lenty. So Joseph rhymed off the count from one to twenty, in his own, the West Cumbrian dialect, singing it almost, as the words demanded :

'Yan, tyan, tethera, methera, pimp, sethera, lethera, hovera, dovera, dick. Yan-a-dick, tyan-a-dick, tethera-dick, methera-dick, bumfit.'

'Bumfit!' Mr Lenty interrupted ecstatically. 'Oh, thou Bumfit! My Bumfit. Now why can't we *still* say Bumfit. Fifteen doesn't hold a candle to it. Bumfit! Oh – go *on*, Joseph.'

'Yan-a-bumfit, tyan-a-bumfit, tithera-bumfit, methera-bumfit, giggot.'

'Giggot!' said Mr Lenty. 'Twenty. And-the-days-of-thy-years-are-tethera-giggots-and-dick. Now isn't that better than three score and ten? Tethera giggots and dick. It *sounds* like a life-time, doesn't it? I could hear you repeat that all evening – but pass the paper back and listen to *my* count.'

He took the paper, held it at arm's length (a short distance as his head tracked down the shoulder to bring his myopic brown pupils nearer their target) coughed, smiled most mysteriously at Joseph and began:

'Now Mr Kirkby wrote this out for me. Remember that. Mr Kirkby. I'll take this one. Yes. "Een, teen, tother, fither, pimp, een-pimp, teen-pimp, tother-pimp, fither-pimp, gleeget (yes, Joseph: I too prefer "dick": but forward): een-gleeget, teen-gleeget, tother-gleeget, fither-gleeget, bumfra ("fra" for "fit", you'll observe, but same base – bum): een-bumfra, teen-bumfra, tother-bumfra, fither-bumfra, fith-en-ly." (Twenty. Rather slippery along the tongue.) Well then. So what? – you might ask?'

Here, Mr Lenty really did tremble with excitement, even to wiping his brow, calming the nervousness, unable to bear the strain of it all.

'Joseph,' he said, solemnly. 'Some of those other lists you saw on that piece of paper were sheep-scores taken from different parts of England and one from Wales. You will admit that they were most remarkably similar to the one you say, ours, in Cumberland. But the one *I* read to you, Joseph, and one *other* on that list, Joseph, now listen, hold the nails for a moment, yes, the one *I* read, Joseph – that one is used by the Indians in North America.' He paused to let this revelation have its full effect. 'Indians of the Wawenoc Tribe,' he said, 'and it was recorded there in the year 1717. In a land 3,000 miles from our own. Joseph, across that mighty ocean, there, over there,' he pointed, 'are Indians and Cumbrians counting sheep in the same way – give or take dick and giggot. It says something about man, Joseph: but what? That was my immediate question to Mr Kirkby – and he traced it back to the Garden of Eden. *Extra*-ordinary though, isn't it?' he continued, delightedly, 'really, as information goes, that's the most extraordinary specimen that's come to me for a very long time. And I have you to thank, Joseph. And I do thank you. I've asked Mair to make a copy of this for you. It's something you'll be able to keep all your life.'

Joseph had not the heart to hazard the possibility that the Red Indians might have learnt the count from the Welsh or English settlers. And indeed, though this suggested itself to him, he dismissed it as a piece of unnecessary cleverness. For he, too, *wanted* it to be true, wanted there to be this tangible yet mysterious connection between different peoples: and besides such a desire, his observation appeared as a trivial irritant. The two men sat in silence, feeling the world spin them about, deeply content that all over it there were men counting sheep with the same numbers.

After he had left, Mr Lenty took advantage of the shop being empty and came into the kitchen to take up what was obviously a well-worked topic:

'Yes,' he said deferentially, standing at the kitchen door and thus halfway between his domestic and industrial self, 'Yes, I think I shall most certainly ask him after this Easter holiday. He never speaks of the House with a *great* deal of affection and he is already fairly useful in the shop. He could be a prize cobbler. I shall ask him.

'And he can live in,' said Mrs Lenty. 'He's very useful about the house. He can have the spare bedroom.'

'Do you think he *will* come, then?' Mr Lenty asked – for the thousandth time.

'I'm sure of it, my dear,' replied his wife. 'We'll all be really snug together.'

'Good,' said Mr Lenty. 'Then it's settled. I'll ask him on his return.' He smiled happily. 'We'll have some good talks together.'

Joseph had worked for Lenty for two months when Mair got

married. The marriage, once announced, was rapidly concluded and it took only another three months to explain the rush of it all.

In these circumstances, Lenty was forced to offer his new son-in-law both shelter and a job. He accepted both and Joseph was again out of work and parted, probably forever, from someone whose geniality had secured him most happily.

May also married at that time and he was glad he had some money saved to send her a decent present.

Having lost after having had was worse than never having had. He felt the pressure of John, his father, on him, who could not face a man without work, and tore around the district between panic and despair. Nothing, nothing to be had. And once more he left his own County, this time on an impulse come from fear.

Chapter Four

Twenty now, thin-faced, small-framed, watchful, having lived through the first pangs of real hopelessness and yet managed to retain a capacity for pleasure – the blue eyes suddenly wincing, the laughter ringing out in the industrial Midlands, Joseph was out on his own.

After leaving Lenty, his only regular work had been with a road gang – mainly Irish – who had started to dig a new route between Walsall and Birmingham and then stopped after two months. 'The money ran out' was the extent of the explanation granted to those who had done the labouring.

The gentle fantasies had retreated, yet their romantic imprint remained on the pattern of his ambition. This was 'to be his own man'. The phrase had been overheard casually and instantly fixed in his mind. He wanted ease, yes, and time for play, for thinking and dreaming – but they were on the other side of the wall he was building for himself : first, to be his own man, first, first and last.

Because of Stoddart. The Foreman. Tall – over six feet tall – big-boned, heavily muscled, gaunt from his longing for violence which clashed ceaselessly with his will to control everything; he had taken Joseph on and then disowned him, the very next day, for mimicking him in front of the others.

He had neither fired him nor hit him. Kept him there to torment him. Called him 'Runt'.

It was a big coal yard : Briggs Bros. had more than twenty lorries and they delivered over most of the city. Joseph had been taken on to work in the yard where the coal was stacked from the mines and loaded into the lorries. His job in the first week was down the 'hell-hole' – that is, under the grating which covered the loading bay. Here the coal dust piled up and had to be shovelled away and put in sacks. Until Joseph arrived, the way of it had been for half-a-dozen men to dig it once a fortnight – on a Friday when there would be some lorry drivers around after short runs, and the drivers would put the stuff in sacks. A new boy was always sent down there first, of course (everyone accepted that brutal necessity) and made to work in it for a week. But after that, he was put on normal work and the usual routine re-introduced.

Stoddart set up a new 'system' after Joseph's first week. One man alone was to be responsible for the 'hell-hole' to get in there every day and shovel; to do the sacking himself and also sort out the useful small lumps which had fallen through the grating so that they could be sold directly at the gate with the cheap 'slack'. Joseph was to be the man.

'Yes, Runt, you! Any objections, Runt?'

The insult had been swallowed at the beginning when it could have been a joke. There were worse nicknames than 'Runt'; Joseph had not smiled but he did let it pass. Even that day he regretted it, and soon Stoddart was using the word like the lead tip on a lash : forever flicking it at the younger man, enjoying the fleck, the blood.

And 'Runt' became his name to the others in the yard – who used it in a neutral manner, though, and he did not mind so much; except that it was always an echo of Stoddart.

The man began to obsess him in a distressing way.

In that first week, unused to such concentrated work, Joseph's hands had given way. The blisters on them were like pouches and he could press them so that they wobbled from side to side under the black membrane of skin. For him, hands were grained with coal; and to get them clean meant bursting the blisters.

The lodging house he lived in – and which took thirteen of his twenty-one shillings for two meals a day and a bed – had no bath and a very erratic, always limited, supply of hot water. Washing averaged two hours a night that first week; on top of a ten-hour day and one hour's travelling. And alone in the cellar with the two tin basins – one full of cold black scum, the other a black sludge of tepid grit, there on the damp flagstones, he cried to himself as the blood came out of the raw blister patches.

Lonely there. And every other thought of Stoddart whom he dreamed to smash and murder, garrot and flay; and feared to confront.

He was not afraid of a beating; of that he was reasonably sure. It would be a severe beating because Stoddart would not fight unless he really meant it and then would have no hesitation in using to the full all his physical superiority. He was not afraid of that, he would tell himself, perhaps a little too often, too emphatically.

As he saw the face, the jaw, the hands, the walk, the look of Stoddart; every other second. Slept and woke on him.

The only impulse which had any power at all to interrupt this spell which was cast on him was the regular droning of his hope 'to be his own man'.

Stoddart terrorized him. Down there in the hole, his mouth and nose most pitifully protected by a length of rag which he tied at the back of his head, he would look up and there would be Stoddart, feet astride on the grating, bending almost double, sometimes squatting, so that he was thrusting himself into Joseph's face. And always 'Runt'. 'Runt.' 'Give over, Runt, there's a lorry coming.' 'Is that the best you can do, Runt? I've seen a sparrow spew more than's on that shovel, Runt. Runts have to work, no?'

The shovel was broad; he could have been out through the tunnel and up the steps in a few seconds; Stoddart would not be expecting it and go down; for good if the thing was swung hard enough. Why did he not at least attempt that?

It was his indecision which helped to paralyse him. For he had never had much cause or opportunity to hesitate before.

In one way he felt that Stoddart would have loved him to lose control of himself and try to fight; recognizing this occasionally gave his passivity the colour of obstinacy; and the more he was provoked, the more he could regard his self-control as tenacious. But though Stoddart would have enjoyed seeing Joseph break, he was quite willing to torture him without the bonus of such an outbreak.

54

The work itself was terrible. Besides the muscular exhaustion, there was this dust which, after a few weeks, felt as if it coated the inside of Joseph's body. When he coughed, the spittle was black: when he breathed, his lungs felt caked and clammy. He lost weight, could scarcely find the energy to wash, spent all Sundays in bed – nor would he have eaten on that day had not some of the men brought him up a plateful from the table.

In another room in the lodgings were two men who worked in the pit and were active in the unions. Late in the evenings, when he had half-eaten his supper and almost crawled up the stairs to bed, he would listen to them arguing as he tried to forget how he ached, to forget Stoddart squatting on that grating 'Runt! Runt!', to obliterate that face from his mind. They spoke of 'action' and 'comradeship' and strike-funds, protest, hours, benefits, Rights: it all sounded so strong, so worked out, so fair. He envied those who could be in unions: no one in the coal yard was; no one in the Big Houses had been, nor on the farms, nor in the road gangs. If you had a job that took you into a union, he thought, then you would have no problems: you could complain about being in the 'hell-hole' for ten weeks if you were in a union; that was the sort of thing you *could* do there. And they would listen.

'Listen – Runt, you work there or you work nowhere.'

The other men grumbled and one or two even worried about the young man now literally almost staggering around, bloodshot eyes, hands bandaged in oily rags. But what could they do?

He knew what it was, in the end; what it was that kept him at it. His father – John, yes. John would say 'What's a bit of hard work? What the hell. Stick it.' And he couldn't lose another job. 'You can't just quit, anyway,' John would have said – Joseph heard him now. Him and Stoddart talking: never arguing against each other – just one talking after the other as the lorries backed onto the grating and the dust fell down onto the heap. 'Call that a sackful, Runt?' 'Good God, man, it's only work.'

Joseph could not say 'God' nor 'Christ'; not aloud. But whatever it was he could swear by, he did – but it was neither an oath nor a vow he swore. 'I'll work, I'll work all right. But it's because I'm bound to. When I'm not – I'll forget it. I'll set up on my own.'

He got a very bad cough which kept him shivering in bed for three days. Then he got up and went back to work.

Stoddart had replaced him.

Chapter Five

Once more at home, he settled for a desultory drifting. He had been hurt by Stoddart and needed time and a little peace to attempt recovery.

Thurston was well placed to sustain him. There were slabs of days numb with boredom but ... gradually ... it was an interesting time. He spent almost all of it in the town. He had not stayed long in one place in Cumberland since childhood, and discovering the town, gradually sorting out the names and relationships, becoming familiar with the gossip and private histories, this street-corner study was to be remembered as a happy time. It seemed a town so packed with life and yet so comprehensible. You could walk from your house to any important building – church, school, pubs, auction, shops, post office. There were about four thousand lived there – a manageable number.

Because of its position, just in from the coast, it was much less badly affected by the depression than the mining towns of West Cumberland. Thurston had been a very plump little town at the end of the nineteenth century when its location – as the natural centre of that mid-western part of Cumberland – had made it such a successful market-town. It was still fed by those farmlands, but the increased use of trucks and lorries was taking trade to the bigger centres – Carlisle, Dumfries, Hawick. Yet though decay was slowly making its way through paint and prospects, there was still layer on layer before the bare bone of a West-Coast Maryport where 85 per cent were unemployed. Only between 15–30 per cent unemployed and of that percentage, a fair proportion of unemployables.

It sat very well, the town, and only to the west did you leave it down-hill. Otherwise you dropped into it from Howrigg

Bank or Standing Stone, Station Hill, Longthwaite or Southend.
Two main streets which formed a T at the Fountain in the
centre: the cross-bar was West Street and King Street; the
upright High Street. There were many versions of how it had
come to its nickname, 'The Throstle's Nest'. The one which
Joseph favoured was that of Gally Wallace who said that his
father and some other Thurston men had come back after the
First World War and found that the train from Carlisle to
Thurston was delayed: so they walked the eleven miles and
as they came over the hill and looked down at the churches,
Highmoor tower, the town with fields and auctions in the
middle of it, with farms just a few yards from King Street and
all shapes of courtyards, alleyways and passages – Gally's father
had thrown off his pack and declared: 'Away, lads – it's the
Throstle's Nest of All England.'

Though knowing people in the town was a matter of pride
to most of those who lived there, Joseph had little clear idea of
the middle-class lot: the solicitors, bank managers, teachers and
doctors; those who owned and ran the small clothing factory
where the women worked or the paper mill where the men
were employed – these drifted around the edge of his landscape,
suits of tweed and white weekday collars, high black prams and
changes of clothes.

He was on nodding terms with some of the shopkeepers;
with George Johnston who had a large shoe-shop and bred
Basset hounds, Toppin the butcher and Pape the ironmonger.
With Mr Harris, one of the three clock-makers in the town,
a white-haired, waxed-white-moustached man, courteous and
thoughtful, who sold no watch he could not mend and served
voluntarily in the public lending library. He knew Joster Hardin
who was a carpenter and old Mr Hutton who took most of
the coffin trade; Harvey Messenger he knew who had a paper-
shop and was never once seen by anyone out of temper; and
Ginny McGuffie's bread-and-cake shop, the best vanilla slices
he had tasted, so fat with sweet custard that just to touch
them was to make them ooze. Soon he could run around the
town in his mind, marking it by shops and houses and faces –
see the old women in black who would greet each other by two

Christian names 'Hello, Mary Jane,' 'I saw Sally Ann,' and the old men on the wall of Tickle's lane, carving wooden ships and daggers for the little boys; and he would deliberately not go to sleep at night so that he could see again the faces of the men on Water Street corner, the women coming out of the covered market, the farmers beating their cattle to the top auction, small boys everywhere running around the town in endless chases.

He hoped for work at the paper-factory, but so did about two score others. While waiting and doing odd jobs which brought in the extra few shillings, he began to make friends: there had not been the leisure for this since early childhood, for at eight or nine he'd become his father's apprentice. He did not find any special friends, though he would have liked a 'best friend', a man to whom he could have told anything, from whom he could have asked anything; but had to make do with acquaintances. Decent at football, game for any scheme, useful at all sorts of work, he was not short of company. And when his father shook his head and regretted the solitary trudging of his son from no to no, the son would like as not be living, as John thought quietly himself, the life of Riley.

Early in winter he took up with Dido and his gang. In Thurston there were many like Dido, called 'Potters' or 'Squatters' or 'Gippos' by ordinary people; others called them rascals or criminals or vagabonds; respectable old people who feared and disliked them referred to them, if at all, as 'wastrels' or 'scavengers': children who idolized them, daringly whispered that they were the 'boyos' or the Hard Men.

For generations, an important gypsy camp had been set up near Thurston every year – at Black Tippo, just beyond the cemetery. Hundreds of gypsies came, for weeks, sometimes for months, and the women would sell their pegs around the district and accost people with demands for silver on the palm; the men would trade in horses and dogs, be accused of every crime and accident there was, and move around with their animals and children at their heels as wild-looking as a tribe of Red Indians. Romany words came into the Thurston slang – 'scran' for food, 'mort' for girl, 'parney' for rain, 'duckel' for dog and 'cower' for anything at all – already the local dialect was notorious for its impenetrability. And some of the gypsies stayed, to squat in abandoned houses; to live as free as they chose, it seemed, as daily they scoured the countryside for the leavings which sustained them.

Among them were all sorts, from the Hard Men who were up regularly for theft, fighting and assault and sometimes sent down to Durham Jail; through all the sports and boasters to those near to jokers, like Dido and his two pals, Lefty and Glum – who were yet clever enough to float where others were sinking.

Joseph had been walking back from Waverton after playing football one night when Dido had come up in his pony and trap and stopped to give him a lift. Then instead of going Joseph's way, Dido had turned off and made for the Wampool, for a part which he'd heard was full of salmon. On private property they had poached, Joseph keeping a look-out while Dido walked into the river with boots, socks and trousers on, and tried to tickle them by moonlight. Something relaxed and careless about Joseph at this time had sealed an attraction which he had always felt towards the boyos, ever since he'd first heard tales about them. And their nicknames were never to be forgotten: there was a Diddler besides a Dido (and to each other as to the world in general they appeared to have no other name but this, none) Patchy the brother of Lefty; and Gripe the father of Glum; a Nimble a Nosher and a Tont: Bloss, Tuttu and Swank; Muck, Fly, Old Age; and Kettler, the star – way out of Joseph's reach. In some families there were three generations of single-minded unemployables, now the clowns, now the villains, but all, to Joseph at that time, a great relief.

They were outside the struggle and he too wanted to be detached, for a while, for a rest.

Chapter Six

He had first taken notice of her when coming back from Mickle-thewaite with Dido. They had cleared some old byres belonging to a Mr Purdom and the trap was high with broken mangers.

It was evening, about half-past six: February, dark, snow-covered; hedges and roads black threads on the downy surface. The moon came up as he turned on to the main Carlisle–Thurston road and the cold rays lit the snow so that he could see clearly. The pony walked steadily, the mangers swaying perilously on the cart. Joseph and Dido took alternate puffs at a cigarette and they went slowly through this level spread of snow.

He heard the voices, the noise of the bicycles, and then the bells as they came up to pass. It was a gang of girls who worked in Carr's Biscuit Factory in Carlisle and cycled the eleven miles there to start at seven in the morning; now on their way home. As she passed the cart, Betty turned and smiled at him. Her face was white, pinched, would later, in warmth, smart back to life; her headscarf had come loose and her black hair blew around her neck: she rang and rang again her bell then pulled ahead of him, the others following. He could hear them free-wheeling down the hill, the rubber tyres crushing the crisp slush, and the laughter as they straggled up the next rise until he saw Betty again, cresting the skyline, circling on her bike, a silhouette waiting for the other girls to catch up. They straggled to join her and all seemed to stay still for a moment until, with shouting and more ringing of bells they swooped out of sight and finally out of hearing.

Betty's mother had died a few weeks after her birth; un-balanced by this her father had left the town and gone south where he was killed in a fire without ever seeing his daughter again. One of his brothers had given a sum of money to Mrs Nicholson and she had brought the girl up.

Mrs Nicholson had then two sons but no daughter: she so longed for one that she gave Betty her own name and treated her as a daughter – quelling every reference to the girl's real parents in those early years.

Betty was bright, active and amiable: Mrs Nicholson took in washing and the girl used to deliver it for her when she grew big enough to manage the baskets: she did the shopping for the woman she always called 'Mother', and in various ways got to know and love Thurston – every alleyway, house and row of steps, the halls and arches, yards, side streets and shops. She was a pleasant girl, not at all shy, and soon became well known, well liked. For the rest of her life she remembered those childhood years in the town as a capsule of perfect happiness.

Mr Nicholson, whom she always called 'Uncle', had worked at a factory where he had had an accident; there was no compensation and for two or three years while he recovered and then looked for work the house was in trouble. His wife decided to 'take in' unwanted children; not uncommon as a source of income. Many mothers who could not afford to or find the circumstances which allowed them to take care of their own illegitimate children would pay a married woman a weekly amount to do so. Mrs Nicholson took in three.

The illegitimate children arrived when Betty was eleven; the fact of their illegitimacy frightened her, for though the town accommodated ten different churches from Catholic to Quaker, people of Betty's sort – the respectable working people, the majority – were united in a ferocious puritanism. The little girl cared for the new arrivals as devotedly as if they had been lepers.

And when she herself was told that Mrs Nicholson was not her real mother, she nursed this knowledge secretly for almost a year – and throughout that time she daily believed herself to be one of the paid-for children. When she could no longer contain it and burst into terrible sobs one night, her 'mother' corrected her mistake but the new information, that both her parents were dead, only deepened the wrong and the damage was confirmed.

About a week after she had 'been told', Betty who was a strong swimmer, got into difficulties in a dammed-up part of the river and almost drowned. She ought not to have found herself in such trouble – she had swum there many times.

Later as the girl became more timid at the edges of her experience, more fragile, Mrs Nicholson smiled to herself with relief: she saw it happening to all the girls of about fourteen, this preparation for the leap into courtship. She was relieved to observe that the business of discovering her real parents to be dead had had such a temporary effect.

The first time they were alone together was just before Easter after a Pea and Pie supper and social in the Congregational Hall. Betty stood at the top of the steps leading out of the hall, waiting for her girl friends, and glanced sharply at Joseph as he bounded up towards her, the look accusing him of trickery in catching her so on her own. But he was as surprised as she and stood away from her, leaning against the railings, trying not to shiver in the cold night.

He had first hunted her in the expected places, circling the town on his bike in the dark evenings, seeing her come out of her house, the pictures, a friend's, the Guides – and at that stage she had accepted to be the prey and run away from him, slipping down an alley which he would turn into to find himself bumped off his bike by steps or jammed against a wall with the escape wide enough only for one. And when he left his machine to race after her he would always lose her in this town riddled with tiny sideways, interjoined and dark.

Then he had joined the male gang which was the counterpart of the female gang in which Betty concealed herself; but here she was no longer single prey, and gave every appearance of her preference for numbers. As immediately as she had sensed the weight and urgency of his first intention and manoeuvres, as sullenly now did she seem to have no notion of it. Any attempt he made to single her out was instantly defeated.

So they stood outside the Congregational Hall and looked

down Water Street, waiting for the others. Nor was it until a full five minutes had passed that they realized that a plan had been made to leave them alone.

Each recognized this at the same time and, answering together an unuttered question, Joseph said, 'I'll go and tell them to hurry up.'

But she shook her head. To be the girl who had demanded that the others give up their scheme would be far more shameful than an accommodation. Already she could hear the giggles from the cloakroom at the bottom of the stairs. 'I suppose we'd better go,' she said gloomily. 'But just to the end of Water Street.'

He wheeled his bike in the gutter and so kept to the outside of the pavement: she walked beside the house-fronts: the street had no lights and they were guided by the lone gas lamp at the end, where it joined the High Street.

And they came to that High Street without having exchanged a single word.

'Well,' said Joseph sternly, as one who has kept his faith, 'you said just to the end of Water Street and this is it.'

'Yes,' her tone was penitent.

'Good night then, Betty,' he said, and slowly but decisively he wheeled his bicycle out into the middle of the road and prepared to mount.

His use of her name gave her no option but to use his if she wanted to call him back. She watched him bend over his back wheel to put on the red light.

'Have you ever thought of going *away* somewhere for work, Joseph?' she asked, timidly. He turned and smiled at her. 'Or the army,' she asked, more confidently. 'They always want people – why don't you go and join the army?'

'Well, others can, that's all,' she said.

'And some others can't.'

Betty was not interested in argument. Most men in Thurston had jobs: it made her uncomfortable to qualify references to Joseph by saying that he was out of work. Had they lived in Maryport where unemployment was almost universal, it's likely that she would have been just as uneasy if he had been *in* work. As in dress, manners, ambition and tastes, so in this matter also, she would not have anything out of the ordinary : would not do anything to draw special attention to herself.

'Look,' he would say. 'What else can I do? I say I'll go south – but you won't come with me.'

'I should think not. We aren't even engaged.'

'If I *did* join the army I'd never see you.'

'They have holidays sometimes.'

'But Betty . . . !'

'And you should think better of yourself than to go around with Dido and them.'

'Why?'

'They're dirty.'

'O God!'

'Well they are. Nobody's *that* poor. Soap's cheap enough.'

'It isn't that important.'

'Is it not? Well they pinch things, Joseph Tallentire, you know they do, and it doesn't matter if they don't do it when you're there, it's not right.'

She hated any hint of illegality and thought Joseph was determined to see Dido and the others a few more times, to maintain his dignity, her clear opposition confirmed some of his own inclination and he knew the roaming was at an end.

'Well I'll try farm-work again.'

'Not *farm*-work!'

'What's wrong with it?'

'Nothing.'

'Well?'

'Once you get started with it, you can do nothing else,' said Betty, rather desperately.

'So?'

'*I* don't want to be stuck in a cottage in the middle of nowhere.'

'Ah! So that's it.'

'Yes it is.' She hesitated. 'I'm sorry, Joseph; I'm not much help, am I?'

'Never mind.'

One of the proofs of love, he thought, was to serve; and though Betty seemed demanding she wanted little. To stay in Thurston with those she had known all her life, engaging her, protecting her; he could give her that at least.

He would have given her much more. His life until now seemed a procession leading to her: the figures along the way no more than those who had to be passed by on his way to this ...

He decided on the big rayophane paper factory. The managing director lived in a most spacious and grand manor house set in its own large grounds in the middle of the town. Joseph stationed himself outside there every morning and every morning followed Mr Lancing through the town, down to the factory. It was a walk of about half a mile which Lancing used as his constitutional. Joseph kept about three paces behind him, having looked him blankly and silently in the face as he had come out of the large wooden gates. In the evenings, Lancing was driven back, and when the car stopped for the chauffeur to get out and open the gates – there would be Joseph, standing beside the right-hand pillar, making no attempt to help the chauffeur, looking directly into the car at Lancing.

After a fortnight, the director's curiosity awoke, or his nerve broke. He got out of the car and came across to the waiting man.

'Who *are* you?'

'Joseph Tallentire.'

'Why do you follow me about like this?'

'I want a job at your factory.'

'So do a lot of people, young man.' Mr Lancing's use of 'young man' was cutting: he himself was just in his early thirties. 'I think I could do a good job,' said Joseph – the words forced out, throwing off coils of embarrassment and self-consciousness.

Mr Lancing smiled. 'Do you indeed?' He paused. 'I suppose you'd better come and see me on Monday. Eight o'clock sharp. And *don't* follow me down the bloody street again!'

Joseph swallowed all that.

He began work on the Monday as a junior slitter, and in that factory found his place in industrial England.

At that time the machinery was antiquated and the men needed to be mechanics as well as do the job they were paid for; the conditions of work were foul, with chemicals clogging the air, long barely lit sheds, rarely cleaned corridors, freezing in winter, broiling in summer. A noise whose first impact must have sliced most of the more tender nerves leading from the ears and after that hammered at the mind until it was a wonder the men did not come out with pulped brains dripping from their nostrils. All had the knowledge that the job must be held to at whatever price, whatever humiliation because there were plenty of people ready to take their place and they were lucky to be in work.

To this place Joseph came for eight eight-hour shifts a week, one every day but Wednesday when he did a double shift, and his going in and his going out were attended by the punching of his card into a machine which registered to the minute his daily span of servitude and rang a bell.

When he went there you got the same rate (in his shop) for the job – 4d. an hour – whether you were a boy or man. The foreman got 5d., otherwise differentiation according to ability, output or age was unknown. There was much talk about the injustice of it – but no action. There was no single union which embraced all the skills in the place and such union members as there were knew that to call in their branch secretary would be worse than useless : there was nothing he could do in such a place of varied trades. Not one shop steward was there in the entire place. Troublemakers were fired and no questions answered.

Joseph almost enjoyed the work for the first year or so – enjoyed getting to know the machines, enjoyed being in work. He had a flair for mending the big machine he worked on and made two improvements on it. One was to invent a roller which worked in synchronization with the feeder and so enabled the paper to roll along steadily in even lengths, thus making the slitting much simpler; this saved time, increased production, cut out a great deal of irritation and passed without notice from the owners. The other thing he did was to make a much more efficient passage for the rolls of paper from the machine to the stacking bay : this involved the simplest mechanical adjustments and gained its chief effect from a reorganization in the system of stacking itself : for this he was given five pounds.

Now he could start courting Betty, slow and hesitant it had to be, but her need for him showed itself often enough for him to forgive the reluctance.

At the end of the year, Betty found a job in Thurston's cloth mill, starting at 9s. a week; top wage (after five years) 23s. a week. She gave 8s. 6d. of the 9s. to Mrs Nicholson and to supplement her pocket money worked in a bakery for two nights a week.

Her move gave them more time together.

Chapter Seven

They met on Sunday mornings beside the Fountain at about eight. This fountain was a gift to the people of Thurston from the man who had given the town its swimming baths, helped found its boys' grammar school, restored its Anglican church, sat on many boards and helped many people, lived in the huge and fantastical house on a hill to the south of the town, kept a deer park there always open to the public and died bankrupt just after the First World War.

The base of the Fountain was like a tomb and it was defended by black, pike-topped railings. Small gaps to east and west led in to wizened heads of bearded old men from whose black bronze mouths water dribbled when a large button was pressed on their foreheads. Above this funereal base, there was a shape something between a thin pyramid and a fat spire – about twenty feet high; a stumpy cross had been stuck on the top. It stood in the centre of the town, at the junction of the three main streets, and was the natural place to meet, especially if you were on bikes. You could circle around it, hold on to the railings without dismounting, do any last-minute checks and repairs on the triangle of space which lay to one side of it like a parking place for its shadow, and watch for the others coming along one of the three ways, cheering at them in the distance, the full sound like a reveille along the empty morning streets.

It was not a cycling club but a gang who liked to go biking together. People Betty had known all her life – John Connolly and Jack Atkinson, the Middleton girls and Mary Graham. They were ten this June morning and Betty and Joseph, like two of the other couples, rode a tandem. Sandwiches, a big bottle of lemonade, capes and a football in the large bag which rested on a frame of its own over the back mudguard: they were set for the day. The bicycles circled the fountain, waiting for the church bells to strike eight, and then they peeled off down the main street, down Burnfort along the Carlisle road, making for Whitley Bay, the East Coast, about seventy miles away.

Within a couple of hours they were well on the road which ran parallel to the Roman Wall: bound straight as a ruler for Wallsend, but dipping and rising like a switchback. The tandem was an old model, bought second-hand and built for survival rather than speed. It required heavy pedalling, for if anything was to be got out of the day, they could not loiter. Nor did a slow pace appeal to any of them: the idea was to go as fast as you could without breaking your back.

Now that he had been at the factory for over two years Joseph could claim one Sunday in two in winter and one in four in summer: he took them all, luxuriating in the strange dimension of a full day with Betty. Strange Sundays they were too at his home. Frank stayed in bed – the garage being closed. Joseph got out the tandem to bike into Thurston and collect Betty; only John went to work – to the farm where he mucked out the stables and helped with the milking.

Joseph rode in front, Betty behind. He preferred it that way – because he could set a steady pace and stick to it. When she led, they would be forever drawing ahead and then dropping back; sometimes she would decide to get off at quite a small rise, or she would accelerate as they approached a big hill and he knew that there would be no stopping her until they got to the top of it. You could not forget yourself and day-dream or look at the countryside or chat comfortably to someone riding alongside you: not when you were liable to lurch forward any second or suddenly find that she had decided to free-wheel. In none of their time together, despite the usual quarrels and disagreements, had anything even begun to approach the irritation he experienced on those rides on the tandem. What made it worse was that she appeared tireless. There was never the prospect of calm which could have rested on a knowledge of ultimate superiority. He had tried to exhaust her once or twice and ended up blowing hard, turning on his saddle to meet such a mischievous and pleased smile as made him want to dump the damned tandem in the nearest river. But he could not do that, nor could he sell it – to do so would be an admission of defeat.

At the time he bought it Joseph had thought it a romantic idea. He had seen them spinning along through country lanes, bound together, the idea of two in one symbolizing and strengthening their affection.

> Daisy. Daisy.
> Give me your answer do,
> I'm half crazy,
> All for the love of you:
> It won't be a stylish marriage,
> I can't afford a carriage,
> But you'll look sweet
> Upon the seat
> Of a bicycle made for two. (Ta-ra-ra-ra-ra ...)

But from that point of view it was a disaster.

What it did do was to refine Joseph's attitude towards Betty. Again, he thought it ridiculous that she should learn about her through a tandem – his fantasies had told him that he would learn about her as they sat side by side on a river bank, or in 'the nook of an inn-parlour' or they would be given knowledge of each other 'on fairest days under whitest clouds'. But it was on the tandem that discoveries had been made.

They biked along the desolate road and stopped at Housesteads, the Roman cavalry camp, to have a breather. There were a few sightseers looking over the site but though Joseph urged the others to go up and have a look, he was outvoted. It would take up too much time. He insisted a little and so was howled down. As they set off, Betty slowed the tandem's pace so that they fell back behind the others a little.

'What did you get so worked up about?' she whispered to the back of his head.

'I wasn't worked up.'

'Well?'

'You should see things like that. *You* would have liked to, wouldn't you?'

'I might,' said Betty after a little hesitation. Then, honestly, 'Yes, I would. But nobody else wanted to go.'

'We'll come on our own one day.'

'Yes,' she replied, unexpectedly. 'I'd like that.'

He twisted around fully towards her to make confession of a dream private to himself for years until this moment: 'I would like to have been a village schoolmaster, you know,' he said.

Betty smiled and he leaned back to kiss her. 'Watch out!' The bike swung towards the ditch and he only just managed to get to the handlegrips in time to swerve away from it.

Through the towns along the Tyne they went, and quickly, silently, for there, writ large, were circumstances but a thread-snap away from their own. The towns were as in mourning – Jarrow, 'the town they killed' – and at this late morning hour the streets were lined with miners waiting between the shilling for the football match the previous afternoon at St James' Park and the threepence for a gill when the pubs opened, for many the span of their week's entertainment. There was an injustice and shame about it which Betty felt as directly as the cold. Such misery as could plainly be seen oppressed her and she was made sick by it, so that her stomach tightened, her hands sweated and she bit at her bottom lip nervously, feeling ashamed to be biking so carefree past these men. Joseph turned around to say something to her, feeling the drag on the pedals, but seeing her expression he guessed precisely what she was thinking and this sympathy overwhelmed him with love for her. He changed his remark.

'It's terrible, isn't it?'

'Yes,' she said. 'They should be shot for letting this happen.'

The words brought the relief of anger to her and the thought of what should be done to those who were responsible for governing the country helped to displace the weight from her feelings. She wished that she were old enough to have a vote: when she was, she would throw it down for Labour like a weapon for them to use.

They raced the last mile or so to the sea, heads down, rubber handlegrips warming to the clenched fist – a spontaneous rush for the coast. The weight which had clung to their legs over the last twenty miles fell off as they sprinted towards the holiday resort, along the front to the grassy banks at the northern end of the town where they turned their bikes upside down on the ground – to keep sand and dirt from getting in the chain or hubs – and lay down to eat their sandwiches.

After the sandwiches they went to the beach and played in the cold North Sea. There was only one way to go in – full speed and altogether – and they joined hands and raced across the wet sand right into the water, running until they were thrown forward by the pressure of water around their legs. They splashed each other, the men duck-dived and grabbed the girls' legs, heaving them clear and throwing them up into the air. They swam but a little way from the shore and kept as closely together as a school of dolphin. The beach was filling up; it was the afternoon and all along it were thin white bodies, men in black woolly swimming trunks, women in full covering bathing costumes temporarily balded by their white rubber bathing caps, children paddling along the edges of the sea, grandmothers deep in sand and packets of food, bundles of clothes, the whole a shivering exposure to freedom as if they were not holidaymakers so much as refugees, the very movements jerky and over-strenuous as if the most had to be made of this day for there might be none like it to follow.

So the gang from Thurston, having dashed along the seventy miles, bolted their food, bashed into the unenticing waves – now raced from the water and started a game of football with the girls as energetic as the men, and then a form of handball, men against women.

Afterwards when they had changed and dried themselves came those embarrassing moments when they split up. For an hour or so they would wander off in pairs, alone with their girl-friends – and yet the hesitation and false starts involved in bringing about this uncomplicated and unexceptionable situation gave them the appearance of being set on an insoluble problem. They hovered around the bicycles, the women wrapped up what was left of the meal and put it in the bags, a bottle of lemonade was passed from hand to hand, it became imperative to move a few yards away from each other and look out to sea unblinkingly, broken mutters and glances tore at the even weave which had held them together all day and eventually it became a matter for courage. Who was going to make plain what was on the minds of all, and make himself the target for mumbles and jokes by over-heartily announcing that he felt like going for a walk on his own, and did she (his girl) fancy coming along? Before this happened the men and women split into two groups and the bicycles between them were like a magic line – once crossed new laws would operate.

Joseph always held his peace. He was irritated at this procedure and would have seen that it did not even begin to happen had he had his own way. The situation was clear and obvious and it was stupid to waste time in this way. But he had learned his lesson: when he *had* gone first and abruptly to propose to Betty that they should go off on their own she had said no. Which had turned muted awkwardness into an open argument, with *everyone* feeling in an impossible position. So he waited.

At last alone with Betty he feared even to put his arm around her so much did he want her, so afraid to frighten her. More than just accepting her strictness about making love he believed it intrinsic to her attraction. But even in his kisses he feared to bruise her. Lying with her, there, in the high grass in a hollow of the dunes, his body melted to hers and a slow intoxication suffused him, the world became this deep drift of coloured, tasted love and all that was hidden and trapped in him broke free at this time and found a place in the pressure of his lips on her cheek.

Though they were not yet engaged, they intended to be and Joseph wanted her to be seen. Boxing Day was just right.

Everyone was waiting for them. The smaller children in giggles, Frank determined to see that Joseph was given fair play, May, who had come with her husband and baby for the day, trying rather unsuccessfully to forget the sharp clash she had just had with the 'step-mother' as she always called her. John had his good suit on and was looking very conscious of his 'smartness' there in the kitchen.

Joseph had wanted to come out on their tandem – but she had insisted on walking.

She got as far as the end of the lane, saw the cottage, felt the eyes peeping through the windows and refused to move further. Nor would she go back. Joseph argued – but: 'I *can't* go there,' she said. Then, half-derisively, allowing room for her to see that he would have no objection to being followed, would quite welcome it, in fact, if she cared to come along with him, he drifted down the lane alone; and was still alone ten yards from the cottage. He turned and saw her stuck to the same spot as if her feet were in cement.

Smarting under this – for he had *seen* as well as felt the eyes at the windows, he marched back and lectured her on her responsibilities to herself, to him. 'They'll think I've taken up with some half-wit,' he said. 'Good God, Betty, if thou's frightened of this – how'll we ever get married?' 'Well I won't get married, then,' she said, 'not if it's as bad as this.' It was a cold day: she had on her only coat, bought the previous spring and intended for the summer. Her face was beginning to turn blue. 'My mother's *expecting* you,' said Joseph. 'I'm sorry,' Betty wailed '– but I *can't move.*' 'I'll bloody well push you then.' Joseph went behind her and pushed. She stumbled a few yards forward and then stopped. He pushed again. Again she trotted a few steps and then halted. Once more. 'We must look right fools,' he said. 'I'll walk on my own,' she said, 'but don't hold my arm, now *please*, Joseph, *please* don't: it makes us look like an old married couple. And not like that. That's not what I meant at all.' (His arm had gone around her waist.) 'Now just walk normally – and I'll go without pushing.'

'Mebbe we should march,' he suggested. 'Don't be silly,' she answered, speaking out of the corner of her mouth. Joseph imitated this and put on an American accent: 'Do you think they'll shoot before we can draw, baby?' he asked. She giggled. 'Don't make me laugh, please,' she said. 'I'll whistle, baby, to throw them off the scent.' He began to whistle *Dixie* and marched in time to it. 'If I had a handbag, I'd clatter you with it,' Betty muttered. 'I'll buy you one for your birthday,' he replied. 'Ooh! You're awful, Joseph Tallentire.' 'Ooh! You're lovely, Betty Nicholson.' They were now but a few yards from the cottage, Betty as stiff-shouldered as a guardsman. 'Give us a kiss,' he said. '*Joseph*: please!' 'Just a quick one. To show everybody how much you think of us.' 'I'll show you what I think when I get you on your own.' 'I can't wait,' he replied. 'Let's just walk right on and go down to the tarn.' 'Do I look alright?' 'Smashing.' 'But *really*?' 'Really?' He paused, they went through the gate and were almost at the door. 'Really,' he replied slowly, 'there's a bit of soot on your nose. Mother!' He opened the door. 'We're here!'

And she looked so solitary, so fragile in her determination as she entered the kitchen before him that it was all he could do to stop himself folding his arms around her and holding her to him.

It was May who ran to meet Betty and in that action was both a generosity to see the girl of her brother's choice properly welcomed and a pointed declaration of the fact that she stood closer in relationship to Joseph than his step-mother. May, even plumper now, took Betty's hand cordially, scrutinized her quite frankly and nodded three or four times with unmistakable significance. Having *seen* her, the younger children bolted until tea-time. Mrs Tallentire took her coat, Frank took her gloves, Joseph took her scarf, May took it from him and, in very plain dumb-show indicated that Betty ought to be found a seat. John had already found a seat, May's husband searched for a match, Joseph gave him his box, and as the waters of the Red Sea closed over the Pharaoh's army so that where there had been movement there was none so as Betty sat down all sank into their positions and there was a deep silence.

Then. 'It's quite mild,' said May to the rescue, 'for the time of year.'

'T'lass looks frozen,' said John.

'Put some more logs on't fire then!' May rapped out to Frank who leapt up – and obeyed.

May nudged her husband, wanting him both to help her at this time of need and to show his form.

'Is thou any relation to 't Nicholsons o' Warwick Bank?' he asked.

'Shurrup dad!' said May, buffeting him with her elbow this time and glaring at him for taking his cue so crassly.

'There was a fire in our garidge a fortneet ago,' said Frank, clearing his throat, manfully.

'I heard about that.' Betty turned to him with gratitude.

'Just small,' he said, his effort spent. 'Nowt to talk aboot.'

'Tea'll be ready in five minutes,' said Mrs Tallentire.

'Aa'll gaa and see what Aa can do to bring it on faster,' said May striding out to the scullery.

'That's a very nice dress,' said Mrs Tallentire. 'Did you make it yourself?'

'Yes,' Betty whispered.

'I wish I could make them like that. Where'd you get the material?'

'Studholmes. They were having a sale. One and a penny a yard.' A reasonable price; already colouring that she might appear showy.

'*Very* good quality. Can I touch it?'

Betty nodded and went across to the older woman who felt the hem with unaffected admiration.

'That *is* nice. I've never seen such nice material.'

'*What's* nice?' May demanded, hands on hips, filling the scullery doorway.

'This material,' said Mrs Tallentire.

'You'll waste it if you keep rubbin' at it,' said May.

'I don't mind,' said Betty.

'Hm. They'll have it off your back if thou's not careful lass. Off thee back!' and she turned back into the scullery where she could be heard haranguing the jelly. She blamed herself for her twistiness, laying all manner of strictures upon herself, but she could not bear the other woman to take her mother's place; again and again she came back as full of good resolutions as a New Year choirboy and – within minutes – she was lost to her temper.

Tea made things easier because there were things to do – but even so it would have been a poor do had not John taken the matter in hand. He spoke to all of them, but looked at Betty, and they took to each other from then on. Of what came most

77

easily he spoke to her – the work he did with the horses – and described the big Shows he had been to that autumn.

After tea May claimed her, and did it so sweetly and skilfully that Joseph, who recognized the effort involved, was moved that she should be so concerned about him. His mother took the smaller children and May's baby for a breath of air; his father took off his stiff collar, poked the fire, stared a while at the flames and then fell asleep; he himself went with Mary's husband to see the progress of a van which Frank was building from scrap.

The two women talked over the dishes: May washed. 'You'll not be used to such a gang,' said May, using a delicate tone and using it tentatively as if she were handling the very best china.

'Oh, there were a lot of us at home – at Mother Nicholson's –' The girl .paused and May scrubbed a plate severely, already furious with herself as the apparent cause of Betty's distress. But Betty felt the woman's kindliness and rushed to heal the breach she herself had made. 'When anybody else came we had to have two sittings.'

'*Did* you?' May was delighted. 'So did we.'

Later, May said, 'It doesn't matter if you have money, you know. We had nowt – Michael and me – we had nowt then and we've nowt now but we got married.' She paused and then, blushing, added softly, 'Mind, I was older than you.'

'Where did you meet him?'

'At this big house where Joseph used to work. Michael was assistant gardener – he came after Joseph went away and it was just luck that I'd decided to stop on a bit because I was that mad the way they got rid of Joseph, he was the best footman ever! And *smart* . . .!'

'So Michael came to work in the gardens . . .?'

'Yes. Well you see I'd been told he came from Cumberland – "a native of your county, May"' (a mincing imitation – so off-key that both women giggled, though quietly, not to wake John) 'and he came from Wiggonby, see, that's where Joseph and my, our, that is, *real* mother was born – not meaning to be nasty to anybody but that's where she was born. Mind, he's older than me, Michael.'

'But that right,' said Betty. 'I'm glad Joseph's older than me.'

'Ay, but *considerably* older.'

'He doesn't look it.'

'No?' May smiled proudly. 'I'll tell him that,' she paused, then frowned. 'Mind, it'll make his head swell.'

And as they stacked away the dishes, 'Now look after him!' For the first time, May spoke sharply and Betty drew back.

'No, no, please, don't take offence.' May put out her arms, took the hands of the younger woman in her own. 'But, you know, I helped to bring him up, you see.'

Though rather frightened by the urgency of May's emotion, Betty was impressed by its sincerity and making an effort, she stood her ground, even let her hands lie in the grasp of the other woman though she longed to pull them away.

'I know,' Betty smiled; but her lips were dry and so the smile restrained.

'If you love him,' ignoring her own nerves, May broke from the knots which so often bound her – 'if you love him, look after him : and if you don't, tell him. He's a good man, Betty, and he deserves that.'

'Yes.' Betty nodded, eased her hands free and then had to glance away, away from May's open gaze.

At first, Betty was reluctant to talk about the visit; or rather she was reluctant to talk about it as incessantly and at the length demanded by Joseph's 'What did you think of father? and May? and Frank – isn't he a *good* man, really? and May's husband – he'll be right for her, don't you think? she gets hurt so easily, he looked a kind man, didn't he? He works in the woods up near a place called Crossbridge, in the fells – we could go and see them. May says it's marvellous – and our *real* mother lived there once.'

It was his innocent reference to his 'real' mother which unsealed her reticence. And it was that missing woman who marked that visit as something final in Betty's mind; for Joseph must have suffered too and yet he kept his face open to the world. She would marry him.

*   *   *

As the time of their wedding approached he was conscious of all sorts of impulses which had been forgotten or never before appreciated, and walked feeling that his legs, his eyes, his taste, his body, everything about him was freed and tingled as freshly as if he had just raced out of the sea. Merely to walk that summer, and see the sun slant down between the trails of cloud, a blackbird landing on the tip of a bough of hawthorn, springing the bough, the leaves waving, the pulse beneath the feathers – with his mind creating its senses and then slow-plunging back into them, that was enough and a wonder.

These sensations drew on his past, thickened his present, obscured the future. And at his father's cottage he culled the pauses in the routines of activity, watched the small children play unawares, drew from his father not the positive claims on circumstances which he liked and admired but that dedication which threaded through the older man's tussle with life like gold through a dull tapestry.

Sometimes he thought he was walking in a waking dream and was surprised to find that he did things, that he set off for a place and reached it, that he talked and made dates, that he played cricket and went biking. So static did he feel, so slumbrously, voluptuously still – and there was no guilt, no worry – no concern other than his own living. I am here now. That underlay all he did. Without stress or accent on any of the words, each one the simplest declaration, murmured softly when alone – I am here now.

He saw a man walking with his child towards the town, and slowed his pace, would have stopped had that not brought attention to himself who wanted to be unseen before this sight. The man was a labourer, old, possibly the little girl's grandfather. She held up at his hand and skipped, using the hand to steady herself. Then she wobbled away from the man and went through the long grass on the verge, pushing her bare white knees against the long sheen-backed blades of sweet grass, picked up a dandelion, trotted back with it to the old man and made him stop and blow the time away – until only the dry bleached heart was left, and the shrivelled petals. Joseph saw this and it rolled into his mind like the slowest wave which had travelled across a long ocean and still would not break but forever curl around his senses.

He began to look out for such moments, for expressions on people's faces, for the shape of a cloud, for the wind in the candles of a chestnut tree, the glide of a perch in the water, drizzle cold on his warm face, muscles pulling so slightly in his legs, the light on Betty's face, the moon quartered against the empty sky, a dog curling slowly on its tail before setting its muzzle on its soft paws. There were times when he felt like a man who had contained all the earth's feelings, times when he felt that each pleasure was a gift loaned him, a nest half-hanging over a gutter, beer sliding through the froth to part between his lips – he must look for them and remember them from the past and make a store of them, not as a miser, to gloat, but as a man who had discovered that if so much is necessary, then there is so much more unnecessary, for merely in looking and feeling he was conscious, and the more conscious he could make himself, the more alive he would be.

And in this mood, which sometimes weighed him down with such a surfeit of pleasure that he thought he would never move from that spot for fear of breaking the spell, with this and Betty's love and her to receive his own love, then nothing more from the world could be wanted. So he swam, floated, drifted, was still, and the matters of the world struck him not as challenges and exclamations, demanding a spark from the flint of his desire, but lapped him around and made even more intense the richness of his perceptions. Later, he was to look back on this time and wonder that he could have passed so long in such a state, and at times he could not understand it – thinking that he must have entered a long dream.

It was the same feeling which had gathered in him as he dreamt through the summer afternoons while the sounds and smells from outside the school had intoxicated him as he sat at his desk, his legs weary of idleness under the coarse weave of his patched trousers; which he had drawn from the land he grew up in and dragged out of it as he had worked at the farms in that first eighteen months; which had spun at the back of his mind while he cleaned the heavy silver in the gloomy big house.

Now his love for Betty made it so powerful that he was convinced that this was what his life would be, that marriage would intensify it still more, that he and Betty had found the perfect way and so would keep to it.

Late autumn, 1938, married for about a year and a half, Douglas six months old. She had insisted on that name though it was most uncommon in the district; it came from the fictive world of films and magazines which had nourished Betty's secret, repressed feelings : in the naming of her first son she planted her groping claim on that world.

Joseph had changed jobs and worked in the 'Stores' at the new aerodrome about six miles away; a five and a half day week and now, this Saturday dinner-time, free for the longest regular break he'd ever in any job enjoyed. But he ate his egg and potatoes with no pleasure and at each sip of tea glanced across the dark kitchen to the corner where Betty was feeding the child, bottle held firmly against his mouth, such a bitter silence about her that the sound of his eating was a taunt and the child's suck a provocation.

It was dark enough to warrant putting on the gas – but it always made Joseph feel uneasy to have a light in the day.

He still did not know what was the real cause of the row, but he would have to get it out of her for it would just sink deeper and deeper, the longer he left it, become increasingly difficult to discover, result in one of those marks of their life, like the white trace of a scar. Though his own temper was quick, it was short : hers seemed to ignite areas unknown to him and they would feed the temper exhaustingly, sometimes against her will. 'C'mon, Betty,' he said, as lightly as he could manage. 'Get it out.'

She said nothing. He hesitated and then imagining himself to be making a heroic effort (it was this which tired him – so soon did her defences demand the very last ounce of his attack) he repeated.

'Come *on*, Betty.'

But she would not.

He pushed his plate away, the food he had eaten already

heavy and disagreeable. There were no more cigarettes in his packet – Betty did not smoke. He needed a smoke, he thought, to settle down for the fight – to sustain himself through all the tedious sparring necessary if she was to be drawn. Yet to scramble about the kitchen for a stump would undercut his position.

(He liked to think of it in such terms; to pretend it was a contest which he enjoyed. For a contest had an end, and if he pretended to enjoy it then the despair which fled into him would pass.)

'What did I say?' No answer. '*Was* it something I said? I said nothing.'

She took the bottle from the child, sat him up in the correct position and began to pat him for the wind. The half-bald head joggled uneasily in shoulders hidden under two mounds of white knitted wool.

There was nowhere he could go but the back kitchen: the house had no sitting-room. And to go upstairs would be to sulk. 'C'mon, Betty. You know you'll tell me sometime – tell me now. Eh? Will you?' Gently said, those last words – a final effort.

And though realizing this, understanding that Joseph would now move beyond patience, recognizing that his cautious approach invited some reply and feeling rather foolish now that such a situation should have arisen from what at this moment appeared a mean cause – still Betty could make no answer. Something inside her luxuriated in the sullenness and would not be revealed.

'Well,' he said, jumping up, his eyes rapidly scanning the top of the mantelpiece to see if there were any stumps (there was one behind the clock), 'I might as well go and talk 'til a stranger as talk to myself.'

He took his jacket from the back of the chair and pulled it on. Betty still patted the child who had not yet passed wind. 'No wonder the poor bloody thing can't burp,' said Joseph, using this facetious observation as a bridge to bustle him over to the stump behind the clock, 'it's got a mother that's dumb.'

'And a father that's selfish!' she returned.

'A-Ah! – it can talk!'

'Don't be nasty.'

'I wasn't being nasty.'

'Yes you were.'

'No – I – was – NOT!'

'All right then – but you were.'

And later, as always after such occasions, Joseph would be unable to explain how such childish altercation could lead to such murderous feelings.

'I – WAS – NOT!'

'You'll upset the baby.' Calmly said; uninterrupted, the patting.

Joseph felt himself urged to go forward, his arm pulled to be raised and smack down some compliance into her.

'Don't you dare, Joseph Tallentire,' she said. 'It'll be the last time you *do* touch me.'

He put the stump between his lips: some of the tobacco flaked onto his tongue immediately and, in his nervousness, he spat it out, spat too forcefully; it landed on the child's clean wool cardigan.

Betty stopped trying to wind the child and for the first time looked directly at Joseph.

'Get a towel,' she said, 'the one next to the sink.'

He went through to the back kitchen and did as he had been told, hovered around her while she cleaned the garment, took up the scarcely blemished towel and returned it to the sink.

'I'm sorry about that,' he murmured politely, as he re-entered 'but it doesn't change things.'

'Oh – go to your football match.'

'Who said anything about a football match?' It dawned. 'Aha? George Stephens has been round pestering to see if I would go and see Carlisle this afternoon – hasn't he? And you thought I'd hop along and forget I'd promised to let you have time off to do some shoppin' – didn't you?' He was smiling now. '*Well* – didn't you?'

The child burped.

'*He* knows what's what any road,' said Joseph.

And she used the child once more as an excuse – but this time to slip out of that sulky imprisonment.

'*You* hold him,' she said. 'You can always make him laugh.'

'Does he burp better when he laughs?' Joseph took his child and cradled him in his arm.

'I wish you wouldn't say "burp".' She stood up and smoothed the front of her cardigan and the skirt she was wearing. 'Are you sure you had enough to eat?'

'I didn't but let it be. I would have choked myself with you glarin' like that.'

She cleared the table while Joseph had the satisfaction of feeling this child warm on his arm and against his chest: he gobbled at the face which peered back and then opened into a laugh, a sucking sound accompanying it which, if simply heard and not seen could have signalled pain as well as pleasure.

'Why *don't* you go to the match with George?' she asked in as earnest a tone as she could manage.

He stepped aside to let her carry past the tablecloth which would be shaken in the backyard: there was so little space in the house that unless you were seated you were invariably in the way of someone walking around.

'I don't feel like it,' he replied; and to the baby he sang while he joggled him:

> 'Gee-up jockey to the Fair
> What will you bring your man from there?
> A silver apple and a pear
> Gee-up jockey to the Fair.'

'I could do what *I* have to do in half an hour,' said Betty, helped in the easier expression of her generosity by the song which half-hid her words.

'No – you have your afternoon,' he insisted, not to be out-done – and indeed the current changed and both now were charged with affection for each other.

'It's no good my going with George anyway. He *talks* all the damned time. When I go to see a thing, I like to watch it in peace and quiet and enjoy it in my own way.'

'His *father's* a quiet enough man,' said Betty. 'Old Mr

Stephens. "Old Father" he used to be called, by the boys.' She paused and then, as a confession, she added 'He wanted me to sit for the Grammar School you know. He thought I might have a chance of passing.' She tailed off, confused by what might be interpreted as vanity. 'Anyway I liked *him* – he did beautiful drawings of birds and flowers – I would have loved some of them to keep – they were worth framing.'

'Well, George is a blabbermouth,' said Joseph, addressing his son.

> 'Blabbermouth, Blabbermouth
> Send him back to Cockermouth.'

'Oh – George is all right.'

'There's worse,' agreed Joseph, now shuffling into a dance with his child:

> 'Georgy Porgy Pudding and Pie
> Kissed the girls and made them cry
> When the boys came out to play
> Georgy Porgy ran away.'

'When does he get teeth? Twelve months is it?'

'About then, I think.'

'You should *know*.'

'I'll know soon enough; so will you.'

And when George came, boy-like standing on the step asking if Joseph was coming to Carlisle, Betty said 'no' with a warm heart: Joseph was upstairs rocking Douglas into his afternoon sleep.

She shopped and took her time about it – but the streets were not full and she did not meet as many people as she had hoped.

Her life since the birth had changed so much that even now she could not quite believe it. The child chained her to that dark and damp little house: the loss of her wage had meant a severe domestic economy. She could never go out in the evenings and though her friends dropped in to see her it was almost as if they were visiting an invalid: while she herself, even given such a completely free afternoon as this, would soon be tired, have to return home, feel even that small heap of provisions she had been able to buy too heavy.

Joseph made a cup of tea for her – a rare and tender treat – and she insisted that he go out and watch Thurston play, at least. He needed little persuasion: they had a good team this year and he liked to watch a game on Saturdays. He himself no longer played.

It was about half-past three and the town was dead. He passed the shop which had bought the tandem from them – still not sold – even though the shopkeeper had knocked down the price to £3; past the pub where the bus used to pick up the aerodrome men in the mornings, past the church – a glance at its clock and above to the scudding clouds. It began to rain. He pulled the mackintosh tightly round his neck and with difficulty did up the button; shivered a little, stepped out. And in the house Betty huddled over the child and tried not to think of the future.

Chapter Eight

Joseph ran up to the top. The thinly ridged rubber which covered the diving steps pressed damply and pleasantly on his bare feet, almost tickling them. There were two others on the top step, tussling, each trying to push the other in; Joseph got behind them, rested his arms on the back-rest, heaved up his feet and shoved against both of them. With mock-death cries they fell off and down into the water. A cheer went around the swimming-pool, damp and booming, and Joseph took a pace forward and clasped his hands above his head like a boxing champion, bowing and nodding to the applause. But someone had crept up behind him and the next second he too was hurtling down, to land on the choppy green water with a skin-smarting belly flop.

They were at Blackpool for square-bashing. He had applied for air-crew and been sent to a place near Edinburgh for the written examination. Five hundred of them had gone, two hundred had passed, and he had come seventh overall. To say that he was pleased with himself is to describe only the reaction he felt it proper to register. There were men there straight from school, college and university, from office jobs, the civil service and business – and in those tests he had beaten almost all of them. Nothing in his life could ever be the same, he thought, for now all the threshing in the shallows was over – he was out on his own, had found his way.

Although in common with the others he had adopted a dismissive and downbeat style with regard to the business of being in the services – effing this and effing that until the word performed grammatical miracles and was waved like a magic wand; making a bee-line for the NAAFI as soon as duty was done, cards out, drinks in; sceptical of the society of most of the officers and of the sense of most of their orders; trooping around Blackpool of an evening with a deliberate though furtive slouch which cocked a snook at the rigid shoulders of drill – in fact he was enjoying himself enormously. He worried about Betty and the children – but qualifying the anxiety was the certain knowledge that he was doing more for them by being trained to fight than ever he would do by staying at home with them. Besides – that was what happened in war-time.

You waved to everybody on the street in war-time, you pooled the pocket money you allowed yourself and went around in a gang in war-time, each one prepared to battle for the other, and some even sought out the opportunity to display this physical loyalty, you knew exactly where you were in war-time and forgot all those self-entangling days of brooding, you had an aim and an honourable one, a place and that set, a cause which could draw on all your instincts for romance, and a sense of active justice in war-time.

Joseph now clearly saw the Germans as the Enemy. He had never so totally and unreservedly had an enemy, not even Stoddart; it gave him clarity. And now that he was actually doing something – even though it was only training – he felt a duty to the rights he saw that England was defending. Rather shyly, in secret, he felt that there was something to be fought for greater than any cause he could have imagined. As the news came of German victories and advances, and he felt the shock waves as things began to grow worse, so his belief in the liberties he was defending grew stronger and he wanted only to be safely through this preparation and out there, among it.

He had decided to try for navigator. He would have preferred to be a pilot but that seemed to be pushing too hard. He could not, he thought, be that lucky. A navigator or a gunner. As long as he was in the plane – that was what counted.

In the pool the men – all of them naked, their bodies very white and boyish – flung themselves into enjoying the last quarter of an hour which was 'free time'. Some soared in dives from the boards, others, like Joseph, clowned around and jumped into the water in freakish poses, a water-polo ball had been thrown in and a game had started up across the shallow end: everywhere the men ran rather self-consciously, as if enjoying the nakedness but not absolutely sure that it was quite right.

Some of them started to try to swim a length underwater. Joseph watched them stroking silently beneath the surface, their short hair swept back from their scalps, arms and legs moving with a slow-motion effect which gave to the white bodies a strange, attractive appearance in the green water. He went down to the shallow end where they were lining up to try it. All along the length of the bath, heads bobbed through the water like lifebuoys suddenly bouncing up from behind a wave.

Joseph took a huge breath which swelled his chest and dived in. Under the water his hands seemed to draw through thick feathers. The chemical in the water stung his eyes and he closed them. It was marvellous this easy weight to be displaced, his legs kicking against the faint resistance, his arms drawing through as if massaged by their contact. His head was under pressure, he opened his eyes, his ears sang, he felt the breath come into his mouth and push against his lips. He saw the wall at the end. Pulling with all his strength he felt himself surge forward to touch its white surface.

There was a terrible pain in his ears. He shot up to the surface and shouted out in agony. His hand went to his right ear and he felt something trickling out of it.

He spent the rest of the war on non-combatant service.

Betty posted the letter in time to catch the 5.45 collection. She wrote to him every day.

The streets were already dark. Douglas walked beside her. Harry, almost a year old, was in his pushchair: they made a bustling compacted figure going through the town. Harry was the son of one of her 'brothers', a professional soldier who had been killed at the outset of the war. His wife had died of pneumonia soon after the birth and Betty, remembering her own beginnings, had taken the baby in and would adopt him, already thought of him as her son.

She collected money for an organization which sent gifts to the prisoners of war in Germany. People gave a certain amount

a week, a shilling usually, sometimes sixpence and the sub-
scription was entered in two account books, her own and theirs
– each entry concluded by a double signature. At the end of
the week she took the money to the post-office, got a postal
order, and sent it off to an address in Liverpool. Tuesdays and
Thursdays were her collecting nights. On occasional Wednes-
days she went to the Labour Party meetings in the late afternoons, and on Friday she made up her weekly parcel to Joseph.

Wherever she went, she took the two children with her, even
to work. She cleaned for people who had big houses, two mornings a week for two of them, and two whole days – Mondays and
Thursdays – for Mrs Rogers, who lived three miles away. The
other two houses were away from the town also, and she went
there on her bicycle, with Harry in a small basket affair at the
front and Douglas behind her on the carrier-seat. She loved to
ride so, Douglas commenting on all that took his notice, herself
safe and protected by their presence, freer than ever she felt
when alone. As now, walking up the street with them, secure,
free and contented. They were very tidily dressed. Faces washed,
noses blown, hair combed, socks straight. And however hard
Douglas would try to make himself untidy, he would be kept
neat until they had visited all the houses and collected all the
money.

She went around the dark town like a secret messenger, bringing proof to all that things were still going on, help was still
needed. Throughout the country at this time, penetrating each
hamlet and city side-street, nosing out solitary farms and reaching even to the centres of labyrinthian slums, came such messengers coaxing more and ever more for the war. At night, in
their homes, in factories, people worked for the war – and each
day in the battle their work was spent and more was demanded.

Mrs Askew, Mrs Graham, Mrs Sharpe, Mrs Hetherington,
the Misses Snaith, Mrs Ismay, Mrs Wilson, Mrs Beattie – she left
Mrs Bly to the last and had to be firm with herself, reiterating
all Mrs Bly's good qualities as she walked down the street to
her house – she *was* a good woman, gave to everything, was
very nice, was very nice, nice, yes, yes. Betty detested setting
foot over the woman's threshold.

Mrs Bly lived in squalor which, as it was patently avoidable, Betty abominated. There were old people in the town who had neither the will nor the means to clear up after themselves – but Mrs Bly was in her forties, her husband brought her in a decent wage, there was no need for dirt to be thick on the floor, meals left on the table, a stink throughout the house. Mrs Bly liked a gossip – but again, Betty told herself, there was nothing wrong in that, she herself enjoyed talking to people, in fact one of the compensations for the embarrassment of such an obtrusive job was that she was building up her connection with the town once more, unafraid of it, loving all the details and nuances in it – yet Mrs Bly's gossip was a deliberate search for malicious reports. Betty was almost afraid to open her mouth, so aware was she that Mrs Bly could spin whatever she said into a reflection, a sour or damaging one, on the person concerned.

Finally, Edwina Bly was dishonest. And that was awful.

Betty took a deep breath of the cold air and knocked. 'Always come right in,' Mrs Bly said. 'You needn't knock.' But Betty always knocked. She pushed the children in before her.

Mrs Bly stood beside the fireplace, a tea-caddy in one hand, in the other a spoon dropping treacle on to the mat.

'I'm making treacle tarts,' said Mrs Bly. 'Do you want one?'

'No thank you,' Betty replied, over-quickly.

'I'll give some to Douglas then; Douglas'll eat it: won't you, Douglas?'

The boy stepped forward. Despite the gaslight, the kitchen seemed dark. Behind him he could feel his mother willing him not to go : before him was the tipsily enticing figure of Mrs Bly now holding a treacle tart between her long mucky fingernails.

'Thank you,' he said and bit at it. Mrs Bly watched him bite, saw the pain go across his face as the hot treacle touched his tongue and then said :

'They're hot, Douglas. Be careful.'

Betty wondered where she had got the sugar.

Douglas let the treacle cool against the soft flesh of the inside of his cheeks and then he slid it painfully down his throat : he held the tears at his eyelids.

'Oh dear, I can't find my purse,' said Mrs Bly.

The purse was on the sideboard, clear to be seen by all. Betty did not like to point it out.

'It's there,' said Douglas.

Mrs Bly shed a small smile and put her hand on Douglas' head as she passed him : as if wishing to screw it into his neck.

'He's going to be a clever boy,' said Mrs Bly. 'You'd better watch him, Mrs Tallentire.'

'I will,' said Betty, abruptly – then, realizing that she could have sounded rude in that she made retribution. 'Mrs Beattie's back's bad again,' she offered, and regretted it immediately for Mrs Bly turned on her, holding the unopened purse, and pounced on the news.

'Did she say *why* it was bad?'

'Is it – because of the rain?' Betty faltered.

'Ha!' Mrs Bly replied. 'That's what she would like you to think. Did you see Ted?'

'Yes.' Ted was Mrs Beattie's lodger.

'You mean you saw Ted and she said she had a bad back and you thought it was because of the rain! I wonder she has the face! Fancy trying it out on a woman like you, Mrs Tallentire. You wouldn't think badly of anybody, would you Mrs Tallentire? That's not like you, is it, Mrs Tallentire. But *I* can make two and two of what you've said, believe me.'

'Now then, Mrs Bly,' Betty replied, 'I said nothing.'

'That's right, my dear. But it was the *way* you said it. Oh, you can't kid me. I know you'd be the last person to cast blame, but the *way* you said it, Mrs Tallentire, I could *tell* you'd been upset by that woman just the *way* you said it.'

'What way?'

'Now then, Mrs Tallentire.' Mrs Bly shook her head. 'Enough said.

Betty was without an answer.

Next, Mrs Bly got on about Mrs Hope, and so on as before with others, each time prying through keyholes seen only by herself, winkling out secrets secret only to herself until Betty felt like the Dutch Boy trying to stop a whole dam from bursting with only his thumb as a defence : and yet so ruthless and swift was Mrs Bly that Betty was completely thrown, for

at times she thought that she was merely imagining all the badness, that Mrs Bly was simply chatting away as normally as
anyone else would. 'Well I'll have to be off to put them to bed,'
said Betty, indicating the children, so determined to be gone
that she cut right across Mrs Bly's speech. Which did not go
unnoticed.

'Oh, rushing off, are you? I thought you might stay for a cup
of tea.'

'No thank you.' She took out her collection book. 'I'll just
enter it in and then I'll be away.'

'I haven't given it to you yet,' replied Mrs Bly in a tone which
might have been teasing.

Betty smiled and took out her pencil – indelible ink – which
she dabbed against her tongue.

'It's poisonous, you know,' said Mrs Bly, 'that stuff in pencils.
Poisonous.'

'Is it?'

'Don't they tell you that?'

'No.'

'*Don't* they?'

'No.' And again Betty felt that somehow she had betrayed
someone.

'Well now,' said Mrs Bly, 'you'll be wanting a shilling, I
suppose.'

'Yes please,' said Betty, brightly.

'I'll see if I can make it.'

The coins were tipped on to the table and she sorted through
them, very slowly.

'I'll tell you what,' she whispered. 'I can give you it in eggs.'

'Oh.'

'Here.' With her first rapid movement of the encounter, Mrs
Bly turned, bent down and came up with a large cardboard
box. Inside were a dozen eggs.

'Oh,' said Betty. 'You're lucky to get hold of them.'

'Lucky?' Mrs Bly laughed. 'You need to be better than lucky
in this world, girl. Four do?'

'Do what?'

'Four for the shilling?'

94

It was reasonable. Betty could easily put in the shilling herself. The eggs were new-laid. Two each for the boys. Of course four would do!

'I have to take the money,' said Betty, speaking as if through a lump of wool in her throat.

'*You* put in the shillin'. And you get the eggs. Hard to get, believe me.'

'I know.'

'Tell you what – Five.'

But there was the book and a shilling had to be entered. Mrs Bly's book and a shilling had to be entered in that. Though it would not be cheating – it would not be right. As soon as Betty felt that word come to her, she felt much more sure of herself, everything became much clearer.

'I'm sorry, Mrs Bly,' she said, 'but my job is to collect a shilling.'

'All right my dear. But after you've collected it, would you like to buy four of the eggs for a shilling?'

It was all perfectly in order. The shilling would be handed over : handed back.

'I'll do without the eggs, thank you, Mrs Bly,' Betty muttered.

'Will you now? Mean to say you're going to deprive those two little boys of fresh eggs?' To Douglas. 'You would like an egg, wouldn't you?'

'Yes please, Mrs Bly.'

'There you are. I'll wrap them up for you.'

She reached out for the newspaper and began to wrap up the eggs. Betty hesitated.

'I've some eggs coming,' she said, eventually : not a lie, at some time she would get some eggs. When they came, they would validify the statement.

'Oh,' said Mrs Bly. 'Who from?' She paused, an egg halfwrapped in the photograph of a tank.

'From – *some*body,' said Betty, faintly.

Mrs Bly grinned.

'Good girl! Don't tell! I knew you had it in you. Still waters, Mrs T., still waters. Here's your bob! Sign the book. Small handwriting. But clear – very clear. Good girl. Mrs Rogers, eh?'

Back in her own house, Betty washed the children and put them to bed.

'One kiss from me, and one from your dad.'

'Is he coming back?'

'Yes. Of course he is.'

'When?'

'When they've finished the war.'

When she felt particularly lonely, she brought the two boys into the double bed with her. One on each side, rolled down against her.

Easing himself out of the hard narrow bed, Joseph swung his feet on to the cold floor and waited. All the men were asleep. Outside he could hear the booming and the whines. In the dark he reached out for his socks and pulled them on. He took a blanket as a dressing-gown and walked quietly down the long room to the door. Sometimes he woke up Norman, his mate, but tonight he wanted to be alone. He felt rather selfish about it, but he was more able to dream, alone.

Up the back stairs and into the attics. He had brought a torch. It was a big house they were billeted in – rather like the Sewells'. The sergeant had put them on the top floor. Joseph had two stripes now and argued freely with him : if a bomb drops the top floor's bound to get it most badly, he said. The sergeant would not be convinced. Perhaps he thought that others might be coming and wanted to establish superiority over them in the most undeniable way. Whatever it was, they were billeted on the top floor.

Joseph pushed open the window and got out on to the roof. It was cold and he pulled the blanket around him. Carefully he walked to the turreted edge of the roof and sat down – looking across to London. He got out a cigarette and lit up.

An air raid was under way.

He saw the lights raking the sky, like shimmering scissors snapping at the aeroplanes. Fires, the red glow, a furnace in the night. Flak, deadly morse, flicking rapidly through the dark, shrill silent screams of protest. All he could hear was hollowed by the distance: as in the swimming-pool, the sound boomed strangely. Sometimes an aeroplane came back in his direction and he ducked, for occasionally they off-loaded any remaining bombs. He saw some drop about two or three miles in front of him. Again, it was like a display.

Nothing of screams or human agony: to see and hear that he had to shut his eyes and remember the photographs in the newspapers, and then he saw London burning, the cranes and ships in the docks like eerie models, looking artificial in the bleeping light; imagined the Thames stained red and yellow-white: saw the houses crumbling as if the stones had suddenly rotted, and people surging to the shelters, ambulances like refuges in those uncertain streets, the grey, smouldering desolation at dawn. He was safe from that: he twisted his body on the stones, jabbed by the word; safe. The stars were obscured.

They could not be seen in the sky, the enemy planes. Like the plagues which had come to London in the past they struck the people down with crude decimation: you were spared by luck which flung itself from street to street.

It was terrible – like a sight of the end of the world or a distant pattern of hell. Yet – he would not admit this to another soul – there was something compelling about it. It was a dream and he was part of the dream.

He sat there and smoked a full packet of Woodbines. The cold settled slowly on him and he did not move, becoming as fixed on the turreted ledge as beneath him were the crude, Victorian gargoyles.

When he did go to bed it was about dawn.

He woke up, startled, as a bomb dropped in the grounds. All the windows of the bottom three floors were shattered. Doors were blown in, furniture inside the rooms smashed against the wall.

But the top floor was untouched. Not a pane of glass cracked. The sergeant took full credit.

Douglas was Montgomery. Jackie Paylor was Rommel. Harry (3 now) and Lionel Temple were the Eighth Army: Jackie

Paylor's two sisters were the Germans. William Ismay was a Soldier.

The battle was fought between Station Road and New Street with Moore's garage where Frank used to work as the bridge-head.

Douglas was tireless. Up and down the ramp, the wooden machine gun raining a forest of bullets before him – 'de-de-de-de-de-de-de-de-de-de-de-de-de-*de*! Drrrrrrrrrrrrrr – de-de-de-de-de-de-de-de-de-*de*! RRRRrrrrr – you're dead, William Ismay! And your Mary's been dead since it started.' 'I'm not!' 'Yes you are. De – de – de – de – de – de! There! You're dead now, any-way.' 'That wasn't fair.' 'It doesn't matter.' 'I wasn't ready.' 'You should have been.' 'De – de – de – de – de – de. There *You're* dead.' 'All right,' said Douglas lying down. 'Count to a 100.' 'In 10's?' 'In 5's.' '5 – 10 – 15 – 20 – 25 ... Harry! You were supposed to stop in that tyre.' 'Mr Moore said go away.' 'But it's our headquarters!' 'De – de – de – de – de – de! You're dead again – and you can count 200 this time.'

The songs on the wireless which made him wince when they said 'love' – turned away from the wireless and looked at the wall, sure that everybody must be as embarrassed as he was – but at night he murmured the words to himself, licked them in his gob, shuddered at their power. The town seethed with strangers – evacuees who used the school and came in buses; orphans at the convent, girls, cropped hair, green dresses, walk-ing down to the park two by two, the nuns fore and aft like the daughters of Noah; airmen come to the local airfield to work on the maintenance of the planes. Douglas moved through a shimmer of love, people shouting hello to each other on the streets, songs from the pubs, the horses coming in scores to the horse-fair, the organ at church and the words at Sunday school. Football, cricket, running, running everywhere, catching tid-dlers in jam jars, getting lost in a field a quarter of a mile from home and the man he asked the way was an American who carried him back on his shoulders and gave him some chewing-gum. His mother gave him tea.

Then the war. On the news, at the school – 'will children whose fathers are in the war stay behind?' – swollen with pride

– war against the Southend lot, war against Michael Saunderson who thought he was cock of the form, fear of the older
boys who could turn when he gave them cheek and then he
had to run through the riddling side-streets, right through a
shop once, for fear of being caught and hit. Picking up stumps
in the gutters in imitation of Alfie Coulthard who was ten and
fought at the matinees. War on the news at the pictures.
Coming out sick with fear, running home for the wooden gun
– de – de – de – de – de – de – let them come here, he was ready.
His mother's father had died and they had moved in with his
Grandma. He had been taken to see the man laid out in the
parlour. Musty, dust risen. An aunt had taken him to see.
His grandfather's face was the colour of porridge : and lumpy.
He had wanted to touch, dared not.

His uncle Frank had been killed in North Africa. That was
why Douglas was always Montgomery.

So they had moved out of the cottage and lived now with
his Grandma. His mother's mother : he had to say it slowly
at first until he had practised. The house was full of people
coming from the war, coming from work, lodgers, relatives,
people put up for a night : Harry and himself slept in the
same room as their mother. Deeply calm there – and yet in that
calm the coldness of his mother's tears at things that had
happened. He was sent to that room to be alone when he was
bad. Not locked in – but he could not go out.

Tanks came, one dusty afternoon through the town, real
tanks, scores of them. Soldiers were always there, left-right, left-
right, marching in the gutters; but these great long-snouted
tanks which shook the very ground – they came and fastened a
menace and awe on the town. One of the soldiers let him have
a ride. They left the tanks on Market Hill and the men went to
drink. Like all the other boys, Douglas followed the men, asking
for sweets and chewing-gum. He saw his aunty Helen with
them – and that gave him the confidence to stay out much
later than he had ever done before. She had Lester with her
and pushed him across to play with Douglas – but Lester was
about a year older then he was, beyond Douglas's childishness.

He stood around the pub doors and heard the men laughing

and singing. His father was in the air-force, so was his Uncle George, so was his Uncle Donald, his Uncle Pat was in the army, so was ... The black town was full of enemies and loved faces. Oh, he rolled about that town the boy, blind and drunk with the endlessness of it. His mother did not keep him in. There would always be someone who would know him, someone he could talk to if he felt anxious.

Later and later he played, exhausting the others – daring himself to stay out longer.

Before going home he went down to see the tanks once more. Cold and massive in the dark. The Jerries could never win. He touched the tracks of the tank, hard, impenetrable under his soft, shivering hand. De – de – de – de – de – de – de – de – de – de – *de*! You're dead! You're dead! You're dead!

Helen was Joseph's cousin. The daughter of Seth, she had been brought up in Maryport and after her mother had run away from Seth, been spoilt by him – turned into the little darling of Socialism. Her interest in his politics had died when, aged sixteen, she had taken up with a married man and refused all pleas, resisted all pressures, staying with him long after he had grown tired of her. Then there were others.

She had arrived in Thurston just after the war started: with her was Lester, three years old and carrying her name, Tallentire. She had lived with the man for two years and then he had gone back to his wife. She had tried to force him back to her, going around to his house, fighting the other woman, screaming, promising – but he had stayed with his wife and found another sweetheart. Then Helen had broken down, shifting around the West Coast like one homeless, though Seth had followed her devotedly, patiently. During that time, her reputation became a public joke in the mining towns and so Thurston was a retreat.

There she had married George Stephens, son of the schoolmaster, a damaged man who failed to match the sweetness or scholarship of his father and insisted on attempting to be one of the 'boys', the 'Hard Men', working at the factory when he could have found an office job or been articled. George had known Betty since childhood and she'd always felt sorry for him especially as his father was so widely admired. Having been taught by old Mr Stephens, she was full of affection for him; but this reinforced her feelings for his son. And she worried when he married Helen who saw him off to the war with relief and turned to a boy-friend again.

This time, she said, it was serious. She was going to go steady with this man and tell George straight out when next he came on leave. But would Betty look after Aileen for a few days? Lester could stay with the Cleggs but Aileen needed mothering still. They were just going to go to Blackpool. He had leave and he wanted to take her to Blackpool. She had never been. Would Betty, please?

Aileen was indisputably George's daughter and this may have had something to do with Betty's immediate acceptance. But she could not blame Helen: nobody could blame her after what had happened to her. Yet it was not right, not at all, to run around while George was away: just not fair. He had no chance.

Helen's reputation in the town was bad. No one ostracized her partly because her retorts and her liveliness were too good to be deprived of. Betty would never tolerate any gossip about her, went out of her way to see her, talk to her: the two women got on well – both were fiery though with one it was on the surface, with the other below it, both liked to laugh, both were energetic and had definite opinions about what they thought good and bad, right and wrong. That in one area these opinions were totally contradictory provided occasional trailing silences in their talk ... but a recovery would soon be made. Helen cleaned the lavatories for the parish council and also scrubbed down the offices five mornings a week. She was a great one, too, for organizing herself when there were rose-hips to be picked or raspberries, hazel-nuts or potatoes: she managed well and if Lester was scruffy, it was after he left home that he got into that state.

Yet was *she* not deceiving George, also, by looking after Aileen and so making it possible for Helen to rush off to Blackpool? The question posed itself to Betty as badly as the riddle which precedes the solution of a thriller. She wanted to laugh at this rattling interrogation – but not for long because it sank into her mind like a cold needle and could not be withdrawn. For days she thought of little else but Helen: more of Helen than of her children, her husband or her work.

And when Helen returned with the announcement that 'it hadn't worked out', Betty felt even worse. The more so because there was no way out. Having given her affection to Helen, she could not nor would she withdraw it.

Yes, Aileen had been very good. She had played with Harry. Had a fall – but been more scared than hurt. She listened to the tales of Blackpool's nights. Betty hid her confusion in work.

Both the boys were at school now and she had taken on the cleaning of another house. She liked working in these houses if the people were pleasant. The new woman was not, alternately snobbish and over-confiding, curt and over-possessive. Betty dreaded going there but would not give in her notice. She could not bear to break with people, to allow the possibility of having enemies. Alongside that was another feeling – that she had openly taken the job on and was not going to give it up: not going to look like somebody who could not stick out a difficult bit of work.

Alone in a room – with a duster and polish – then she would bring it to life: what was dirty became clean, the dull shone, the messy became tidy, the disordered ordered.

She was scrupulous but not fussy. She did not run after muddy feet with a dustpan. The houses she cleaned – as her own – were cleaned for their own sake, not as an example to those who lived in them.

She liked the furniture and the space in these houses. The large and deep armchairs with flower-printed coverings, the long dining tables, the pictures on the walls, the lovely china and cutlery; yet she felt no urge to imitate this when she thought of her own ideal house. This was not at all to do with the notion that she must 'keep her place': on the contrary, her own tastes were firm and inclined to what was neat and easy to clean and modern, light, simple-lined.

But work could not solve everything. Lying awake on hot

summer nights, the windows wide open behind the blinds, no sound from the town but occasionally a dog barking, she grew conscious of the forces which held her so rigidly to the town. She felt, as much as saw, that they grew out of the fearing part of her and she was tired of them. Now that she had the children, now that she had 'paid back her mother', there was no reason why she should not leave the place altogether.

If Joseph again asked her to move – she would.

At the new place, the Stores were in chaos. The Sergeant met him at the door, gave him the keys and told him to take over: he was off to England. For a time Joseph lived almost as a recluse, never called to parades and drills (sometimes he thought it was unknown that he was there at all: one day in the canteen he heard a Flight Lieutenant say, 'There's a man called Tallentire supposed to be here to do our stores.' 'No need for that,' someone replied, 'chap called Joe down there, working like a beaver.' Joseph said nothing) and at the end of two months the huge buildings were clean and organized, their contents checked and catalogued, the method of withdrawal regularized and efficient.

For that he was offered sergeant's stripes. The condition was that he should sign on for another five years. There would be a house provided for him in Germany, and the Air Force would pay for his wife and children to come across. He was very tempted but did not write to Betty about it. He knew that she would not move and saw no point in upsetting her by relaying the offer.

John was silent. With Joseph he had walked from the cottage towards the road that Joseph would take back to Thurston. The afternoon was hot and Joseph had suggested that they sit on a hedge-bank for a few minutes to relax.

He had seen his father the day after he had come home, but this was the first occasion on which he had had time to talk to him. Talk they did along the road, the chat that concealed the real statements while yet allowing them to be pointed to, but there was a severity in the old man which nothing but straight talk could do justice to. A severity in his manner, in his tone, in the way he refused to look at all about him on this bright day but walked with his head slightly bent; he was past his mid-sixties now but the years seemed to make him only more hale, bright-eyed, deft in his movements.

Now they sat on the bank, Joseph in his still unfamiliar 'civvies', John in the same sort of working clothes he had worn his life long. He lit up his pipe, having silently refused the cigarette Joseph offered him. A car passed by on the main road. There was some wind that day and the full-leafed trees shivered gently. Near them was a chestnut and its large leaves seemed to Joseph to be cut out of foil, so exactly were the lines shaped. He watched the leaves, supply lifting on the slow shifting branches. When John spoke it was all of a piece, very quiet, as much to himself as to his son.

'Frank went.' He padded the rising ash of his pipe down with his thumb. 'Just like that. He was driving his tank, thou knows. Always was mad on cars. In the letter *we* got they said he hadn't a chance. A direct hit. So mebbe he didn't know much.' He screwed up his eyes. 'He wasn't me own, you know, Joseph, nowt to do with me really, but I thowt a lot on that lad. Straight as could be.' He paused. 'Then Donald. What can a man mek o' that, eh Joseph? There's a lad went right through – and then he dies of food-poisonin' two days after it's all over! It would mek you laugh if it didn't mek you cry. And he was a real warrior, Donald, a bit like our Isaac – your uncle Isaac. Frightened before no mortal thing.' He murmured once more. 'Food-poisoning.' Then, more steadily, 'All of them, our Isaac, Sarah, Tom that was killed int' last war – one of his lads – they've all got somebody gone or hurt for ivver. And we've lost touch. There's brothers of mine I wouldn't recognize, and full cousins o' thine thou dissn't know exist. We're blown like chaff, man : there's neither sense nor purpose in it.'

Part Three

The Throstle's Nest

Chapter Nine

He slid into the peace, half-dazed, half-heartedly euphoric. That a few months before he had been prepared, if given the chance, to shoot at and drop bombs on people now appeared as an unreal hiatus in his life. Yet he knew that it was part of him, and that he wished he had been given that chance. The only way was to forget it : but the act of forgetting was numbing.

When in the services, he had thought of his demob as a release from a bow : he would soar with unrestricted energy, driven by the clear knowledge of what he did not want, straight to the target. But he had slipped out almost reluctantly at the end, sad to leave the chains which were also supports. Arriving in Thurston on the double-decker bus he had looked at the streets half-nervously, wondering that he had lived there and would live there. It seemed a stranger place than the foreign country from which he was returning. Stepping off the bus, the people in the streets were in a glass, he knew them all but would have to break the glass to talk once more to them. More than ever he wished he had taken the offer of the sergeant's stripes. There had even been a hint of an eventual crack at a commission.

He went back to his job at the aerodrome and within a few months felt as if he'd never left this treadmill and never would. As usual, he looked outside the job for more driving interest but his glance went no further than the old crowd, George and Norman, John and Lenny – a few drinks, a little gambling, some sport. The real interest of the town was in community efforts – and Joseph was always rather detached from those.

One of the things which was clearly a drive, seen in Thurston as elsewhere, was that the children should be given their chance. The Butler Act legislation had made it possible for children from poor homes to go right through university, the

National Health system would see that they were fit, school dentists would check the teeth, school milk and school meals see that they were looked after, all over the country homes were endowed for those orphaned or deprived, articles about child-rearing appeared in every sort of magazine, films were made in such a way that the majority could 'safely' be seen by young children; though far from being a stampede a movement for 'giving children their chance' was well under way.

Directly out of that came the vivid, post-war carnivals. In Thurston after the war, you could whistle up a carnival in a week. There was little money spent on the dresses or the organization of the affair, yet by sorting through old cupboards and by borrowing and 'all piling in together', these carnivals became, for a few years, occasions of marvel and excitement. Made for the children, on a shoe-string, corporate and yet neither hierarchic nor informal, they wove together many of the strands of the post-war mood – and everybody turned out for them.

There was a man called Kathleen who was to lead it this year. It had all been a mistake, Betty explained to Douglas. His mother had wanted a girl so much and everything had been prepared for that: little dresses made with 'Katie' embroidered on them, Kathleen painted on the brand new cot, K on every handkerchief and even on the panties – yes – Douglas need not laugh – it was all true. And the woman was broken-hearted, but she would not give it up. Kathleen he was called, and as Kathleen he was dressed until he went to school: it took a terrible threat from her husband to get the boy into trousers for his first school morning. Douglas, who was now eleven, suggested point-blank that the woman had been a 'stupid old fool': Betty clattered his ears but later admitted that perhaps it *was* a little too soft of her. She ought not to have burdened the boy so.

Douglas, who had immediately fantasied himself into the situation and saw himself walking up High Street being called 'Kathleen' (writhing with embarrassment at the image but hugging it to himself again and again) persisted through days on this questioning about Kathleen. At night, he looked out for him and followed him through the streets.

Understandably, said Betty, Kathleen had grown up very quiet: too quiet really: in fact, almost completely silent. He grew very tall and people got used to the name – people who had known him all his life – but there was always somebody who found it a joke or children (she glared at Douglas, demanding a confession and at the same time daring him to make one) who thought it clever to run after him and shout his name. Douglas closed his lips firmly: the chanted taunt rattled against his teeth – he wondered that his mother did not hear it: only last night, he and a gang had pursued him, shouting:

> 'K – K – K – Katie!
> Ain't 'e a matey
> His mother couldn't tell
> A knob from a door!'

The lyric was now traditional. It was shrilled in cockatoo – film-cockney – and the boys longed for Kathleen to turn and look at them – then they would scatter, the terrible consonant – K – K – K – Katie – kicking through the streets. So, Betty continued, it was no wonder that he didn't talk to anybody. But if you said Hello, nicely, then Hello would come back. Or Nice Day, or whatever it was: back would it come. Always pleasant. A very good worker. Very *strong*. (This, too, said with admonitory emphasis and Douglas swallowed and nodded.) Always did labouring jobs and always did them well. Never short of work. Handed his pay packet over entire to his mother. People had occasionally told him to get his name changed (you could do it, though it cost a lot, said Betty) but he just smiled and did not answer.

But, recently, aged about forty, Kathleen had begun to open out. He had started to drink a little, to go to hound trails, was seen at the local football matches, smoked cigarettes. This metamorphosis had reached its climax the previous year when Kathleen had appeared in the autumn carnival dressed up as Mae West. Where he had got the idea, the nerve, the wig or the other things, no one could guess. But there he was. Immaculate.

A long cigarette holder and high heels, silk stockings, the lot.

Of course he was put at the front. A position which he had accepted very calmly – almost as of right – and then the walk! The works. Talent stared everyone in the face. He got first prize for Gentleman Individuals and shared the Certificate of Originality with the woman who came dressed as King Kong. Many considered he ought to have won it outright.

This year he came as Two-Ton Tessie O'Shea. Tessie O'Shea's bulk was always balanced by a lightness of foot, slim ankles, and her fatness was jolly, almost a prop. Kathleen was six feet two. His legs very heavy. (For Mae West he had worn an ankle-length gown in silvery material.) Moreover he had increased his bulk by employing some of the methods of mummification: sheets had been wound around him and pillows used, though sparingly, between the sheets. In outline he was a circus Fat Man – grotesque. But such was his talent that there *was* a recognizable likeness of Two-Ton Tessie O'Shea peeping through. *He* needed no card on his back. And to allow for no misconstruction, he had a ukelele which he strummed continuously, singing Tessie's songs. He could not play the ukelele and made no attempt to. The instrument was held firmly and his right hand swept across the strings without pause. He knew about half a dozen songs and these he sang through and then began again immediately with the first one. When the organizer asked him once again to lead the procession, Kathleen nodded without interrupting his performance, and took his place in front of the band. His mother who was again with him as she had been the previous year stood nearby on the pavement and prepared herself for the long walk to the park.

It was a silver band – about twenty-four piece. Uniforms navy blue with silver buttons. Music on small rectangles of cardboard stuck into a holder on the instrument so that each man marched rather myopically, head hunched over mouthpiece, eyes peering six inches in front of them. The bottom half of their bodies strode in time. Johnny Middleton played the big drum this year, temperamental but unrivalled at twirling the large, mop-headed drumsticks. He had found a leopard skin and already, before the procession had begun, was swelter-faced.

Another speciality of his was the slow march of Guards where one foot paused as if to touch the other as it moved forward. He had not been tall enough to get into the Guards himself but had learnt it all the same.

The carnival was in a way a fantasy. That this was constructed out of very limited means only made it more poignant. In the four years after the war it became a very popular affair, calling in competitors from villages and towns all around the neighbourhood made it more powerful. The town was not too big (Carlisle could never raise a respectable carnival) nor was it too small (the village carnivals always resembled fêtes). And in these years after the war, relief at having passed through the thirties, triumph at having been victorious in battle, dread of the Atom Bomb, carelessness encouraged by the ominous warnings of future struggles, all perhaps were combined with a half-mythical memory of community display, of those sun-bursts of earlier times when the festivals were explosions at the end of a thin and narrow trickle of months of dry-powdered existence.

For though there were no great traditions such as have part institutionalized CARNIVAL in many countries – carnival day in Thurston did disjoint the town : people set out most purposefully to get drunk; those who dressed as conservatively as all England did at that time suddenly put on wanton plumage; others, like Kathleen but not only him, played out a personal vision or desire at once harmlessly and at the same time challengingly. For many it was a day of outrageous expense to be saved up for like Christmas; for others it meant a very rare Saturday morning off work. Children abandoned themselves to it, shops closed early, pubs stayed open late, traffic, such as there was, was diverted and overnight the men who had organized it became Officials with a large brass badge and the word in green letters. The park-keeper mowed the long stretch which would be used for the sports and did what he could to station a few boys around the more important flowerbeds. Shopkeepers gave prizes, farmers gave sacks for the sack-race. Where the procession passed there was bunting so that the upper stories of the street were rigged like a ship and all morning the man with the Tannoy tested his equipment beside the tennis pavilion.

Behind the band were the dancers and following them the procession proper. First, those on foot, Walt Disney was a great influence and so were the Nursery Rhymes – Donald Duck walking with Old Mother Hubbard, Three Men in a Tub and Mickey Mouse, Snow White hand in hand with Little Boy Blue: people of all ages, though children were in a majority. Hollywood provided much inspiration – Indians were very popular with boys of about nine or ten who loved to be covered with brown boot-polish. Occasionally, personal likenesses were traded on: there was someone who looked exactly like the Prime Minister, someone else who did Max Miller. The Arts were under-represented, though there was Robinson Crusoe, a Laughing Cavalier and an idiosyncratic attempt at Fagin. Sport was strong with boxers and footballers numerous among the boys. There was a Pope, an Aristocrat ('The Duke of Knowall'), Al Jolson, a farmer with his dog, policemen, apemen, and various circus stars like the Trapeze Artist and the Strong Man. These formed the backbone of the walking procession – to be judged according to known and established standards in relation to their known association with reality. Threaded through them, like ribbons through a mane, were the surprises. A girl dressed as an Ice-Cream, a man who was the News of the World, a Lamp Post, a Tree, a family who were London under the Blitz, a Tin of Corned Beef, the Spirit of Charity, a Tea-Cosy, Songs of Praise, a Haystack, a Fiddle, Man of the Future, a Grandfather Clock, the Evils of Drink, Heroism, Mount Everest and Poverty. And, finally, there were a few people bursting to dress up, incapable of fashioning an idea to fit the costume they had made, roving about the edges of the procession, as novices to the priests who bore cards.

There were about twenty wagons. Even at this time there was an annual horse-market in Thurston which lasted for three days. The horses without exception were well-dressed. The rear was brought up by four lorries – two coal lorries and one from the West Cumberland farmers and one from the Co-op. The wagons and lorries became small stages on which were groups from streets or churches or clubs. There was the Old Covered Wagon, of course, and Beside the Camp Fire; the Grand Piano, as usual, with the boys in black and the girls in white representing the notes, jumping up and down while a woman played a real piano. The Carnival Queen and Attendants, the Flower Queen and Her Maidens, The Darby and Joan wagon. And then, again, the free-wheelers: In the Trenches – the lorry stacked with sandbags and mud, the men in their uniforms singing 'Pack Up Your Troubles'; a Packet of Woodbines – a truly colossal piece of work, the wagon made up entirely of small woodbine packets built up to make one monster carton, with four people in white tubes, their hair powdered brown, poking out of the end; English Heroes (the Methodist wagon): Jonah in the Whale; the Old Woman who lived in the Shoe; the Test Match; Heaven and Hell; the Bank of England; Alice in Wonderland (C. of E.); Inside Big Ben and the Spirit of Labour (on a lorry provided by the Co-op). Neither Catholics, Quakers, Methodists nor Salvationists had an individual wagon but the Congregationalists had their own carnival. The winning wagon was 'Liberty or Death'.

What made it the stuff of fantasy was not so much those of the entrants who had thought up unusual costumes – but the thing itself, stretching for three-quarters of a mile along Low Moor road, the hedges dull green just before autumn, the town which they would march through a grey, rather battered place, with little new paint, only the very smallest marks of any prosperity, where five pounds a week was a very good wage and the long reach of the war had stretched even so far from the battle to pluck lives and cancel ambitions. Thurston was no place for tourists or day-trippers, too mournful even for some of the inhabitants who wanted only to leave it, with the clouds grey and the people watching the assembly of the carnival almost all dressed in navy blue, black, clerical grey, brown – in this place the fact of the procession was like a dream made tangible and quite unexpectedly laid over a normal waking life. The colours were bold – yellow, red, green, purple, orange – and the whole fragile, well-ordered noisy procession could have descended on Thurston from another age and climate. Yet the faces were the same as those in the crowd and this gave the dream its lush substantiality.

Betty was in charge of the dancers. There were about thirty girls, dressed in white, with four bells on a white handkerchief, bells on their wrists and bells around their ankles, small, on grey elastic, shining like little bubbles of silver. The girls walked in pairs directly behind the band – jangling in the wind – and danced every four hundred yards when the band stopped. The dancing was called Morris Dancing but had long lost any relationship it might have had with the Maypole and yip-haw, the dialect and sticks of those revived original·dances which are a mixture of pedantry and Swedish drill set to slender melodies that often shudder at the impact. No, the girls danced a very formal, very simple, skipping and chain-making dance nearer to a Scottish reel than to the pure source of Morris. The band accompanied them with Scottish tunes, 'A Hundred Pipers', playing slowly, being the most appropriate.

It was only this day, the actual day of the Carnival, which made Betty nervous. During the war, particularly through the Labour Party, she had become quite used to organizing things : because everybody else was mucking in, that had been all right. Even when proposed as treasurer of the party she had not objected. It was the war – the men were away and everybody seemed to be on some committee for this or that. It was the same with the collecting of money, and when the Carnival Committee had asked her to take charge of the girls, she had agreed immediately. A hand-written notice in Harvey Messenger's shops and it was done :

> Will all girls between the ages of 7 and 15
> who would like to be in the Morris dancing
> please meet at the West Cumberland Farmers
> Building at 5.15 next Monday.

Everything about it appealed to Betty. The girls took their places in accordance with age, the younger ones leading – and so it was fair. The dance was so easily learnt that there was little nervousness. The business of getting them all to move at the same time was difficult enough to make it exacting work, but not so difficult as to make it hard work. Most of the girls had white dresses and if not, they could easily be made – while J. & J. Airds sold the bells for a penny each – so few could possibly feel barred through poverty : and if there *were* girls from large families who came along rather sadly after the announcement about the white dress and said they could not afford it, then it always proved possible to get hold of some material (from somewhere) and run one up in an hour or two.

It was pleasant down there during the rehearsals, beside the West Cumberland Farmers, on that quiet, narrow road, this horde of little girls, all known to Betty, their mothers and grandmothers known, dancing away, singing the tunes to accompany themselves, grey cardigans, loose ribbons, ankle socks. Sometimes Douglas would come down with her (Harry would never go near the place) and sniff about like a wasp for pollen. His mother's position gave him a reason for being there – but he could never quite believe his luck, at large among so many girls. He fell in love with most of them on sight and his Monday evenings were powerfully intoxicating. Almost eleven now, he had just passed the scholarship for the grammar school, but interest in the new uniform he was to get, the satchel, even the two weeks of extra holiday, waned before this occasion. He soon picked up the dance and so further established himself by being able to teach it to some of the more tardy girls. And when a set was one short, he would fill in. Had one solitary boy ever appeared, as once did happen, then no matter if he was totally unknown to Douglas – that particular boy was very well-known to him – he would shrivel with embarrassment and run, not considering even looking back until he was well into the town where he would halt, abruptly, shove his hands into his pockets and kick something into the gutter.

At six o'clock the factory hooter went and she could see the first men on their bicycles going up into the town and it was then that they stopped. For Joseph's bus came in at six-thirty and she liked his supper to be hot and the table laid.

Those early evenings there, with the girls, like herself when young, remembering the Girl Guide evenings, seeing the moving phenomenon of well-known characteristics inherited by yet another generation, the quiet town up Toppin's field, the clothing factory where she had worked, and about her the fields she had played in and dared in and courted in, these times gathered together her love for the town which she had never lost, though fear had overlaid it and misery had once seemed to dissolve it. She loved the knowledge that at the end of this road there would be Hill's showrooms and some of the same furniture would be in the window as had been there before the war. And there was still the black corrugated-iron of the shed, with one panel loose, which she had crawled through, and her feelings lurched as she saw Douglas crawl through it. Truly there were countless places, expressions, smells, tones, tableaux, intonations and memories all crushed and contained with ease in this town. Such a small place – but still she loved to go along Bird-cage Walk with Joseph and the children in the evenings, still loved to look towards the fields and watch the clouds move across them, see those luridly painted sunsets drawn down a few miles away to the Solway Firth. The town was her life but it was also like a grand, endless and deeply thrilling book. For not only did she live there, she saw herself living there: not only met the people but appraised them; not only heard of what they did but felt for them. She had never lost the absolute love given to the place in her childhood. Oh the steps at the end of market hill where she had played with Anne Bell's dolls and the smell of the Co-op, wheaty, bacon, musty vegetables, of the bakery in which she'd worked, the girls arm in arm singing as they came from the factory – sometimes she could have hugged them to herself as she wanted to hug the two boys : but only rarely did so, fearing that she might spoil them.

Gone, now that the war was over, was the desire she had felt to leave Thurston. To have been tired of it seemed now, to Betty, to be tired of life. There were so many people to talk to, weddings, births, gossip of all kinds, shows, sports, carnivals, meetings, auctions, markets, strangers, a new building, a new vicar, a story about one of the boyos, a breath of legal tattle, and herself able to go back to cleaning in the mornings now that the boys were at school. Just approaching thirty, she could still enjoy dances – when they could get Joyce Ritchie to come in and baby-sit – could still feel the flounce of a new dress as she walked up the street on Easter Monday; though not vain she was pleased with her figure which had quickly returned to its slimness after the birth – and the lipstick red, bright on her lips, the hair waving on to her shoulders – dare she try the New Look? Sometimes it was as if she were taking part in a story. Betty at this time moved in a world heightened and made more dense by its relation to that rhythm in her mind which took pleasure in extending what she saw and did into a form dependent on but different from the accepted reality – fictive, dramatic, sometimes fantastical, sometimes tragic. And Douglas was charged with this feeling of hers.

The preparations over, the day arrived, and then Betty was nervous. She had to walk at the head of the girls – lead them in fact. However hard she tried to walk very closely to the crowds on the pavement or drag a little behind, there was no doubt that she was prominently in charge and this upset her. This doubt transferred itself to everything and What to Wear? became an enormous problem – all the more disturbing because her wardrobe was meagre and she never otherwise hesitated for more than a few seconds. But 'Would a dress be too showy?', she would ask a totally indifferent Joseph – or 'Would a coat – the black coat, the wine one was for going to shop or cleaning in – would this black coat be too formal? or too hot? or too gloomy? or too short, anyway?' And should she wear 'sandals or shoes – what do you think?' 'Whatever you like,' Joseph replied from behind the paper – his response to many of her questions. 'Whatever you like.'

This day she wore her second-best dress, the green and white striped one – which did not suit her as well as her best dress, not even as well as her everyday dress. Despite it she looked lovely : eager, sparkling at the thought of so much enjoyment about to be had, the tension giving a little glow to her skin.

And she felt so well about this carnival. There was nothing 'laid on' about it, neither from hands of the mighty dead nor from the hands of the rich living. In that way, Betty thought, it was like the Labour Party which proclaimed that people were now equal with regard to their health and their basic livelihood, and more equal than before in regard to education and the systems. She would respond emotionally for the Labour Party on any subject – but especially now, at this time, when they were in power with Clement Attlee as Prime Minister and 'making a really good job of it considering the mess there is to clear up after a war'. Somehow, the carnival was directly related to the Labour Party's term of government – but more importantly it was related to people peacefully enjoying themselves. She loved to be in crowds but feared it terribly when the slightest ripple of nastiness stirred. Here was a time when there was none.

So, grasping her handkerchief in her left hand – for this dress had no pockets – she did her best to forget her feelings of unease – (she was *not* showing off, she had a legitimate reason to be there – and nobody noticed her anyway – who did she think she was?) and nodded cheerfully when the official came and asked her if the girls were ready. The bandmaster muttered 'Men of Harlech, quick march tempo, get them going, plenty of cornet in the chorus,' lifted his baton, turned his back on the band, prodded Kathleen – and away they went.

> 'O'er the hills, thro' night lies sleeping,
> Tongues of flame thro' mists are leaping,
> As the brave, their vigil keeping,
> Front the deadly fray;
> Then the battle thunder
> Rives the rocks asunder
> As the light falls on the flight
> Of foes without their plunder:
> There the worsted horde is routed,
> There the valiant never doubted
> There they died but dying shouted:
> "Freedom wins the day." '

The music stirred Douglas to uncontainable excitement. So clear the sounds from the silver band, with the drum-beat lifting his feet in time and so much to look at! Douglas had never yet been in a carnival. Each year had been the same: overwhelming intoxication at the thought of it, a thousand ideas as to what he could be and, in the end, almost drowned in his multitudinous waves of emotion, tears and the decision to 'go as nothing'. He loved dressing up : in the choir he closed his eyes with pleasure as he slipped the pleated surplice over the long but- toned black cassock, and when the vicar had introduced ruffs he could hardly bear to take his off, would have worn it in the street if he had dared. At the primary school, also, a new teacher had set them all doing plays in the last year and the doublets and hose, the sword and Wellingtons for top-boots, the character to be assumed and the lines remembered, all put him in a daze comparable to that which came on him when he felt that Pauline Bell was looking at him with interest. And each time he read a book or went to the pictures, then for at least a day afterwards, he *was* the hero : either a quiet, strong, honest schoolboy with deep talents, too profound for the superficial observer – someone from the Fifth Form at St Dominic's – or he was Errol Flynn or Johnny Weismuller going O–o-o through the streets, calling the elephants to his rescue. When his father took him to watch Carlisle United, then he was Ivor Broadis for the rest of the weekend, and in the cricket season he was Denis Compton. He was forever imitating the gait, expressions and attitudes of those boys older than himself and longed to wear long trousers so that his roles could be further extended. Douglas had a hundred masks a day, swung between ecstasy and despair hourly, ran everywhere – even going up the street to do the shopping – was now the leader of a gang, now ex- cluded from it, lived in a daily pageant of bonfires, Christmas, Easter, football matches, films, the Cubs, the choir, the auctions, the horse-sales, exams, swimming, hounds and hares, fishing – he was played on by the town and its images each day of his life.

When it came to squashing all this into one costume for one carnival day – the effort was beyond him. Besides, he liked to be alone, watching, hovering, out of it yet marching perfectly in step with the band, seeing all the people, alternately proud and ashamed of his mother being so pretty and so prominent, looking at the new people come into town for the do, hugging it all to himself, lonely and at the same time feeling himself to be almost the spirit of the carnival, for he had been down to the park every night that week to see them get it ready, had stood outside the Temperance Hall to hear the band practise, had explored the yards to catch a glimpse of the wagons being decorated on the Friday night, had asked practically everyone what they were going as, had dreamed of the carnival, entered and won the races, won the hearts of the crowd, met a beautiful girl, had his mother smile and congratulate him.

Sometimes he had to close his eyes and look away, for it was all too much, too many people he knew each carrying a different scent which he breathed as he passed them by, too many alleys and lanes, walls and doors he had played in and done something he would never forget or never be forgiven for. So he was charged with his past and flooded by his present, his moods winking as rapidly as morse, and sometimes he had to dive down a side-turning to be alone in the empty street and hear the carnival in the distance because it was too much to bear.

Harry had dressed up as a boxer. He had wanted to be Joe Louis but Betty said it would be much easier to be a white man. Joseph had suggested Bruce Woodcock but Harry was not convinced until he had started to rub soot on his legs. The sight of his legs turning black had unnerved him. So he was Bruce Woodcock. A pair of shorts, his goloshes, Douglas's dressing-gown, a pair of boxing gloves which Joseph had sent back from Belgium and, last demand of Harry's, a black eye. The costume was not inspired but Harry felt very pleased with himself and was quietly convinced that he would be among the prize-winners, though when he arrived and found five other boxers, he was prepared to concede that he might just miss the award for originality. He was a little chilly because he insisted on the dressing-gown being open so that people could see his shorts, and he rather resented having to stop every so often while the girls up front did their dance, but on the whole he was very happy about it all. He wished that he had not been put quite so far back because he liked to hear the music and could not be sure of keeping in step when it was so faint; that was his only complaint.

In the Lion and Lamb, Joseph was keeping an anxious eye on George. He was annoyed that he should be doing so, but by now it was a habit he could not break. Even while playing darts, he would find as he pulled his arrows out of the board that his first glance was for George, sitting in the corner of the room, almost drunk, belligerently arguing. It was impossible to avoid being with him, for George clung very tightly; and even when Joseph had been directly rude, George had bounced back – into the welcoming arms of Joseph's regret at his loss of temper. Moreover, since George had married Helen, Joseph felt obliged to be somewhat responsible for him. Helen was treating George so badly now : she drank around the place, most probably slept around, no matter how many the evasive constructions Betty put on her actions, she was careless about Lester, her son, and always short-tempered with Aileen, and George's only defence was to pretend to be ignorant. For he always loved Helen and it was that which bound Joseph to him.

As he heard the band approach he, too, as Douglas, felt the rhythm penetrate his skin. He finished off his drink quickly and went out into the street to get a good view, George tagging along behind him.

Kathleen passed to ironical cheers which he acknowledged gaily by even more furious strumming on the ukelele. Then the band stopped, bumping into each other like a falling pack of cards. An official ran ahead and tugged Kathleen to a halt.

The girls held their handkerchiefs in the air, the bells tinkling lightly, and the bandmaster nodded at Betty who turned and by the most unobtrusive of gestures, informed the dancers that they must be ready. Joseph was near her but did not try to catch her eye, knowing it would unnerve her, though she looked so cool, so tranquil in command. The music began, the girls dipped forward, sweeping their handkerchiefs to the ground. Joseph looked for the boys.

He saw Douglas on the other side of the street, squeezed between two stout women with shopping baskets, his head just above one of the baskets so that it looked as if he was being carried in it, live, as a turnip on top of the groceries. He was staring at the girls, so completely absorbed that he looked almost shocked to attention. His hair was mussed up, tie askew, cheeks red. When he did notice his father, he gave him a most peremptory nod, and though Joseph knew that this came from the annoyance many boys of that age feel at *having* a father – especially one who was to be seen in public – and understood that this was compounded by the intensity of his concentration on the dancing, which could not tolerate even the temporary intrusion of a brief recognition – yet he was hurt by his son's lack of need for him. The hurt came and went no more painfully or powerfully than passing muscular twinge, but it added to the muggy isolation already encouraged by the beer: his wife there, and his son, untouchable. He looked along the line for Harry and eventually spotted him, standing quite still, looking up into the sky as if praying for an aeroplane to pass to give him a diversion while all this dancing about was going on. Joseph smiled, and forgot the hurt he had felt.

The dancing over, the procession set off once more, passing the fountain, turning into West Street and going down the hill towards the park. Joseph stood and watched all of it and was delighted when Harry saw him and waved a glove.

More pleased, however, with the gang at the very end, behind the lorries and wagons. For after the procession had left Low Moor Road, this gang of boys – aged between eight and fourteen, about twenty of them, all very poorly dressed – had joined on and wagged like a tail. Lester, Helen's son, was the leader, and he carried a stick on which a large square of cardboard was nailed, with the words 'THE CADJERS', written in charcoal. Some of the boys wore trilbys, others wore old scarves around their neck, most, even the smaller boys, wore long pants and boots.

Joseph did not quite know why they pleased him so much, this gang. The cheek of it was something, for they scattered whenever the band stopped and with threatening and barefaced determination held out their hats to the crowd, taking a collection for themselves. Perhaps, also, after the artifice and work of the walkers and the wagons, this higgledy piggledy – 'Let's see if we can get away with it' – mob of boys came as a relief. That they came from very poor families made poignant their rapacities over the coins – usually pennies and halfpennies – which were thrown at them. These were the children of people as poor as you could be without deserving the description 'destitute'.

Most of all, Joseph was glad to see Lester out there in front. He had taken to Lester ever since Helen's arrival with him and lost no opportunity of giving him a treat or bring him along to Hound Trails and football matches. Lester repaid this by never wavering in playing out his own part which was that of a reckless, daring ceaselessly active boy. Whereas Douglas sometimes got into trouble, Lester went out looking for it. Whereas Douglas seemed to plunge into himself on occasions and be inaccessible, Lester appeared to act on every impulse that took him. He had not passed for the Grammar School and only longed for the day on which he would leave school altogether. Then – he had plans! Joseph threw him sixpence and Lester caught it, beaming and, waving at the others to join in, began to sing a currently popular cowboy song which came out from those twenty liberated throats with shrill jest and menace.

The procession passed, Joseph went back into the pub. He would get down to the park later, Or perhaps not at all: there were three races on the wireless that afternoon and he could not really miss them.

Douglas became magnetized by a girl with long corn-coloured plaits whom he had never seen before. He schemed to stand near her and yet be unobserved: tailing her like a 'private eye': jostling with others so that he could stand behind her on the steps to the banana-slide and touch her; rewarded by a smile; then together on the American Swing – love, marriage, at last; her father called her, and she ran away nameless.

Harry saw a man who had been in Thurston the previous year with a small company of repertory actors who had taken over the parish rooms for the autumn. A very lugubrious, rather paunchy, myopic man. He needed chatting to, Harry thought, and cheering up. So he went and stationed himself nearby, edged closer, explained things, asked him how he made himself look different on the stage, and finally asked what he had withheld for fear of a negative answer – whether the actors were coming again? They were. Harry was struck dumb with pleasure and allowed himself to be bought an ice-cream.

Betty took charge of those girls whose mothers had not come, went around the wagons with them, looked at the costumes, encouraged them to enter for the races, looked out for Joseph who did not arrive.

Lester ran in every possible race and when they were over began the intensive operation of finding empty lemonade bottles and taking them to the stall to claim the twopence return. Single-minded in this, he was also light-fingered, and many a mother placed a bottle neatly beside a tree and found it gone at the next glance.

The girls did one final dance on the lawn just before they were given their tea and then Betty's work was done. She had five of the little ones hanging around her, but she knew their older sisters or brothers and could disengage herself from them whenever necessary. For it was now that the husbands drifted down; not the dutiful or interested kind who had been there all day, nor the fellas who would never be caught in public with their wives, but the ordinary type, who'd had a drink or two in the afternoon, or been to a match, or worked on the allotment. Not Joseph.

He had gone into the back room of the pub to listen to the last two races and drunk more than usual because it was rare that he was in with the clique who drank out of hours. When he came out, even this early autumn sunshine made him feel a little dizzy, and by the time he reached the top of Ma Powell's field and looked down at the park, he knew he needed a little snooze. He went back home for it. Besides, it was one way to get rid of George.

Having given up hope of Joseph, Betty felt lonely. Douglas was not to be caught nor stay for longer than a minute anywhere near her – plunging through the dying carnival in a state of exhausted over-excitement, he was too rootless even to wait while she searched her handbag for a promised threepence for an ice-cream. Harry was not to be seen anywhere, but Betty did not worry because plenty of people knew him and the boys had been able to find their way home from anywhere in the town ever since they had started school.

Though there were other wives there without husbands, she

thought it mean of Joseph not to put in an appearance – if only for the children's sake. He never took them for walks or anything like that; the most he managed was to let them trot beside him as he went to the bookie's or along to a match.

She had come to expect so much during those years alone while he'd been away. They had not been all that easy, despite the children to take her mind off things. There had been too much time to think about herself; to listen to the radio and think; and wonder about Joseph and indulge frightening thoughts. She remembered the kitchen, the blind down, not a sound from the town, news of war and the consequences of war, the pulley heavy with clothes which would never dry out in that damp weather, the gas mantle which needed renewing, blistered brown paint on the corner cupboard. At least he could have stripped or scraped those cupboard doors since his return; at least that. *She* would have painted them.

When she got home, she was so disgusted to find him snoozing on the sofa that she had not even the energy to wake him up. The boys had not come with her but she did not expect them until dark.

George came before Joseph woke up and his presence was a stopper to the argument which silently tore between them; as the men went out the boys came in and Betty got ready their supper, determined to wait up for Joseph and face him with his life.

Chapter Ten

He came back after closing time full of beer and guilt, gave the door a slight kick to show his independence and caught it with his hand before it banged against the wall to show his consideration.

Betty was in the corner pretending to read the *Women's Illustrated*; she had knocked off the music on the wireless as she had heard his step down the street.

He turned his eyes aside, pretending that after the few minutes between pub and house the gas-light was hurting them. Already the cheerful memory of the evening's roving – with the tailpiece of the carnival trailing enticingly through the pubs and dark streets – curdled to a thin trickle which might have been fear; and so he deliberately 'lurched' forward to provoke an accusation of drunkenness. None came.

O this silence of hers! He could have murdered her just to hear the sound of it.

He sat down 'heavily' opposite her, thrusting out his legs as if wanting her to get up and trip over them. She did not even glance over the top of her page. Joseph then glared at the fire and behind the over-masculine gestures cringed, then reproached himself his weakness and willed his real feelings to match those assumed.

Betty had begun to read the while and one tired part of her mind was quite interested in it, curious to turn the page. What was the use of arguing?

'Do I not get a cup of tea then?' Joseph's right foot kicked at the air as he shouted this question.

'You'll wake the children.'

'You always say that.'

'I shouldn't have to.' She had glanced up but now looked back at the magazine and with loathing added : 'Coming in drunk.'

'I'm not drunk.'

'Well stop acting it. Anyway you are.'

'I – am – not,' quietly emphasized.

'They just have to whistle and you go wherever they want.'

'Who?'

'Anybody.' The pause was her burden and having lost the advantage of her silence, she was too irritated to bear it long. 'Look at George – he just has to come and you're away.'

'You could come with us.'

'Who wants to go drinking every night?'

'Nobody *goes* drinking every night.'

'You might as well for all we see of you.'

'Put that bloody paper down.'

'There's no need to swear.' She lowered the magazine but did not let go of it. 'Sometimes the boys wonder if you still live here.'

'I can't help that, can I? I'm up before them . . .'

'I have to drag you up.'

'. . . and when I get back they're out playing.'

'And when they get back you're out enjoying yourself.'

'Why shouldn't I? You would do the same.'

'Don't be ridiculous – I need the nights to keep this place in order.'

'I've told you before – drop one of your houses and use the time for this : there's no need for you to work so hard.'

'You don't say that when I buy Douglas a new suit out of my own money.'

'Betty!' Far from being offended, he used her tentative reproach as a means of gaining sympathy for himself. 'That's a nasty thing to say. Really nasty,' he added, complacently.

'I'm sorry.' She put down the magazine and went into the back kitchen to make a pot of tea. To get there she had to step over Joseph's legs and as she did so he made a grab at her. His touch restored her disgust and she pulled away so forcefully that he knew it would be asking for trouble to hold on :

but he hummed to himself and still rested on his little victory.

'Anyway who would look after the boys,' she asked, hidden from him, 'if I came out with you?'

'That's stupid, Betty. You can always get somebody in. Anyway, they're old enough to look after themselves now.'

Betty nodded to herself – her point proved – and stood beside the gas cooker, waiting for the kettle to boil. She heard Joseph pull off his shoes and then take the poker to riddle the fire, over-energetically : that would be another shovelful of coal which could have been saved.

The tea mashed, she brought in the two cups and handed his to the outstretched hand – he was lying out on the sofa.

'Is there a biscuit?' he asked as she was about to sit down.

'Yes. There's a full packet.'

She had the cup on the arm of her chair and went again to the back kitchen, found the biscuits, brought them, handed them to him, sat down, still holding to his words 'they're old enough to look after themselves now.' Watched him sip his tea and felt a passing regret that he should so be letting himself go that at his age he had a beer belly; if only he knew the effort she was forced to make time and again as he took off his clothes for bed – there was a lack of delicacy about his undressing; and the clothes were left where they dropped – but that was unimportant, she told herself, doggedly, appearances were unimportant : though she lived by and for them.

'Harry was upset this afternoon,' said without apparent provocation. 'Hm?'

Betty did not press for the moment, concerned to control the anger which bobbed into her throat. Joseph, cigarette, tea and comfortable displacement of stomach, blew unsuccessful smoke rings at the ceiling and relaxed in anticipation of a Sunday lie-in.

'I said Harry was upset this afternoon.'

'Was he?'

'He wouldn't say why.'

'Can't have been much then ... they usually say, kids, don't they?'

'Do they? I shouldn't have thought you knew much about them. Kids.' Still evenly delivered.

'I helped to bring up four brothers and sisters – remember that! – I could change nappies when I was ten years old.'

'Yes, I've heard all that. It seems to have sickened you for life.'

'O now don't *start*, Betty. Just when we were peaceful.'

And there was some justice in his complaint, she thought. 'But if *I* don't say anything – nothing ever *gets* said.'

'That would be a relief sometimes. Everything I do's wrong.'

'I only said that Harry wasn't himself.'

'I know. But you meant that it was my fault. I should have come to the car-niv-al – oh, deary-me.' He blushed at his own meanness, shifted uneasily on the sofa as if something was sticking into him. When he began like this, he could not stop himself; yet all the time, a calm voice was singing inside his head the incongruous sentence: 'You love her more than you could love anybody: if you left her you'd be lost.' He turned to her and accused her face to face. 'So what was wrong with Harry?'

'I don't know. He wouldn't tell me.'

'And what do you expect me to do about it now? Go and wake him up and ask him a lot of questions?'

'Don't be silly.'

'Well why drag it up then?'

'Because these are the things that people do bring up,' she said, desperately. 'Those that don't spend every night out drinking.'

'Once and for all you could have come with me!' He swung his legs off the sofa and saw them land on the carpet, soft under his woollen socks, knitted for him by May: that fact reminded him of how unquestionably he was appreciated elsewhere. 'You're welcome! You know that. You're welcome to come!'

'I never ask where you've been,' timidly. Betty darted to the glow of another suspicion, once warned by a whiff of gossip.

'I always tell you.'

'But you needn't. I don't want to know.'

'What's that got to do with it?'

'It has.' Her face set, defying what, she was not clear, but defiant. 'It has.'

'You can't carry an argument – that's your trouble. It puts years on anybody talking to you. You've no idea.'

'If I was clever you would find something else to shout about.'

'I'm not shout – O, I hate all this. I do. I really do. I come home, it's been a carnival day. I've had a few all right so I've had a few, and off we go into arguments. What a bloody life it is. It is! It really is.'

'There's no need to swear.' Upright on the edge of her chair, her back straight, the cup and saucer poised in her hand as if she were being observed at the very politest tea-party: miserable.

'I mean, I saw you this afternoon,' Joseph had moved himself rather deeply by his previous speech and wanted to consolidate the feeling of noble suffering it had given him. 'I did – just outside the ... District Bank ...' his tone sentimental, he stopped to let it take effect.

'You mean opposite the Lion and Lamb.' The sentence popped out and then her lips snapped shut, as if they had suddenly parted to allow her tongue a rude gesture and, too late, were shocked at what they had done.

'All right,' Joseph groaned and eased himself back into the horizontal position on the sofa. 'Opposite – the – Lion – and – Lamb. That's what I mean about you! I've forgotten what I was going to say now because of your stupid interruption! And where did it get us? Eh? Eh?'

The challenge fell between them and grew cold in the silence. His voice had sounded so querulous and old; Betty was a little frightened by it.

Some dream broke through and in an entirely different accent and manner, thoughtfully, as if speaking for someone else, Joseph said:

'This is what happens to you if you haven't been educated, see? I *feel* all these things, but I can't explain them. And *you* certainly can't – no, I didn't mean to be nasty, really, I didn't, really. But if we'd both of us, if we'd stayed on at school and maybe gone on from there – we would always have something to talk about. Something sensible and interesting to talk about instead of these arguments that don't get anywhere. I mean, I would have read an interesting book or something and I would tell you all about it and you would be interested to listen to me talking because I would know how to put it, see? Then we wouldn't – I mean I wouldn't *have* to go out, at all. No – but –' he closed his eyes and the beer seemed to be stirring around inside him, soaking through him as through paper and in his mind he saw the papers, the comics and magazines and self-declared 'rubbish' which served his large appetite for reading matter; and felt ill at the thought of it. 'What we read is trash! It *is*. Trash! Like that – that thing you're reading now – I mean, what's in it?'

And again, though he had made her sympathetic to him, there was something too demanding about it all.

'There are some very nice things in it,' she replied, promptly. 'Patterns and things –'

'*Patterns!* Who could have a conversation about patterns?'

'You're not supposed to talk about them – you're supposed to knit them.'

She smiled: Joseph would start to laugh at her, she could see the beginnings of it in the corners of his mouth. 'And anyway, there's the serial.'

'And what's in that?' he demanded.

'Well . . .' She had forgotten. Her mouth opened, and realizing that it could be comical, she took care to parody herself, lightly, hoping that Joseph would be affected by it but would not notice so that she would find a way out of this trying argument without having been seen to seek one.

'Sounds a great story if you can't even remember it.'

'O yes. There's this young doctor. And he's working for his exams.'

'What's interesting about that? That's what they all do.'

'Ah. But there's this nurse as well.'

'Don't say it! Don't say it!' And Joseph lifted his hands as if he was beating off a wasp. 'He starts to go with her but he can't see her often enough because of these exams of his and she thinks he's running around with another nurse and so she sets herself up to another doctor who isn't as clever as number one but has more money – what's wrong?'

'You've read it!'

'No I haven't.'

'Why did you ask me what it was about when you'd read it?'

'I – haven't – read it. I just made that up.'

'You can't have done. That's the story.'

Joseph giggled – very well pleased with himself. 'There we are then. Your husband's an author. That's another reason you could do without that magazine.'

'You *must* have read it.'

'Don't you believe me?'

'But that's the *story*?'

'I tell you I DIDN'T READ IT.'

'You'll wake the children.'

'You always say that.'

'You must have read one just like it.'

'Maybe so ... maybe so.' He was tired now. 'You give me credit for nothing.'

'Why? What have you done?'

'You would drive anybody crackers, Betty. Really. I mean, we started by talking about education.'

'I'm sorry.'

'Never mind.'

'I'm sorry though.' She hesitated. 'Well then?'

'Yes?'

'Well?' She nodded, smiled encouragingly, 'let's talk about education then.'

'What about it?'

'Douglas is always top,' she said.

'*I* was always top as well.'

'Hm! I didn't say it proved anything.'

'Why did you say it then?'

'To get us started.'

Joseph shook his head and tasted his tea, pulled a face: 'See? This tea's cold now.'

'Oh blooming heck!' Betty stood up, took his cup and went towards the back kitchen. 'Anyway, Harry wasn't himself.'

'I'll talk to him in the morning – Oh! That reminds ... can I borrow your bike for Tommy Mars tomorrow morning? His own's bust and I said he could borrow yours.'

'Why?' She resented lending her bicycle; partly because she depended on it so much for her work, but also for some of the same feeling which made her unable to drink out of someone else's cup.

'What d'you mean – why?'

For goodness' sake, Joseph, stop taking up everything I say! No wonder you're bothered about education if you don't know what "why" means!'

'Keep your hair on.'

'I hate you saying that.'

'I know.'

'There's your tea : drink it hot this time.'

'We thought we might go to Bothcl.'

'For cock-fighting. Don't try to kid me, Joseph : everybody knows what goes on in Bothel on Sunday mornings.'

'It's a good job everybody doesn't.' He laughed; a forced and unnecessary laugh.

'You'll have a fine lot of chance to talk to Harry, then, won't you? By the time you've had your lie in and read your blessed *People*, it'll be Tommy Mars and Bothel on my bike.'

'I'll talk to him.'

'It doesn't matter.' Her tone was sensible and calm : as if she had realized this all along but thought it not worth mentioning until now. 'He wouldn't take any notice of you anyway.'

'What a thing to say!'

'Well he wouldn't. You never talk to them about anything so why should you talk to him about this? No – I'll get it out of him sometime. Then I'll tell you.'

Much relieved, she sat back in her chair and took up the magazine, quickly finding her place in the story. Joseph looked at her, looked away from her, considered shouting, considered soothing, then shook his head with mock-bemusement and lit a cigarette, the last one in the packet : he must be sure to nip it so as to have a stump for the morning.

She read on.

'Well,' he said, his voice rather nervous – he didn't know why, he wasn't in the least nervous – 'aren't you going to tell us about the carnival, then?'

'You said you saw it.'

'I did.' His curiosity gave him patience. 'But who was there I mean. Who did you see?'

'Everybody was there except you.'

'O for Christ's sake, Betty, give us a bit of chat about it!'

'It's nearly bed-time.' Still her head bent to the page; which she turned over. 'And don't swear.'

'I would've come if I could.' He tossed restlessly on the sofa. 'This bloody – sorry! – this damned sofa's neither one thing nor the other.'

'Damned's just as bad as anything else. Neither one what nor the other?'

'You know – it's too short.'

'It takes up that wall. What else do you want?'

'Was Harold Patterson in charge of the sports?'

'Yes,' her hand went out, unerringly, for her cup.

'He would be. He gets on my nerves that fella. Sets himself up in charge of any mortal thing he can lay his hands on.'

'I think he's nice.'

'Oh – maybe he's nice to you. But you should hear him down at Kirkbride. "Do this Tallentire", "Have you got that, Tallen-tire." *Yes.* No "Joseph" – and he just went to the National school like everybody else. Every bloody – well I *feel* like that! – any blooming job I've been in, somebody's bossed me about. And look at me now – STORES! What sort of a life is it being in STORES?'

'Well change it.'

'How can I? What am I good for now?'

'You're as good as you've ever been and don't whine, Joseph Tallentire.'

'But it's true, isn't it? Even when I was at that factory I was the slave of that machine. I *was.* The Slave of that Machine.'

'Don't be so soft.'

'Why don't we have beer in the house?'

'What d'you mean?'

134

'Well you see them – on the pictures and that – "have a beer", "have a drink" – *they* don't have to go to the pub for a pint of Ordinary do they? Why don't *we* keep stuff in the house?'

'It wouldn't keep long with you around. You've a belly like a balloon as it is.'

'Who's got a belly? Who has?'

'Well if it isn't a belly, it's an illness – I'm saying nothing.'

'You've said enough as it is.'

'I never say anything,' said Betty, most sternly, 'that's my trouble.'

'Trouble she says . . .'

But warmth had come into her tone and he luxuriated in it – how could he tell her how he felt, that there was no need for anything else? Once he would not have needed words.

She yawned and stretched: her arms were thrown to the ceiling and in the act her body was tightened and thrust towards him: had he not known her as he did, he would have thought it provocative. But had *she* not known that he knew her well, she would never have yawned like that.

'Bed-time,' she said. 'And don't you be too late. You promised to speak to Harry in the morning, remember.'

'They've got bikes – they can come to Bothel with me.'

'You wouldn't have them back in time for Sunday School.'

'Promise. Cross my heart.'

'Anyway. What do they want cock-fighting! No.'

'*They* won't have to fight, mother.'

'Don't call me mother. I'm not thirty yet. Look to yourself.'

'I'm no mother either.'

'I can't make you out sometimes.' Again she yawned. 'You say you wish you'd been clever,' yawned again, 'but you say such soft things.'

'Who said he wanted to be clever? Eh?'

'I can't be expected to remember all you said off by heart, can I? You said something like that. But I can't repeat it all back to you like a blooming echo! You're not *that* important.'

'All right. All right. Keep your hair on.'

'I *hate* that ex—, ex— that way of talking.'

'At least I don't take on words I can't finish.'

'No need to be so nasty.'

'Who was nasty?'

'You don't even know you're doin' it. Good night. And don't be long.' The final phrase – though its effect was intended to hasten him to bed – was so far from an invitation to pleasure as to be a parody.

'I can't wait,' he muttered.

'What was that?'

'Nothing.'

She went up the short staircase quietly.

Joseph was happy. He reckoned that he'd got off lightly. Oh – he knew she was disappointed in his laxness but she couldn't know of those unhappy feelings which had been pressing onto his mind for the last few years. Sensations which could not be mentioned: dreadful feelings of his mind in shipwreck, not only hope but instinct adrift, which frightened him and found relief only, only in drink. The times he felt the swell inside his head – as if all that had been ignored and brutalized in him, unused and unacknowledged, suddenly used his uncertainty as the opportunity to show their strength. His head was rocked with fears he could not name.

Chapter Eleven

He thought he had made his 'real' break when he left the aerodrome and got a job with the Insurance. But after a very few
months he knew that it would satisfy only the smallest part of
him; he worked longer hours than at the aerodrome for much
the same pay, and though the hours were more under his own
control and though this collecting insurance and selling it in the
town and the neighbourhood appeared more interesting, he was
soon bored, took pleasure only in the unexpected and looked
for it outside of work.

When the big opportunity came it was only because he was
feeling ashamed of himself that he took it. He had been to see
his father to try to convince the old man to give up work. John
was in his seventies now and his wife had asked for help to
persuade the old man to retire. With small contributions from
their children and the old-age pension they could have about
as much coming in as his present wage packet. His father
had been so contemptuous of Joseph's suggestion that he had
lost his temper, and weakly argued from the effect it had on
other people – that for example and most importantly his wife
suffered because he continued to drive himself so. None of his
business; get back and sort his own life out. He had biked back
to Thurston, smarting at the accusation and angry at the effec-
tive rule his father could still impose on him.

No one at home: Douglas, who was now fourteen, off to
Oxford for a week with three other members of his class and
the history teacher, attending a series of lectures arranged by
the Grammar School and the Church of England. Harry away
playing Rugby for the same school's Under-Thirteen side. Betty
shopping in Carlisle. Joseph had stamped around the house,
unnerved that it should be empty when he wanted to tell

someone what had happened. As if someone were present to be impressed by his action, he had begun to lay the table for tea, slamming down the crockery, barging his way about the kitchen, rattling the slow kettle on the timid gas-ring, muttering to himself, banging the wireless to clear the crackle and only making it worse. He broke the best tea-pot. It had been given to Betty by one of the women she had worked for: not a cast-off, but something gone out and bought – a special thing. Joseph gathered the pieces, guiltily looking at the door in case Betty should come in. When, eventually, she did he could not conceal that though the destruction had been accidental it was somehow intentional, both symbol and retribution for a stupid attack of temper. Betty had winkled that from him in a matter of seconds and from then on he flapped around her hopelessly, until it became obvious to him that he had touched the fuse which fired off a dense and impenetrable mood in her and the only thing to do was to clear out.

It was in the Blue Bell that he heard about it. A pub, the Throstle's Nest (known as the 'Thrush') was to change hands and the Brewery were looking for a new tenant-landlord. In the general mood of the last few years, Joseph would have let it pass. But with the set faces of his father and his wife before his eyes, each in different ways having made him feel feeble and centreless that afternoon, a spark of his former optimism flared, his self-assertion was lit up, remembered, invoked once more. Without telling anyone, he went home that night and wrote a letter applying for the pub. He had nothing to lose. Nothing at all.

A week later, he received a reply asking him to come for an interview. The letter arrived when Betty was out and again he did not tell her, put on his best suit on the nominated morning, caught a bus to Workington where the brewery had its works and offices.

There were five others there – he being the only one who *lived* in Thurston – and the interview was much longer than he had anticipated.

He had thought of the questions they might ask him and rehearsed his answers on the bus. All done secretly, rather desperately, as the red double-decker swept out to the coast road and twisted past slag heaps and pit-heads. His insurance book was heavy in the pocket of his long, belted raincoat. The bus was almost empty. The interview seemed a simple affair. Nor was it much different from what he had imagined : but longer, and as he came back he felt that he was in with a chance.

The Throstle's Nest was the least flourishing pub in the town. Before the first war, when the town had been a prosperous market centre, there had been about forty pubs. Now, with the population shrunk to less than 4,000, there were only sixteen. Yet most of these were run by landlords who made a living from the pub alone and did not have to take a day-time job to supplement their income. The Thrush was badly placed – about two hundred yards from the nearest neighbouring pub, and away from that central cluster which made it so easy for drinkers to change location; in High Street, for example, there were seven pubs on a stretch no longer than fifty yards, which made for concentrated evenings. It required an effort to go down to the Thrush and few at this time thought it worth making. A man called Archer had held it for twenty years; he was in his sixties, his wife was dead, he drank a good deal, the pub was never re-decorated, his beer was poorly kept. It was a difficult pub to run; built as a small inn with several rooms, it required a staff. For the habit then was that unless you were in the bar itself, you did not fetch your own drink : the publican, or a waiter, came for your order and served you. To run the Thrush properly on a busy night would need at least three waiters, which knocked up the overheads and was only worth it if a good trade could be relied on; not to have waiters discouraged trade. Mr Archer had a woman who helped him on Saturdays and Sundays and left it at that. The brewery were grateful for his retirement.

The understanding – and the contract – was that once a tenant-landlord was installed, then he could not be fired unless he broke his contract or broke the law, by serving after time, giving incorrect measures and so on. Once installed, he paid a weekly rent for the house to the brewery, paid rates to the council, was responsible for all his own accounting and ordering and had only two obligations: to buy all his beer from the brewery, and to sell it according to law. Thus, though a tenant, he was very much his own man – remembering Stoddart he was glad of that. Profits came as a percentage of the gross takings. There was no possibility of the tenant's ever being able to buy the pub from the brewery (unless by some misfortune or unexpected change of policy they decided to sell off the pubs) and as very hard work was needed to make a decent living, the brewery were commanding all the energy and worry which goes into small businesses while bearing none of the direct responsibilities. Yet once their choice had been made, then, beyond a little chivvying, there was nothing they could do to force the landlord to work at a pace other than his own.

In the week following the interview, Joseph was very subdued. He came to regard this as his very last chance. Past his mid-thirties – the boys too settled in school to move, this was the best he would do in Thurston. Secretly, he fed it with all the old dreams: that they were still there unnerved him for he realized with what effort he had repressed them. But if he got that place ... then he would be able to run his own house, organize his own life, be his own man.

Still he did not tell Betty – and there was more than pride in that recalcitrance: he knew that she did not like pubs, did not really approve of drinking, would be afraid of 'setting herself up', putting herself even so marginally in a position to be envied. For there was no doubt that the landlords of Thurston were envied. As some did quite well, so all were thought to do, and their income was doubled in the imagination, trebled in the gossip, and finally turned to treasure by a consideration of the potentialities of their situation. That Mr Archer retired to live with his daughter and had nothing but a few hundred and his old-age pension made not the slightest difference to this: and if, as sometimes happened, a man came out of a pub and went back to his former job, swearing he was better off so, he was thought devious, incompetent or both. Landlords did all right – that was the proposition, which was unchallengeable – but the nod and wink which accompanied the words would, he was sure, be distressing for Betty. Yet he knew that she would follow him.

The fact of the Thrush being in poor condition and reputation would help him there. And if the boys were going to stay on at school and even go to university (he dared hardly dream of that) then any possible extra money would be a help. At the moment they managed by not much more than a hair's-breadth and trips like the one Douglas was taking had to be long (though privately) considered, the fourteen pounds involved being no easy sum. That, too, might sway her, though again he knew that she was rather pleased with the fact that they managed on so little and were yet able to get school uniforms for the boys, allow drinking-money for himself (though he supplemented that by odd jobs as always), even, the previous year, take a week's holiday at a seaside resort instead of the usual staying with relatives in other parts of the county. And money worried both Douglas and Harry: Douglas did not want to go into the Sixth Form because he knew that the expectation was for him to be bringing in about £2.10.0–£3.0.0 a week and giving most of it to his mother: Joseph had been forced to argue with him at length on that and Douglas now treated the school as a job, tearing into the work until he exhausted himself. Harry insisted on doing a paper-round before he went to school in the mornings, and the six and six was handed over regularly. That it was as regularly handed back did not disturb him at all.

Yet whatever Betty's objections were, Joseph was determined that he would overrule them. If he got the pub, he would present it straightforwardly. As soon as he recognized his determination, he became self-righteous in it. He would go around the streets, his insurance book under his arm, muttering to himself – 'She *should* agree. I can't be expected to follow her *all* the time; if I think it's right to do it, she should see that.' Overhearing himself he would become rather shamefaced. After all, he could not force her to do something against her will. Yet was not one of the facts of marriage that you accepted to do things against your will? Or at least tempered your wishes and opinions? Again he checked himself, for marriage to him was as 'natural' as work to his father; suddenly to invoke it was proof of a serious nervousness. So he would forget about it. It mattered little whether he earned six or twelve pounds a week, what was that to Betty's peace of mind? He had married her knowing and accepting that she would need protection against certain things: now to abandon that was almost to go back on his word. Well, he thought, he was allowed to change, wasn't he?

What a time he could have there! To make that broken down ruin of a pub into a good 'house'. He saw, or imagined, in the flux of the pub – in the people who came in, the customers to be satisfied, the ordering to be got just so – chances for employing himself in ways prohibited now. You sold an insurance and were glad if you saw it come in useful and that was all. On the airfield and in the factory and the forces, he had got to know his job and then become bored. Yet he had not now the energy or confidence to turn that boredom into dreaming or scheming. Neither of those had pleased him for very long anyway. He had felt that if you came to be so on top of your job that you were detached from it, then there was need of iron somewhere else: some men found it in a hobby, or in drink, women, books, music, talk – none of these gave Joseph sufficient return. He imagined that he wanted a discipline which would, like a magnet, attract the filings of his mind and let him live parallel to his earning life. But he could not find anything outside the job which was strong enough, he thought; or which could truly warrant so much effort. Though he liked to think himself different from his father, he too could not escape work though, unlike the old man, he tried to. He read Harry's comics and lounged around the town supporting the teams, following the dogs, following the horses, following the days. In the pub he would have little free time – he intended to try to get a living solely from it – for there was not one day of the year when a pub was allowed to close and the opening hours consumed the day and there would be an empire for him, as his father's empire was labour.

When the letter came with the news that his application had been accepted, Betty caught at once this longing of his for the possibilities which the pub promised. She did not want to go – for more reasons than Joseph had thought of; but she repressed her objections, dismissed her fears and did as he wanted.

As the arrangements were made – Joseph had to borrow £40 to cover himself against his first order – he had to go through to the brewery and learn about cellar-work for the beer, he had to organize everything just so because there is no closing allowed when a pub changes hands : one man goes out, another comes in, changes of furniture and all the carry-on no matter – so Betty went more and more energetically into it, and her misgivings hardened. Though she would have flinched at the word and most probably denied its accuracy, she was making a sacrifice which disturbed her desperately.

It was not so much that she was well-settled, though the disruption of a way of life which she found both agreeable and full might have helped to lead her to the identification of her disturbance. For she liked the small house – neat now, much the same as it had always been but emboldened by a new set of chair covers, bright flower-patterns, a brass lampstead, two rubbings made by Douglas and framed by Harry strangely peaceful on the busy wall-paper, a new strip of carpet in front of the fender – and she liked to go to the other houses about her work in the mornings and return to have the place to herself in the peaceful early afternoon hours, to arrange it so that all three of the men were well and equally served.

Moreover, she realized how much the present settlement mattered not only to herself but to Douglas whose engagement with his schoolwork had become a battle, following rigid rules, plans, timetables, long spells of solitude each evening in the parlour; and she sensed his fragility beneath the effervescent, prize-winning bumptiousness; knew that he was constantly pressed by the doubt as to whether it was right that he should stay on at school while his mother worked, knew, more, that he could find no secure relationship between the world of his books and that of his daily life and was undermined in his confidence through doubts as to his own value in this new world. A change might throw him badly. His approach to the work often thrilled her by the passion which caught both old and new in vivid articulation, often saddened her by the clash and pull which was in his expression, dogged, almost sullen, as if he thought it all fatal but necessary.

But Douglas was only a part of it. She was nervous at the prospect of standing there serving drink to people, some of them scarcely known to her, seeing some of them get drunk, becoming a 'legitimate' target of envy, tight-lips, and even abuse in a town which, as Douglas had said, 'packed a stiff bible-and-respectability combination punch'. She realized all that and decided she was prepared to take it for Joseph's sake : it wasn't asking much of her. Prepared also for a change which would make it extremely difficult for her to go to church on occasional Sundays (because of the clearing-up after Saturdays and the relentless opening hours), difficult to have friends drop in and see her in the evenings, difficult to be as free as she now was in her movements around the town.

The deepest cause of her misgiving, as she worked it out, the power before which the sacrifice was made, was something she was never in her life more than intermittently and vaguely conscious of. It came from her own feelings but was fed by scraps read, by remarks made by Harry (whose first dawn of adolescence made itself known by a dogmatic belligerence on the subject of politics) and most consistently nourished by statements from Helen. For Helen was very much the carrier of her father's convictions and as her boldness became less of a strain, she found more edge in the notions heard promoted so vehemently throughout her childhood. Fragments rather than statements, to do with the Working Class, the Struggle for Power, the Revolution, Oppression, the Proletariat, the Masses – words which Betty only partly understood, which clarified her feeling rather than her thinking but moved her to considerations of what had for so long been taken for granted. Helen spoke more freely to Betty than to anyone else and her views were expressed with more force and accuracy than Betty had heard at any Labour Party meeting. There similar words had stirred her – but to reassurance. She was not at all reassured when Helen spoke. She realized in a twilit way that there could be more than Reform as an aim, that such changes might even suffocate the real end with good intentions.

And somehow while they were not better off than anybody else, while they were near the brink of their resources all the time with nothing left over for savings, herself obliged to scrub and polish for others every day to make it possible for the boys to stay on at school and so on – still she was on the proper side. To take a pub meant to change sides. And that frightened her most of all.

What succeeded in repressing any show of this misery was her belief in Love – once and for all given – and the commitment of her own love to Joseph.

She moved, she moved, and loaded the handcarts outside the small house (it was no distance from their place; and this way was the cheapest) and scrubbed the floors of the new place, laid fresh lino, planned to re-paper the walls, quietened Douglas, relied on Harry, in public was pleased, in private was compliant, with Joseph was often thrown high by his pleasure and intoxicated by the rush of enthusiasm and fire which came back to him, with those who murmured against her was firm, to her friends who welcomed it all, was grateful: alone, was silently desperate and at a loss.

Chapter Twelve

For the first year or two the pub was even better than Joseph had hoped. He had always done jobs well and been proud of that: this one he did supremely well. And the factors involved were so many and so changeable that most of his resources were needed to make of it what he wanted.

He had a clear idea of what that should be. He wanted it to be the best pub in town. An enormous amount of the desire for this was a matter of sport: the customers were out there, the pubs were open, the race was on: for the first time he had a job where his competitiveness, so far enjoyed vicariously, could have free and fairly harmless play. For he would not do anyone down to get trade. No under-cutting, no over-measuring, no disparagement of others: within the rules. It would be like a fight. Thurston had always been a hard-drinking town and its central position meant that people came in on market days and weekends from miles around. There were plenty of good pubs already: which only increased his determination.

Handicaps: lack of experience, an out-of-the-way situation, small rooms, little 'good will' or tradition of good trade, and certain prejudices (for example against swearing when there were women present) and convictions (that it would not be an area for fighting as many of the more successful pubs were over the weekend) which, in that rough town, would weigh him down. And of course Betty, who thoroughly disapproved of drunkenness.

Advantages: through his many jobs in the area, he knew almost every single person for miles around. Moreover, he had always been exceptionally good at remembering names. And it seemed that the jobs he had done in the past now served him as he had once served them; for there were many who would come out of interest or curiosity to see what he was making of it and that was a start. There was the fact that he was chancing his arm, trying something most of them would have been unable or too timid to attempt – that was worth following. While from his time on the insurance (when he had also run a 'book' for a while) and from all the stories known about him he was scrupulously honest in all money matters and fair with regard to his opinion of others. Indeed, part of the reason for his barely suppressed thrill of those very first days was that his qualities, as his acquaintances, seemed to come out and proclaim themselves. It was a little like a wake, and again that added to Betty's sense of a 'passing-over'. She was glad he was well-thought-of and felt sure he would not change : he had held to himself as he was in many conditions and regarded this as a change of circumstance merely, imposing no mutation of attitudes. Finally, he was fairly young, enthusiastic and as always had nothing to lose. While Betty would keep the place spotless : everybody knew that.

The first thing to get right was the beer. Like every pub in the town (except the Crown and Mitre which, standing near the auction, had the full benefit of the flusher agricultural trade on market days, and sold as much whisky as lemonade some afternoons) the Throstle's Nest was virtually a beer-house. Spirits perhaps for a final fling on Saturday night, a toast to sabbatical superstitions the following day, perhaps after a good win (at weddings, marriages, funerals and 'eighteen' of age parties of course) always at Christmas, necessarily at New Year but for 255 days of the years, the spirit bottles stood, neck downwards, so inactive that when you did take a measure you automatically glanced at the bottle to see if the precious level had left a rim. Sherry, egg flip, advocaat, port – a little for the ladies, very few and a very little unless the occasion or the lady was ripe. So beer it was, and hard work to make a living from – a very steady number of pints to be served before half a crown profit showed : between twelve and twenty, depending on the type of beer and the room it was served in. Mild was the staple – two kinds, light and dark; a tender beer, ideal for long nights of drinking, for slow-accumulating richness of the stomach, sternum, heart, lungs, tongue. It had been kept very badly by the previous landlord.

The bitter had not been kept much better, which was more serious as it was more expensive. Also, this brewery's bitter had a good name and people were inclined to judge the full stock by it. Finally there was porter – less and less sold but still, at the beginning of the fifties, popular enough to be worth a regular order. This porter was rather like draught Guinness but less sweet, less creamy, smacking more of wood and less of peat, heavy, like Guinness, but not as thick in the stomach.

There were bottles of course : pints and halves, light ale, old ale, sweet stout, Guinness, export, lager, brown ale – but there was nothing a publican could do about these. They arrived in their crates, capped and captioned, requiring only to be poured. In this there was a little skill, for it was easy to spoil a bottle by pouring too quickly and making too much froth, or by pouring too slowly and making too little; and there was the question of dregs – for some customers thought that the lees contained 'the goodness' and wanted them in, others wanted them in whatever they contained because they had paid for a full bottle of beer, the more discriminating recognized the bottom as powder, undrinkable, and would frown if they saw the sediment floating down *their* glass. But this was simply a matter of hearing preferences and remembering them. The bottles could be nicely displayed and individually wiped with a cloth – for dust settled quickly on them – they often arrived on the brewery wagon covered with dust – and Joseph insisted that each one be cleaned so that people did not get their hands or clothes dirty if they bought them to take out. It all helped, he said.

Despite the fact that some of these bottled beers were lauded on their labels for having won prizes at Vienna in 1894 and Paris in 1910 and so on, it was not these which attracted custom. Trade followed the barrels.

These came every Friday and were lowered down the cellar on ropes which guided them down, a man leaning back into the ropes, padded, tattered leather gloves to keep his hands from being burnt, the barrels thundering down into the cellar like cannons rolling down a slope. Harry loved to be there to help the men in the brewery wagon. They were big, very West Cumbrian, both had worked in the mines, both played professional Rugby League for their town and had been given a job in the brewery through local fame (for it was regarded as a cushy number) and they had taken it because they could swing the hours and give themselves time for training and the occasional mid-week match. Harry, thirteen, was neither undersized nor puny yet they would pick him up and throw him around like a parcel of laundry.

Once they were in the cellar the two men rolled the barrels across the floor and then lifted them on to the ramps: there were two little boards they could have used for this, to roll the barrels on, but these two kicked them away just a little ostentatiously, gripped the barrel, crouched tensely and then heaved it clear of the ground and set it in position without even the suggestion of a bump: the wedges were put in place and the barrel was set. The very smallest barrels, nipins, empty, Harry could just roll from one cellar to another.

The cellars opened outside the pub, in front of it, a large trapdoor, and he would stand at the bottom, as of a pit, and see the wagon towering with barrels and crates, one of the men stalking over it like a warrior among plunder. The way they swung down the crates was beautiful to watch. Each crate held two dozen bottles. One man on the wagon would pass them down to the other, two at a time. He would stack them around the edges of the trapdoor. Lift one, pause, lift another, swing around, the man below took the first, the second, turned and stacked them, turned back, two more waiting, a slight jostling thud each time a crate was placed. The way a stack of crates was reduced was like seeing someone scything down a field of hay. Then the man who had been on the wagon jumped down into the cellar and the crates were slid down the long ramps, two at a time, and again the coordination. Harry – who was mad on Rugby League and went to see these two play whenever he got the chance – was sure he observed in their actions the same rhythm and balance which entranced him when he saw fast open play.

Sometimes when he was off school and his father was away at a trail leaving his mother to look after the pub, then he would make their dinners – that is, go and buy four fish and two shillings worth of chips, set them out on the table with buttered bread and cakes, make a pot of tea and then have every right in the world to sit and watch them eat! And listen to them talk about Rugby. They rarely spoke of anything else.

When they had gone, Joseph went down to the cellars and checked that all his order had arrived. The making out of this order – done on Tuesdays, phoned through, confirmed by post – was tricky, and here he benefited from having worked in stores. Yet another part of his past which actively contributed to the present: he had thought of all those jobs as so many pegs driven uselessly into the ground – but now they held the guy ropes of his working life. The difficulty about the order (not a great but a real one) was, of course, to get it right. For to order too much meant that you risked having beer on your hands which had been untapped for too long and so was in danger of getting flat: to order too little was unthinkable. Yet to estimate on the amount sold in each department – mild, bitter, the bottled stuff, etc. – especially when you were improving trade and so could not refer to the previous week's figures and were not yet sure of the effect of seasonal variations (Christmas, Easter and Bank Holidays were comparatively easy to judge – but what about August when most men took their holidays in the town, more precisely, in the pubs? – or September when the coach-trips might or might not stop? or a week when there were three darts matches?) this took judgement which, though it might be of a limited order, yet shared with its more interesting relations all the intricate problems of nicety.

The order checked – there were three cellars, good-sized rooms – Joseph would relax and prepare to organize everything to his satisfaction. He liked the smell in the cellars: dank beer. A strong, plain, unvarying, unmistakable smell, which carried in it wood, hops, yeast, and the damp odours from the walls of many years the same. When you breathed in, deeply, the taste of beer swept into your lungs, and when you came upstairs you could feel it settled on your face. The organizing was quickly done : the crates piled in groups, some prepared for the empties, spirits and cigarettes locked in an old Welsh dresser, and then the barrels.

First, the cellar had to be kept clean. Archer had left it as he had found it and there were so many layers of cobwebs on the walls that they were like fish-nets slung there for effect. They had to be scrubbed down and then whitewashed and treated like that twice a year. The flagged floors were hosed and swept out every morning, in hot weather the barrels were sprayed with cold water and covered with damp sacking. It was important to know how to tap a barrel correctly : when, that is, to drive in the iron snout onto which were fixed the pipes. It had to be driven in with a mallet, preferably with one swing bursting the small brown ring which sealed the barrel. A slim peg in the top of the barrel – like the hole a whale breathes through – ventilated the beer and, at the same time, by the froth which came from its edges, indicated its temper.

Cleaning was the main thing. You had to rest on the assumption that the beer had been well-brewed. If Joseph thought it 'off', then he had no hesitation in knocking off the barrel, reporting it, and facing the consequences of an inspection. At that time there were few houses left which served directly from the wood, and few men who would go out of their way to have their beer thus served. For if the pipes and pumps were well attended to, the difference in the taste was unnoticeable to all except those rare men who really did sample beer as consideredly as connoisseurs sample wine.

The pipes were like hose pipes. They went from the barrels through the ceiling to the pumps – snaking up the middle of the cellars like tropical weeds which thrived in the dark, damp place. To clean them you unscrewed them, put them in a bucket of water and went up to the bar to draw through until the water was perfectly clear. Long and laborious work. The pumps had to be stripped down like any other machine : each part scrubbed, polished, re-fitted. It was not inspiring work, nor could it be rushed, but without its being regularly done, the beer suffered. Joseph knew that none of the landlords in the town took as much trouble as he did and, while never mentioning that to anyone, he felt good about it – for it was a fair triumph.

Moreover he hated the thought of anyone being served a pint which was 'off'. At the beginning of each day, he would examine the first glass by the light from the window and if it was not clear – throw it away: not into a slop bucket which would later feed low barrels on careless Saturday nights (funnelling in the profits while the moon shone) but down the sink. There was mileage, of course, in so public an act – for to see a pint of beer poured down the sink would certainly be remembered by the thirsty man who had ordered it, whose hand was still hanging out to receive it, whose gullet had opened in anticipation – but it was for his own satisfaction as much as for his public reputation that Joseph did it. He knew that he could look after beer properly and would not accept less than the due his work owed him.

Finally, he disliked serving a pint which had been overpulled: which had as much beer on the outside of the glass as the inside. He taught Betty and everyone else who helped, including Douglas who looked near enough of age to pop behind the bar for an hour or two, how to pull a pint so that it would not spill. Glass well into the snout of the pump, angled about 45° towards you, first one long firm steady pull which should yield about half a pint, then straighten the glass slightly and with two shorter pulls, top it up, bringing the glass to a vertical position as the last bit went in. About a quarter of an inch of froth, starting just below the rim and then heaping above it, a lovely convex layer to cushion the lips.

Within a week, the beer was better: in a month it was good: after three months it was generally recognized so.

A day.

Late to rise, latest ever, a guilty eight o'clock for Joseph, perhaps even some minutes later; seven thirty for Betty for the boys' breakfasts: the other three moving around while he turned over once more. That lie-in until eight a real expression of privilege: the buses had pulled out with their workers on board, shifts long since started at the factory. The girls clattered up to the clothing factory, farmers coming for their breakfasts after first milking, Gilbert Little, Stan Oglonby and Henry Sharpe long since back from Carlisle with their fruit, the butchers taking in their meat, Arthur Middleton, Bert Toppin, confectioners ready to open, Miss Turner and Noel Carrick, papershops long in business, McMechans and Messengers – and himself still between the sheets. The luxury of that lie-in never palled and for it he traded in the rest of the waking day as work. The bedrooms, sitting room and bathroom were upstairs, the kitchen and pantry downstairs and the scent of razzling bacon filtered through the beer and house smells, the polish and flowers; his favourite smell, and he favoured in bed.

It was a pub-kitchen – licensed for drink though used by the publican and his family. Betty got the boys away, shouted for Joseph and then prepared breakfast for the two of them. Already she was a little tense. Before eleven-thirty – opening-time – there were the rooms to scrub, seats and tables to polish, the lobby to clean and the lavatories, four fires to get ready. Harry chopped a box of sticks every night. The steps to be ruddied. Douglas swept the front before going to school : sweat-breaking, people from the same school passing all the time, unfailingly moved to crude shouts which just missed retributive abuse by being tossed in the tone of wit. The upstairs to be dusted, beds made, perhaps the laundry sorted out. She had accepted to send sheets and clothes to the laundry after a struggle : the decisive argument was that there was nowhere to hang the stuff to dry, for though the pub had stables and outbuildings, these were all cramped around a tiny backyard – a catch-well for soot and also the area containing the Ladies and Gents – no one, Douglas insisted, wanted to dodge through a line of damp laundry to get to the lavatory.

Glasses, which had been washed the night before, were to be polished, the shelves dusted and tidied, brass to be rubbed – the coalman came; she had to slip across to Minnie's for a tin of something – and a dinner to be put on. Helen helped her from nine until eleven. But Betty's mind fled at the notion of someone helping *her* when she had spent years cleaning for others, and she went so far out of her way to make Helen's work light that it would have been marginally easier for her to have done it herself. (Helen stood back : she did not sympathize at all with Betty's passion for cleanliness which was becoming more determined under pressure.) In fact Betty was relieved whenever, as quite frequently, Helen pleaded a minor ailment and did not come. She went through the work at express speed. Joseph liked everything spick and waiting at eleven-thirty prompt : and she agreed with him principally because she did not like to be seen in the old and tatty clothes she kept for cleaning. So she raced and scudded around the pub, carrying before her two small rectangles of rubber, like prayer-mats, on which she kneeled. Upstairs quickly when the doors opened, to wash and change and be down by twelve-thirty so that she could relieve Joseph while he had his dinner.

His morning, though less frantic, was no less busy. Cellar-work, crates to carry up, bottles to put on, bar counter to be polished, backyard swilled, the arranging and re-arranging of teams for this and coaches for that. He had started up a darts team but as yet it had no great reputation (later he was to run two) and it was difficult to get people for away matches : transport to be arranged if the rival pub was not on a good bus route. The Thrush had also become the centre for the Hound Trailers : Joseph had known that they needed a pub. None of the other landlords in the town had sufficient patience to put up with the demands of hound-trailing men who needed impracticable-sized coaches at inconvenient times for all but inaccessible destinations. Or if the landlords had, their wives objected to the dogs which, starved before a race, would howl and quiver outside the pub or, brought inside by their indulgent owners, clamber over the seats without a chastening word, licking the polish off the table legs in their hunger. Or if the husbands had the patience and the wives the tolerance, then more likely than not a member of the executive committee of the local branch of the Hound Trailing Association would have an objection, a grudge wrapped up in a principle. In short the football team had a pub, so did the cricket team, the tennis lot went to one place, the Rugby club was very particular with its favours, so was the Round Table, the pigeon men found a home (in the British Legion) — but there was no place for the Hound Trailers. Joseph was promptly made secretary. This entailed collecting the subscriptions and doing the accounts because the treasurer was nervous about dealing in money, calling the meetings and often taking them because the chairman was either on night-shift or *at* a trail, going around to the houses of the committee members who found it impossible in season to break the training routine of their dogs, and, finally, laying on the coaches necessary to take men and beasts to sport. The recompense by way of increased trade was slight. But the chance the post gave him for legitimate attendance at a sport he loved was the real reward.

Betty was touched that the Labour Party decided to hold its committee meetings in the kitchen of the Thrush. And she was made to realize that she ought to be touched by receiving a copy of the pertinent resolution : 'Seeing that a former worker for our Party is now in a position to offer us a place of meeting at no expense, and seeing that the Temperance Hall costs us five shillings a time with proposed increase to six and sixpence, and seeing that the aforementioned former worker was a loyal worker and is the only landlady in this town who can be said to be openly in support of the ideals of this party, it is proposed in future to hold the Alternate Monday meetings in The Throstle's Nest kitchen. The Annual General and Extraordinaries will be discussed as they arise. Proposed C. Nye. Seconded. D. Muirhead.' Joseph suggested that she frame it. A private word with D. Muirhead beforehand had led to the understanding that there was no *obligation* on members to drink.

Bar and cellar work done, bills paid, coaches booked – all before eleven, Joseph changed and went up the town. There was always a reason – or excuse : the bank, bills, a word here, a chat there – but, like the lie-in, this walk up the main street, dressed in collar and tie, smoking a cigarette, unhurried, unpressed, was its own reward. It was not that he triumphed in not being at work – or perhaps, just a little – but the real satisfaction in that walk was that he gloried in himself. In being alive, cheerful, independent, walking, the sun, the clouds, hello, yes, there, now. On these strolls once more did he experience that ravishment by the external world though not now of things and shapes, colours and animals, but of people, their voices, gestures; and of the town itself.

When the doors did open it was here comes everybody. 11.30 a.m. prompt and he stood on the steps before his prize. Slight attitude of a pirate aboard a captured treasure ship : the engine-room below overhauled, decks swabbed, fresh stores, under his feet the swell, in his eye a twinkle of conquest.

Lunch-time trade – 11.30–3.00 – was slack. Even so he would see about a dozen or twenty men he knew, chat to them, have time to let their characteristics fasten on to the bottom of his mind. Some of the boyos came in and through payment for one pint got access to the dartboard where they practised care-fully : a good darts player could keep himself in drink four or five evenings a week; go out, buy a first pint, stay in the pub all evening, never pay for another, play each game for drinks. Dido came and, older, slower now, decided it was as good as any and better than some and chose to stay. Sometimes a few of the men got out the dominoes – in time the domino school became quite regular at lunch-times and Dido became com-pulsive about it, his first indoor sport. The chief activity, how-ever – for mid-day drinking was low-powered (except on market-day) more a passing tribute than an act of dedication – was in studying the racing pages, assessing the form and plac-ing bets. A 'runner' came down twice, and if someone was stuck, Joseph was always prepared to nip across the street to the phone box and ring the bet through. He himself had a bet every day.

He began to carry around in his mind the people who came into the pub. They were in his house; his job was not only to give them drink but to see that they were happy there. Which is not to say that he played Mine Jolly Host; like every other landlord in the town, he had no time for that sort of affecta-tion. When on the wireless or later on the T.V. he heard or saw such a Jolly Host, he was ashamed for the man. But the fact remained that he stood in a peculiar relation to those who came in. For many the pub was their parlour, they sat in the same seat, had the same type and number of drinks, said the same things, laughed at the same jokes – the pub had become an extension of their own houses. For others it was a place of liberty – where butts could be dropped on the floor, fantasies aired, opinions practised. There were as many reasons as customers, yet within each reason was a willingness to come to another's house: the phrases 'he keeps a good house', 'a poor house that', 'a quiet house' were accurate indications of this attitude. Pubs were 'houses' – and when a man came to your house you could not but be involved with him most closely.

In time, every single person who came was so well known to Joseph that he became a confidant, sometimes a confessor, often a source of material help, sometimes a scribe (particularly for income-tax forms which often caused a near-paralysis of panic) and always someone who could be talked to. Strange that from men who, as a rule, were dour and tight-lipped, who would often use the phrase 'I'm saying nothing: nothing,' and mean it: who found great difficulty in replying to the question of a doctor because they resented his interference and would go through weeks carrying an unspoken burden, who hibernated before icy blasts which might feelingly persuade them what they were – strange that of these men, not a few would tell to Joseph (to a landlord) facts and incidents withheld from wives, brothers, children, even mates. With no nervous demand of its being kept confidential: that was taken for granted.

There was, of many, a retired carpenter who came in at midday every weekday for a light and mild, ten Woodbines, a box of matches and a packet of crisps (on the counter before he had reached the bar, his stick-aided step clearly heard a few yards away): in the matter of the actual buying of drinks, there need have been no talk at all after the first month, for Joseph remembered what they had and few ever changed. He sat in the corner seat beside the fire, unfolding from deep in his coat a copy of the *Daily Express* which he would bend over, putty-rimmed glasses sliding to the tip of his nose, for all the world in his manner, and in the fine mould of his unindulged face, like an ancient scholar breathing life into yellowing parchment. After about half an hour, he would re-fold the journal, stand up at the bar, ask for a sheet of notepaper and then, in meticulous copper-plate, black ink, make out his bets. Never more than four and six (except for the Derby, the Oaks and the National) and all broken down into sixpences, so that with each-ways, doubles, trebles and accumulators the finished sheet would be crammed with names and figures. Had all his fancies come home, it would have rained sixpences for a fortnight.

To describe Mr Hutton's actions and moods would have taken Joseph a week: for he came to know every lift of the hand, the different moods of it as he raised the glass, knew what Mr Hutton was worth, what preoccupied him, what he had done, what he still wanted to do and who was in his will. Moreover, in imagination he could follow him through the town on his way home, knew how he acknowledged greetings, his feet shuffling to a stop, right foot turned outwards; could go into the butchers with him, worry about his dog, follow him home, see him in his blanket-covered armchair – the curl of one of the hairs on his left eye-brow like a lamb's tail. He knew the slight check in his expression when a remark was made which he disagreed with, quite another facial gesture when a remark was made which he both disagreed with and was incensed by, yet another when a remark was made with which he disagreed, was incensed by and moved to reply to, and another when a remark was made with which he disagreed, was incensed by and moved to reply to in tones of anger: yet another when all the foregoing forewent and his reply was phrased ironically ...

Three o'clock close, half an hour to sweep out, mop, dust, bank up the fires, check supplies, tea, read a little, shave again, wash down. Five-thirty open. (Unless he went to a Hound Trail.)

There was one thing in particular which he was consciously irritated by, yet, in that first year, incapable of doing much to remedy. He was too open. It was sometimes said that he was too honest. That is, when some of them asked how much he was making he would tell them. He was doing quite well: very well, in fact. He would never give any actual figures away but after deductions for fuel, light, waiters, help and so on, he and Betty together, from about 160 hours work, cleared between ten and fifteen pounds a week in that first year. Before tax. More than they'd ever had.

He had not been used to hiding his opinions and in his new situation saw no reason to change the habit: instead of pussy-footing about politics or religion, he said what he thought. In this he was unique among the town's landlords. In all things – about someone's action, a buy, a theft, a statement, a beating up, a piece of devious dealing – he always said what he thought; prided himself on it. But, being a landlord, he was particularly vulnerable to challenges to his openness: and there was a pressure to make it outspokenness, bombast, opinionated, a carica-ture. He never successfully dealt with this, however much he practised silence, turned a deaf ear, concealed not by deceit but by omission. A little grit there was, and could not be rubbed out.

Betty was in a similar position in that she was constantly being told (by her woman friends) that she was 'too nice'. This was said with more than a touch of criticism. Yet she acted in no way differently from the way in which she had acted before. Less tough than Joseph, she sometimes felt that her removal to the pub had unleashed a Pandora's box of jealousy, spite, mutterings around the town: and she could not but think that this was the necessary price to be paid. Yet her spirit flared up against the injustice of some of the direct criticism she heard; and in some way, thrown to defend her-self (which she was timid of doing, but not afraid to do) she came to entrench herself more positively in the pub and the way Joseph had chosen. To be committed to it.

Which was as well, for her evenings as her days were spent working in it. She either waited on in the kitchen or helped behind the bar. And she looked for ways to reconcile herself to the new life. Certain phrases, often clichés, which bore on their backs much of the weight of what she thought, fitted her need perfectly.

'Nobody's different' – that merciless egalitarianism which could sound almost brutal and yet somehow accommodate and approve of distinctions in style, manner and behaviour (for the Queen had privileges which Betty would defend day and night and yet, co-existing with this, there was a deeper belief, though but secretly referred to, that even *she* was not 'different'). 'Nobody's different' therefore everybody had to be treated alike – 'whatever you think of them'. She did not like some of the people who came in, would, in private say so plainly and, however hard she tried to disguise it in public, reveal it most patently to those who knew her. But the principle was practised despite challenges which sometimes threatened to overwhelm it, and in the struggle she became firmer in her attitudes. Far from being persuaded that such a turning of the other cheek and blessing those who cursed was impracticable, she saw that without such an idea she would not be able to go on for a day in such a job; while there were always sufficient examples of people changing their attitudes and behaviour to show her how much more supple was the principle than any number of decisive 'practical' judgements. There must be no favourites, and no swearing. Here Joseph objected for her. There was little she could do about it: she hated swearing and always had. It made her feel dizzy, the blood thinned: and again, she did not see why people had to swear in public. If they wanted to, they could do it at home.

Most of all, she was against fights and trouble. Joseph did not like them either. They upset the entire pub, left a bad taste on the evening, frightened people and were bad for trade. 'For every hard man that walks in,' he said to Harry, 'two good customers go out!' Again there was the underpinning of what he believed in by what was good for business; which appeared as a contradiction.

Stopping those fights was a nasty and dangerous business. The town was full of people who went out on Saturday nights expecting trouble and looking for it. There were quarrels between families: there were often gangs of men (sometimes Irish, sometimes Geordies) working on the roads or building the new Secondary Modern school or doing a season of farm work in the area – and they moved in a bunch, challenging attack. Moreover, Carlisle's pubs were state-controlled and at this time allowed no singing: a singing-room was essential to a pub in Thurston, with a regular pianist, Fridays, Saturdays and Sundays, and gangs used to come through from Carlisle for the singing. Again, Thurston had a large, generally rowdy, dance on Saturday nights with quite well-known bands : this attracted a lot into the town, and tanking up beforehand was essential. On Saturdays, Thurston rang and shook and it was a very rare publican who did not take four times as much as on any other night.

Douglas watched these Saturday fights, tense and entranced. After the first house of the pictures. Too young to go to the dances yet. And wanting to be in the pub, to be frightened out of his skin. In bed. A supper tray. The meat and potato pie which they sold at weekends, an apple, some sweet, wireless on, fiddling for pop on Luxembourg, ready at any moment to flick down the volume and rush to the top of the stairs to see what was going on. If seen there, white-faced, pyjamas baggy, full of thoughts of murdering those fighting – then sent back : to peep between the banisters or run through his room to the window where he could see the fight go on across the road, on to the hill. Harry slept through it all.

Betty too was terrified. Yet because of appearances, she would not allow the one thing which could have helped them. Joseph wanted the telephone in. For the bets, for business, especially for Saturday nights when he could then phone up the police. She would not have it. Under no circumstances, yielding to no argument : a telephone, like a car, would, she thought, be a clear and justified object of scorn and envy. She wanted neither. So they were locked in the place when trouble started; for Joseph could not leave to go across to the phone box, nobody volunteered. It marked you – calling in the police. People were afraid to be the one who had called in the police. Nor was Joseph happy to have them around; it would always be held against him that he could not control matters himself, had to get in the Law. *His* authority would be the weaker for it. In that respect, though it contradicted common sense, he was glad that Betty was so adamant about the telephone : for had they had it, then for her sake he would have used it. It was a relief to be able to deal with it himself. Of course, if one of the three policemen who were on duty on Saturday nights happened to be near the pub and came in – that was fair, all in the game. The odds against it were high; sixteen pubs, a dance-hall (two needed there), drunks and the shop doors to check; more than twenty to one.

It was something that he had to deal with himself. In two ways, he was handicapped. Firstly, if he himself got into a fight and was brought up for it, then whatever provocation could be proved, he risked having his licence taken away. Secondly, he knew the men too well. He had been among them until a few months ago. Not as a trouble-maker, and very rarely in the fight; but certainly around. And because of that they thought they could get away with it. Pubs did not change hands very often in Thurston, and most of the younger men who started the fight had been brought up with the present landlords already in power. Authority rested in them from being those who drew the fathers away, pied pipers, magicians, whatever; important men. Not so Joseph. The very circumstances which assured him of an early inquisitive influx also made for a feeling that you could do what you liked down at the Thrush. Moreover, despite the strictness, even severity, of Joseph's 'rules-to-himself', he was a very easy man to get on with; since the age of ten he had knocked around and worked with men and survived with his own ideas about himself bruised but not flattened. This ease, again, invited exploitation. 'Good old Joe – remember when he ...' 'And that time we all went to ...' And *he* remembered and he had been, but there was a different choice now : if he let them have their way, they would take over. That was the fact.

When the fight began, like a glass container under Betty's skin the phial of security and decency broke into fragments. Panic powdered her veins. But Joseph would *not* be driven away from the pub. She cried and dreaded : to herself, but he who loved her had no need of tear-stains on pillows to know. Neither would *she* be driven away. It became a test of her faith in Joseph and her own sense of justice. It was wrong, she thought, for people to come and upset everyone : and if you gave in to them, they would think they could just get away with it with anybody. So though she shivered and had difficulty in keeping herself from fainting – she would not leave for this trouble.

Usually it started in the singing-room. Often over a woman. There were women who came in worse than the men : harridans from the times when it was common in working-class pubs to see women waist-stripped fighting each other, men in a circle egging them on. Times thought to be past : here, only just submerged, like fire in peat, ready to flare again any time. Three or four of them mothers of the men who fought : the men, often in trouble, one or two of them been in Durham jail for three or six months. More stupid than malicious, Joseph maintained : and how could you expect anything other the way they were brought up? Betty excused, with dry bread and jam for all meals. Kicked through the Catholic school and left to roam ever unattended around town and country – often truly looking for food out of hunger.

In the singing-room, glasses break, a woman starts to scream, the music stops. Joseph out of the bar instantly : locking Betty and the two women waiters in it, behind him. With Frank and Tommy, the two men who helped to wait on, straight into the singing-room. Helped by the room being small. Not much real fighting could be done in that space. Girl-friends, people pushing them away; pushing out : furniture baulking, and checking when tables full of drinks go over. Two men in a corner, one holding the lapel of another, bashing his solar plexus with the free hand; the other an arm around the man's neck, trying to grab the striking fist.

Smile, laugh, joke a bit as you go through. Always around the fighters the two or three trying to 'stop it', half-waiting to get in it, a hindrance. Joseph – trying to lighten it – come on lads. One sentence very clear : 'If you want to fight – fight outside.' Repeat. Repeat. As a proposition without a flaw. 'If you want to fight, fight outside.' Clear the room as much as possible : a passage. Then – suddenly dive on them, pull them up together, shout – 'You're going outside! That's that! Now come on !' Dangers : – pub might think it unwarranted interference : if the dive makes your man lose his grip, liable to be dived on yourself. Also, fighters might like excuse to combine and turn on someone else – at this stage everybody hates the landlord : – because he's stopping it; or because he isn't.

Joseph was not going to stand back and let them wreck the place in front of his eyes. A bubble of hubbub from the corridors. What's happening? Who's winning? Tom, a tough little fella, who waits on in the darts-room, used to box – flyweight – in the army : a contender for Northern Command title – wants a crack. Joseph has to leave two men, now humping and swinging more freely – more room now – and warn him off. Tom would make it worse.

Easy now to lose his temper and swing in : so they might hammer him : so what? His body had been hammered many a time. At least there would not be the strain of knowing that everyone might just possibly think he was a coward : and that he might just possibly agree with them. Get right in and *join* in. Want to. Want to now. Hell! – enjoying watching the fight. There'll always be fights. If he took one, Tom would have a go at the other. But consider – a second this – less than – consider – a real scrap : and then all the hard men from miles around would come in to have a go. You can't beat all of them. Nothing friskier than a scrapper for a landlord : like a man on a highwire : everybody rolls up to see the fall.

He, Tom and Jack, together, grab the two men, leave them locked together, push them to the door – blows, on his face – don't retaliate – push, push. Into the corridor – friends coming in on both sides : bottle-neck in the corridor. Now, like a scrum, turn your back to the pack, bar door locked, slam the door of the darts-room – no escape – only the front door, bend your legs and push. Enjoyable again, wink at a fellow watching it all, maybe strike up 'Yo-o-heave ho' – people laugh – the street outside waiting for the fighters – push, push, heave. Out on to the street, down the steps, a big fight now – slam the door and bolt it.

The sorting out of the pub afterwards. Douglas at the window above, curtains flung back, white-faced looking down, fists clenching, his mind shuddering.

Then the men responsible had to be barred. The publican had the right not to serve. Knowing this, the men would make it their business to come down soon afterwards, usually early Monday evening when it was quiet. 'Just a minute, Joe, just a minute.' The two of them into an empty room. Sorry. *He* started it – never again. Another chance. And, depending, sometimes Joseph *would* give another chance. Or he would merely bar the man from going into the singing-room. In those first months, however, he barred more than twelve from ever coming into the pub again. Eight more were barred for six months. It was even more delicate a situation than the first time he had gone into the singing-room. For the men involved in fights were rough, they had a way of fabricating combative tension out of very little. Joseph, small and sturdy like his father, was patient unless long provoked. To stand alone in an empty room, early evening grey outside the windows, the men in the bar silent, listening, and Joseph determined not to give in – it was not something to wake up in the morning looking forward to. And always it ended in the same way : somehow Joseph avoided a fight on the spot and the man would slam out with the words that he would 'get him'. Neither an empty nor an idle threat. The pub was broken into three times in the first year. Walking up the street when the gangs were propping up the walls, late morning, passing them, very much like running a gauntlet, mutters, attitudes, a shout when he was past, spit on the pavement. Douglas saw him walk this way, was himself buttonholed by some of the men – 'Tell yer father he'd better tek us back,' 'Why's yer father barred us then, eh? He's a sod. Go on, say it. He's a sod.'

Joseph scarcely if at all considered the effect all this would have on the two boys. It did not seem to him to be unduly rough. He had expected it, seen worse. But Douglas saw his mother shiver when she got up on Sundays to clean out the Saturday mess, and he shivered with her : Harry knew that his father had not raised a fist, understood, admired, and then despised, condemned him. Whereas if he ever even thought of it, Joseph could not but remember that on his fourteenth birthday he had been sent away to labour, up at five-thirty, a fourteen-hour day : men around to perform brutal circumcision.

Many times, of course, both of them, Harry in particular,

loved the pub. Harry especially liked the early weekday evenings when he whipped through his homework (never a long job for him) and went down, leaving Douglas in sole possession of the upstairs part of the house, locked in his bedroom, lashing into his books as if knowledge could be flailed out, like corn, whipped away from those stems of learning. Most nights for four, five, even six hours, Douglas would be there, muttering poetry, blasting against Latin, singing at the top of his voice sometimes as he discovered something he liked or wrote a passage which had gone well, alternately ecstatic or miserable; slightly mad.

Joseph most liked the early evening. Here the work came at a relaxed pace. Later, when it grew busy, he would accelerate and move very quickly, for he never liked to keep anyone waiting for a drink. As with the keeping of his beer, this was inspired by a regard for a personal standard : people must be served right away. Working behind the bar with him at a busy time was hectic; hellish, sometimes. He demanded the same speed from everyone – and the same rapidity at adding up the figures : furious at delays when someone else was pottering about at the till and he was there, waiting to change a note. Betty often turned her back on the bar, pretending to sort through the glasses, really to regain her balance. But it was exciting working with him – the movement in the tiny bar-space was like dancing when they were busy, rapidly dipping for bottles, pulling the beer, swinging around to the till, knocking the small glasses against the spirit measures, loading the trays.

One thing Joseph had privately dreaded more than a little did not happen. The clinging attitude of George. But George did not want a home, he wanted a base. For the first time in his life, he now had one. He could surge around the town alone, or even with Helen and be secure everywhere – because there was always Joseph's place to go back to for comfort and supplies of confidence. He would never get drunk in the Thrush – such was his fear of being barred. If trouble threatened – he would hop it quick. Besides, he could not monopolize Joseph's attention when there were other customers there, and as he continued to see his friendship with Joseph as being very special to both of them, this rather affronted him. Yet there was nothing he could do about it. Therefore by being rather sparing in his visits to the pub, he thought to emphasize his uniqueness, to assure himself of a warm welcome, to claim legitimate personal attention for a while and to confirm his unchangeable rolling-stone independence.

It was a great relief.

Lester, left school, driving a lorry for a lemonade firm, was someone Joseph could not see enough of. Lester had taken up sport professionally and went all over the place to run, often cadging a lift in the Hound Trail buses as sports meetings were often held at the same place as the trails. Joseph and he enjoyed each other's company : he found that if Lester did not come into the place for a few days, he would miss him.

The pub closed at ten, swept out, glasses washed, Betty away to make supper – then Douglas would come downstairs, taking ten minutes off from his own work to help his father count up. Count the sixpences, threepenny pieces, the silver and the copper, neat piles, ten, twelve, eight, forty. Knowing that this was the boy's tribute, Joseph let him help – though he disliked anyone but himself having to do with the money. Strange, this silent counting, miserly in appearance yet neither of them at all moved by the money. Joseph pleased as he did the day's accounts if the sum was greater than the week before – but the pleasure came from the figures which represented work and victory : not from the cash which was the reward. The bold figures in those small blue cash-books – almost a diary.

A cup of tea, sandwiches, Betty reading her 'book' – a magazine – Douglas, hair long and tangled by his hands, face nervous and exultant at once, his mother's fatigue pricking a tirade of bloody remarks the effect of which brought replies equally lancing. The bursts of argument, the pits of silence, Betty soothing them by reading from the personal column or from an advertisement in the 'book'. The pub in darkness now, top dirt off, waiting for the morning clean. In the town almost all the lights off.

Leadenness along the veins in the legs now. Betty quite

suddenly white-faced and drained. Joseph sat holding a cup of tea, reading a novel, alone in his own family. This was all. And if what had seemed new territory now looked like any other stretch of land, this was all he could do. His stand, his yes, his no to the world.

Chapter Thirteen

Betty could not be bothered to put on the light. She sat there in the upstairs room – called the living-room or the lounge or most frequently, the upstairs room – almost huddled in the sofa, watching the dark clouds massed outside the window. She sat as if trying by an act of will to *make* this room into the centre of the house. The downstairs kitchen was a thoroughfare, people coming in to see Joseph while they were having tea, staying, table quickly cleared before opening time, no centre, no focus. She wanted them all to be together as once they had been: though even before there had been lodgers, half-'brothers', friends staying, but yet for a little while the four of them had lived as an ordinary family. There was a piano there and Douglas had played; gone to lessons, sat for examinations set by the Trinity College of Music, collected certificates (at his insistence, unframed) and then suddenly stopped playing. No one could persuade him to go on. Couldn't even play the latest tune now; couldn't even help out if a wedding party arrived without a pianist and needed entertainment. Waste of money, Joseph said. They both said, to be fair.

Also in the upstairs room, the tea-chest with broom-stick and thick string which Harry pretended was a double-bass when he played in a skiffle group. Sitting there in the corner; could be used as a packing case, hint of moving.

The room had nothing 'lived-in' about it. Joseph never set foot in it. She had hoped he might do his accounts there on Sunday afternoons, but the bathroom was large and he preferred to work in there. The boys had made dens of their bedrooms, small forts they were, and they never thought to come into the upstairs room for longer than an obligatory minute – both of them realizing that their mother so wanted them to come in, neither enjoying it. There was an electric fire, both bars on, a rather stern three-piece suite, a bookcase, a sideboard, the piano, not much room to move in and everything rather badly placed, clean but spiritless. A gloomy room. Betty felt that she was saving it from death by coming in and sitting there. But when she got in she was intimidated; this neglected, heartless room was so like the life which faced her, and whispered intimations of that life came from the walls. She had come into the room to calm herself, to pin-point her anxiety and dispel it – but she found that her mind drifted quite aimlessly.

She would have liked a more ordinary life. More people had better wages now : Joseph served men in the bar who made about as much as he did after fewer hours of work. She was relieved at that; a balance had been in some measure restored. Friends of hers from school now took regular holidays, one or two even had cars, the women would get a new winter coat, wages coming in from the children made a tidy heap on the kitchen table Friday evening. If Joseph had stayed at the airfield or even on insurance, then they would have had a quiet, pleasant life.

Maybe the boys would have been less well off and Douglas might have left school : but she would not have minded that in the least. She would have preferred him to have been an engineer, something like that, where he mixed with everybody else and had a wage, maybe a motor-bike, got out to dances more often. If he wanted to stay on at school, it was fine : but she wished he had wanted something else. Even when the result had come through the last year – that he had won a scholarship to Oxford : even then, behind the pleasure, there was pain that now he would irrevocably be lost to what she did not understand. And Harry was determined to leave school at sixteen anyway, whatever happened. It would not have changed him at all to have had less money available.

Weary, weary she was. As if her life was over though in years it was little more than half-way done. Girls on the street outside, and the heavy shoes of the men walking up the pavements into the town. This town she had run through, retreated from, embraced again – now it came into her house and there was no escape but to this empty upstairs room.

Yes, the old men from the Home which used to be called the workhouse brought her the oranges they were given at Christmas. Joseph let them sit in the bar throughout the lunch-time, often giving them free the one half-pint which was all they allowed themselves so that they could have the fire and the company before trudging back up to the beds in the communal wards. Very clean it was up there; they were given good meals. Well looked after. So why did the thought of it stop her mind like the clang of a broken bell? Such nice old men, some of them – wanly she saw their faces superimposed on the dark window – all well looked after.

The young tough guys who would risk everything in fervour of their sense of victory or vengeance – it was to her they came for advice about their girl-friends and their parents. Alone in the kitchen, low-voiced – 'but really, Mrs Tallentire, when I get a few, I just feel like killin' them all. I nearly killed her again last night. She says she'll leave me, Mrs Tallentire. Talk 'til her, eh? *You* talk 'til her. She likes comin' here. And I'm nivver any trouble in here, am I, Mrs Tallentire?' Maybe because she called them by their full Christian names when all others spat out the nickname or a handy truncation. More likely because she had no advice to give. Trapped, they came to another likewise trapped: smelling out the one who could not help but, who could not refuse.

So she had never done any one thing dishonest on any day of her life. Was ill at the thought of Harry leaping on the trains to Carlisle as they moved out, and ducking out at the other end to avoid the fare. Sent him to the station with the money. Yet Douglas had rounded on her – 'There is no God, it's all propaganda to keep you in your place. Your place is wherever you want to be, mother. Don't let them cheat you.' Weary this load of honesty, fairness, truthfulness, duty, cheerfulness, loyalty, carefulness, self-reliance now seemed. But dreadful and terrifying the abyss with those bridges burned.

She tried not to think of her body. Lying in the bed: Joseph making love to her. That was too secret, too sacred, perhaps.

But the skin was still firm, and when she walked it teased her to push through, push through this self-spun web.

Would not go through. Watched Helen now in fascination and saw the freedom – saw also the sacrifice, the daughter Aileen dumpy, desultory, refusing to follow her mother but unable to find her own way. Fattening as a resistance, a disguise – slowly obliterating herself in heaviness of mind and body. Tailing around Harry most hopelessly with a cringe in her eyes, never erased, made more poignant by his kindness.

Would not go through with the loneliness in the room now. Adrift, feeling so old that she now had boys who would soon be leaving her forever; and this body curled on the couch would soon wither. Looking at her hands – bruised red by the work – she could remember when they were slim-fingered, dainty, that day in the park when she had caught her finger-nail and it had come off. How old then? Nine? Eight? She could see the black finger end, feel the numbness and the pleasure come from waggling the dead nail, like rocking a loose baby-tooth. Dashing back through the town, the pain long gone, holding up the hand like a flag. Yesterday. And tomorrow? – the *weight* of tomorrow.

She heard Joseph calling her. It was not so much that he needed her to help at this hour, but he liked her there. In this working together perhaps he had found a communion. Whatever he had found, she must see that he kept it. And get changed. Stand – it was as if she had to command herself to do that. Stand. Put on the light. Close the curtains. Go to wash and change. Remember Harry's rugby things, remember there were the pies to order for Thursday's darts match, remember the blue glint and laugh in Joseph's eyes as he had swung up to her house on that tandem, remember Douglas crying to have a bandage on his knee though he was not hurt – why had he done that? – remember Mary, her best friend, who had left the town a few years ago and lived down south, going on holidays even at Christmas, it was her birthday soon, remember how often she had longed to talk to Douglas and found no words, remember how she had trembled as she put on lipstick for the first time and Joseph had said – 'better than Gloria Swanson' –

remember her 'mother' who in due measure had loved her, and the way the church looked before they cut down the trees, remember Joseph's father crying at the memorial service after the war, Douglas crying when he lost his first girl, herself crying when Joseph was away in the R.A.F. – would Douglas have to go and fight now in their new war? – and why are you crying here, woman at the mirror in the cold bathroom?

The first hour of the evening. Rare for anyone to come in for longer than a few minutes. The bar smelling of polish, brown wood shining, the oak wall-clock ticking slowly, deliberately. The rubber mat behind the bar still damp from the afternoon swabbing. Shelves full. Joseph pulled himself half a pint: he had all but stopped drinking since taking on the pub, the work demanded a clear head. There was a high green stool which he had had made for him and he sat on it, reading the paper. On the front, the headline that the British army was going into Suez.

He read the news once more – turned to another part of the paper, but again and again came back to it. Harry had already made up his mind – raged against Eden and the Tories for doing this and tried to quench Joseph's flickerings of patriotism and that low crackle mixed of patience and inquisitiveness with which he approached it. Douglas, now in Scotland occupying himself on National Service by shooting blanks, could well be involved if things dragged on as they often did – yet Joseph could not see that, could not see it being more than a skirmish though the hollowness of the prediction ran back through many such and had always been mocked. But Betty would be upstairs, worrying about him.

Joseph could not honestly claim to be worried about Douglas's personal safety. He was more uneasy than anything else: he felt no excitement, no sense of a cause, and yet you supported your own lot if they needed you, didn't you? Not if they were wrong, said Harry. And he had little defence but reciprocal rhetoric just as over-reaching and generalizing as Harry's.

Chiefly, he felt sickened. Another war, more men to be killed, and most of them the ordinary people who'd no hand in the big decisions and all of it played in the shade of the atom bomb. He did not like to feel that the world was mad – hardly any other description had force before the facts. He had met his father in the town in the afternoon – seventy-five John was now, still working, perhaps a little more open to the temptation of retirement but prepared to consider it only if he himself raised it – and there had been no question. Yes, we should go in. Give them a good thump. Hope Douglas and the lads got a crack at them. In a hurry. Quiet nod and away. And then Joseph had realized how myopic he was – between the blind certainty of his father and the wide-eyed convictions of his son.

Like weary dolphins the old question heaved through his mind. Why did men fight? Why could there not be peace? What was the point of anything if there would always be war to destroy all points? He realized now that he had felt this when he himself had gone to war – but had disguised it under timid reflexes of jingoism, buried it firmly underneath his own needs – to get away, start again, trod it down in the name of justice. But, if called, and if he believed in the cause – as in 1939 he had certainly done – he would go again. Which was why those questions came through his mind so exhaustedly, for there were no answers.

He knew his feelings but could not direct them on to a way or thought of life which satisfied him. Between, between; that was his fortune. Between necessity and ease, ignorance and knowledge, confusion and clarity. The past and the future, father and son, met in him and threatened to eat him away.

Patrick O'Brien came in. Liked the full Christian name used. Pint of porter, ten Woodbines and a box of Swan Vestas. Red scarf around his neck. Trilby back from his brow. Builder's labourer. Five children of his own, two more of his wife's from the times she had left him, and now was another such time. To which he raised his glass. Joseph saw the light broken through the froth which lined the top of it. Douglas's last letter – a mate sent to the glasshouse for pinching spuds. Patrick did a stint of tatie-pickin' in the season. Did anything. Believed very seriously in formal conversation. Stood and supped and thought of a formal remark. Did Joseph know that despite hundreds of years of research there had been found no cure for the Common Cold? Had to say no. Yes or no would have been the same, for Patrick ignored the reply and asked for the racing page – his self-respect another day intact. 'The Common Cold,' he added, as he picked up the paper, and he used the two words to feel his way into the palm of fortune as he looked at the runners, 'the Common Cold. Yes – done it again – a mare, "Cold Comfort", 12 to 1.' That was the bet. And a cover on the favourite. No complaints.

Mr Wallace, a Guinness for his health (he was 83) and half an ounce of Brown Twist because he didn't see why he shouldn't. Every day this challenge was thrown to the gods, still un-answered. Joseph grinned as he turned to serve him – that white moustache, like cat's fur, combed and petted for the flattering thing it was. Mr Wallace would shrivel away, but still, he imagined, the moustache would be silky and fat until at the last it would lie across his face like a well-kept smile. Lucky. Same again?

Now Teddy Graham, worked in the estate agent's office, just a quick one, just a quick one, light ale, light ale – close, isn't it? close – how much is that? how much is that? same as yesterday? ha-ha, ah, tastes good, very good, just another, just another, same as yesterday, same as yesterday? and ten Seniors, ten Seniors. Tweed suit: collar too tight: horn-rimmed spec-tacles: small feet. A man to be impressed, Patrick thought, to be engaged in conversation – now take the Common Cold . . .

Farmers from the market, a group, loud, booted, walking-sticks and whisky; a little boy for two packets of crisps with three empty bottles and the men from the Old Folks' Home – the news? The news? – Take two days, Arabs – they are Arabs aren't they? can't fight, with them in the desert – make it a light ale this time, light ale, light ale, – how much is that? Same as yesterday. Same again?

Yes, the Hound Trail bus leaves at 3.15 for Rowrah. It'll be a walkover exercise for my lads. Betty – Betty – hurry up, need a hand, a rush on.

Joseph whirled around the three occupied rooms, serving out

the drink as expertly as a gambler shuffles cards. Betty came down, smiling. One flesh. Lucky. Joseph nodded to her. Brushed his fingers across her arm. Knew she was worrying about Douglas. It would work out.

Same again?

It was easy to reassure her in the pub. The fact that the private gesture took place in public made it easy. For alone together they rasped against each other ceaselessly : they were compelled to live and act in the same place and condemned by custom, habit and the fear of others' judgements to be united; like twin ball-bearings set in motion with oil to lubricate them but the oil had run away. In the few private moments they allowed themselves, each nudge or pulse of mood, each gesture and attempt scraped.

Only in the public place could they show affection and then there was the bitterness of knowing it needed others to help them even like each other. Joseph saw it everywhere : dozens of men had no more than passing remarks to give to their wives : between bed and the bus; between work and the pub; between the house and the match – at the necessary junctions an inevitable sign, the more unthinking the better. It was a desolate expression of the effects of matrimony and he comforted himself sometimes by thinking that you only saw the failures in the bar, those who'd run away : for he wanted to think there was a Happy Land and Marriage had once been that place. Where now?

It was words which failed them, he thought. They could not speak but to remind each other of hurt and disappointment and the misting of the vision which each, as orphans, had polished so brightly in the silence of a chaste adolescence. They could bear neither to be with nor to be without each other. Only moments remained; sometimes weeks would pass and then a light would cause an ember to glow, perhaps a spark would flicker and be extinguished, and that was all that remained of the love into which they had poured every hope and ambition. Having no other deposits and being unarmed with the resilience and irony of self-knowledge, they had tried to capture and claim instinct.

Even Douglas who might have brought them together only defined yet again their separate arenas; in him each of them scored out a territory and declared it a total and private bond; and he was so used to the division that he needed it and went to seek metaphors for it within his mind and in the world. His only reply to them might come in the fiction he was trying to make: this necessary lie his weapon to attack their fears which pulled at him or lay on his face, quivering, smothering.

As with the pub, the town, the news, the customers, the world and their son they found most joy and most relief (the two becoming synonymous) when least personally engaged. They had stretched themselves fully, as they thought, in the marriage and were left outstretched by it. To this exhaustion they attributed a cause – their overwork – and were saved by it as it wore them out.

There came the time when they could not even remember the candles on the chestnut tree that had shaken so violently in the wind when they had looked up after making love in the rain; could not taste the earlier skin, the mouth, nor see the shy glances of desire; shed the other in dreams and in sleep went further back to those root rejections and disruptions which they had sought to correct and heal but failed.

Silently they stripped each other, privately they attacked, publicly held firm and talked of Douglas and Harry late at night in phrases so mild as to lack all passion: but had they said what they wanted they soon would have said nothing. And there were still some matters worth the sacrifice.

Chapter Fourteen

Harry was in his glory. Mid-afternoon, a Saturday in summer, bringing in the last crop of hay. A hot sun sucked the smells from the earth: he could have fallen on his face and let it suffocate him. He had taken off his shirt and the white, rather wandy body rose smoothly from the clammy blue jeans, the thinnest coat of sweat smoothing the skin still more, emphasizing the fluency of his movements.

He was seventeen, been left school almost a year now and had worked on this farm throughout that time. It was where his 'grandfather' John was hired, about three miles from Thurston. He biked to and from work daily, unwilling to sleep at the farm as he would have done even one generation ago. The prospect of spending long evenings in the farm kitchen had been his only reservation about the job. It had not been difficult to find a place nearby. John had recommended him – and that was that: a short meeting with the farmer (it could not be called an interview) where each had stared at the other in embarrassment, terminated by Mr Dawson's abrupt 'So thou's set on it?' and Harry's 'Just about.' He had been hired – though that word stuck in his throat and when asked what he did would never use it: 'farm-work' he said.

Betty and Joseph were a little bewildered by his choice, but kept it to themselves. Since telling Harry they were not 'really' his parents, they had felt shy and, unaccountably, a little ashamed in front of him. Sometimes it seemed to Betty that he had taken the work on as a challenge to their love; for occasionally when he returned from work his very entrance would seem to demand 'tell me I've been wasting my time' – longing for this to be stated so that he could refuse it. But she held her peace. She was not in the slightest worried what job he took, as long as it was honest work. For neither of the boys had she any pecuniary or social ambition whatsoever. She saw that Harry was generally cheerful, looked well on this outdoor work, had plenty to say for himself and was always left with enough energy after a day's work to gobble down his tea and be out in the town. It was this energy which reassured her : given that it was allied to a character which was not harmful – and Harry's was transparently such a character – then she believed that it could be relied on; more than any other characteristic, energy was a virtue, she thought.

It was agreeable to her that both Douglas, now back from his National Service and preparing for university, and Harry – by working at a long learning job like farming – shared somehow in the outward form of apprenticeship.

The tranquillity of her attitude had affected Harry and helped erode the bravado which had led him to farm-work. This was the first hay-timing he had done as a fully paid worker on the farm : and it would be the last.

But it was marvellous to be doing the work. Stabbing the fork in the shuffle of hay, twisting the prongs to grip, lifting with a quick scoop and long swing on to the wagon where Sheila took it and pressed it down. He had never felt so well in himself and almost resented the impulse which was leading him to change his job. Yet, after a year of it, he had realized the inadequacy of doing something in order to contradict a reasonable expectation. So this hay-timing was a valediction; and yet he wished it was not so.

There were seven of them in the field and they moved without rushing, indolently it might have seemed. In the case of John, and Vernon, 'the married man', the indolence lightly masked a very concentrated effort; they displayed with ease what had been gained with difficulty. Among the others, there was real laziness. The day was too fine to squander in toil : there was just the one field left and no worry about bringing it in dry; and once the edge of urgency on such a job was blunted, then laziness was almost demanded by the nature of what was being done. For if you did not drive in the fork fast and whip the hay over quickly, ramming the dead grass into

the trailer like coals into a steam engine – then the next best
thing was not to do it just a little more slowly but altogether
differently : the same jab and scoop certainly, but with pauses
between to chat, look around, watch the others. Watch Sheila.

Harry loved to emphasize the lotus-eating pace of this work :
for at home, in the pub, it was all bustle and rapid actions,
snatches and quick additions, the drive to get the customers
served because 'people must not be kept waiting'. Here the
waiting had been done in the rain; and now that the sun shone,
the hay itself would wait. Unless you were used to fierce and
economic work, as his grandfather was, then it was much
better to go as easily as possible. You lasted longer. And there
was something grand in going about it so slowly. The day
was hazy and in the distance the first line of fells could be seen
a soft blue-grey : from the mosses a few miles north came the
smell of sea; tractors puttered as cosily now as the smack of
leather on willow this Saturday afternoon.

Dawson himself drove one of the tractors. 'Young' Dawson.
He had taken over the land from an austere and hard-working
father with whom John had been hired for over twenty years
and was fat, genial, spoilt and 'bloody useless', John pronounced,
as much in admiration as scorn. Sheila was his daughter, fifteen,
reluctantly girdling herself for one last year at school : Dawson
thought that the easiest way for him to keep her occupied during that leap in the dark, which promised to be short, between
gym-slip and wedding white. Harry had seen her at the farm for
years; he had often worked there in his school holidays. But the
week before this, she had walked down to the field in which he
and Vernon, 'the married man' (it was almost a surname) had
been clearing a ditch. He had watched her walk from the top of
the field, every step seeing her, as he later told Vernon 'for the
first time' : the tight red jeans stuffed into shiny black wellingtons, the white shirt open-necked holding breasts so soft and
steady that the slightest movement trembled them while yet the
most active movement could not disturb their firmness; he had
watched and seen her long brown hair lift and fall at her shoulders, a cloak to her white neck, and he had felt himself go dry;
only Sheila could quench such dryness.

She had agreed to 'go' with him a few days later, and this Saturday night was to be their first real date – at the early show in the Palace Cinema, Thurston.

He had had a number of girl-friends. Letters in school, S.W.A.L.K. pencilled hurriedly on the back; a code to puzzle no-one. First he had gone with Marjorie Barton; then been keen on Lena Brown. Contact – negligible; averted glances in the corridors, giggles from the girls at the milk-crate, forlorn appointments kept by himself alone, speculative bike-rides ending at a row of terraced houses with the house number forgotten, lace curtains drawn against the Sunday-afternoon silence. Occasionally a few kisses after a dance, disturbed petting in the pictures, a brief partnership at a social.

Until now, Harry had not launched himself at girls as Douglas did: perhaps the rapacity of his elder brother had pushed Harry towards the other extreme. For though Douglas had been settled with the same girl for two years now, at Harry's age he had made forays enough to become a passing lordling, limited, but in local regard, a legend. Harry had sometimes felt that he was taking the blame for this when his turn came. But it was more than that. For whereas Douglas could articulate an impulse immediately, Harry burned more slowly and often when the flame showed through the wind had changed and it flickered out in the cool air.

Like the lady of the lake, Sheila had raised her arm through the waters holding the promise of knowledge by conquest. Many times, in those few days, Harry had married her and taken her to a cottage; and his body leapt towards her in reality and dream, so that he was convinced, rightly, that all around not only saw but heard the love he had. In his own head she was celebrated each second, each fraction of a second: she was in the smell of the hay, the beat of the sun, the wind, the leaves. And he hung his head slightly as he walked, overwhelmed by the richness which was in his possession.

The tractor drew away, with Sheila on top of the haycart pressing herself down more to feel the hay pushing up into her body than to achieve any useful effect, her eyes gobbling at the long gaze of her new boy-friend. Vernon, as usual, banged

him in the ribs with the back of his hand and chortled in a
tone compounded of all the experience which a long life of
incessant lechery had secured for him. At twenty-one Vernon
had married the first girl he had courted: they had two children now, and if a single woman ever held his eyes for longer
than that time necessary to a formal greeting, it was he who
blushed – though afterwards he would be intoxicated with the
remembrance of his own brazen flirting. Like many, he was
a once-and-for-all-cracked virgin whose fidelity captured prizes
in adulterous dreams – randy, rapacious unlicensed dreams
rocking him through night and day as gently as a baby in a
cradle – and for these dreams he demanded ransom from mere
'unmarried men'.

'Thou'll be all right there,' said Vernon, said Vernon, said
Vernon, Vernon said, again and again and again. 'Thou'll be
all right there. Clamourin' for it, she is. Clamourin'. I would
be in there messen but – fair do's – thy bit. She'll be hot, mind.
Thou'd better git a haircut. Go to t' barbers,' he emphasized the
point most carefully. It was the only proof of his sexual life,
this downcast purchase of 'two packets' every other Saturday
morning at the barber's. 'An' she'll ride well,' Vernon continued, generously, ruminatively, 'she's a good bum on her and
a fair pair of bangers.' Then, to business – with a little asperity,
'She'll be worth a bit when old Dawson kicks it. Thou's on 'til
a good thing theer. Worth a fair scrap.' He nodded rather
severely, for he could be a grandmother matchmaker as well
as a guide to the cesspool of lust. 'Git stuck in,' he concluded
imperiously. 'My trouble was I was ower fast. The four effs,
Find 'em. Feel 'em – Do t'other and Forget 'em, that was me.
Don't thee be soft, lad.' By another transformation he was the
old wise man around the camp-fire. 'Thou's ontil a gold mine.
And she's not bad, Harry, not bad at all.'

He returned to work. Harry had long ceased to react to him.
He, too, returned to work, shuffling the hay, raking it into a
heap, waiting for the second tractor to come over the field to
join them. He knew all there was to know about Vernon's own
sex life: knew that there had been one woman only, would in
all probability be that one woman only for the rest of his life.

Yet he did not use his knowledge to contradict Vernon's authority. He enjoyed being talked to by a man of the world, as much as Vernon enjoyed being the man of the world. And Vernon knew he knew. Moreover, Harry liked Vernon too much to injure this innocent conceit, and it was because of this affection also that he did not object to the crudeness of his friend's language. For he could well have objected, had he for one moment applied Vernon's words to Sheila and himself. Douglas – he knew, he had seen it happen – went half-mad when people talked of women and sex in that way : relating it directly to himself and feeling himself fouled by the muck of such sewage. To Harry, it was all apart from himself. Indeed, from the bawdiness of Vernon's talk there came most strongly of all a feeling of tenderness. His eyes belied the mouth's contempt.

So the afternoon. They finished the field before tea and went back with the last cartload. The hay was pitched into the loft – enough stacks had been made on the previous days. They sat below the loft and drank from the small white china tea-cups which Mrs Dawson brought them. She had prepared an outside meal and honoured her plans though they could as well have had the meal indoors. Harry soon found an excuse to chase Sheila and they dashed across the yard, in and out of the stables, finally closing to a long, sweet, body-charging kiss, himself pressing her against a white wall.

John watched them play. He squatted on his haunches – the habit remaining from his time as a miner – a short pipe, stem deep in his mouth, a thin wisp of smoke from the Black Twist coming from the small, carbonized bowl, one side of his lips opening slightly, popping gently, as the smoke was released. The pipe emphasized the scar and twist of his face which had ever since borne witness to the accident in the mines which had forced him back to farm-work. He watched them play and remembered some time when he had gone to see his own grandfather – also called Harry – and the two of them had stood that morning in the cup of the fells looking at a couple of hares frisking, mating in the corner of a long field. It had always fascinated him to see birds and animals playing : to see the swallows wheeling to no apparent purpose and swinging across the sky, fox-cubs wrestling with each other outside the den, the hares that distant morning and his grandfather beside him, smoking a pipe, air of a churchwarden in those early months of his retirement. No, he was not as dignified as his grandfather – though he, too, could afford the pipe. Could afford many things which his grandfather would have thought the right of landlords alone in his day : but he had not made himself the man his grandfather had been.

John was just short of eighty now, surly about revealing his age. He feared that he might be 'laid off' work and thought that by keeping his age to himself it might gather around it the protection of secrecy. Everyone knew, of course, and some admired him for it, pointed him out as one of the 'old type', seventy-nine and still going strong. He hated that, totally avoided those older people in the village who sat and counted their years as victories and were kept almost mummified by relatives who loved their age more than their bodies and pointed out with vanity what had been gained, most frequently through modesty.

Harry had already told him that he would be leaving the farm and John had received the news sadly. For though he had daily warned him against the life he was letting himself in for, he had been flattered by Harry's decision to do farm-work. He saw clearly that it was out of love for himself that the seed had been warmed; none of his own would have anything to do with it – Robert was away in the Midlands, an engineer, Annie and Mary had married and gone to towns, one on the west coast, another to New Zealand and so the children from his second marriage had scattered, as had those from his first. He had always regretted Donald, who might have followed him, bold and careless, cut down in war.

Harry had promised a continuation of himself. It did not matter that he was not Joseph's true son : to have been brought up in the family was enough; to have known the boy his lifetime. He liked to listen for the bicycle in the morning. Harry left it at his grandfather's cottage and they walked together to the farm. John slept little now, and would wake before dawn, and came to listen for that bicycle bumping over the cobblestones before the cottage. He liked to talk to the boy, to teach him things – to teach him how to do a thing properly, the pleasure he received from transmitting that knowledge easily as great as that experienced by Harry in receiving it. In all things he liked him to be there – to hear the name 'Tallentire' called and know that there was another to answer for it. He loved the boy *as* a son : and yet had told him he was glad he was going from farm-work.

For there was nothing to farm-work now. Machines did this, engines did that, electricity did the other, you were a mechanic, not a labourer. He knew that one of the reasons Young Dawson had not questioned his right to continue to work there was that he could do things which most younger men had simply never learned to do. And had the patience to do well what they thought irrelevant to their real function. He had accepted that : to be a patcher and mender – well at the end of a life it was something. But there was nothing here now for men to gather to themselves as private strength. Any fool could drive a tractor, he thought, but it took more than a key to drive a pair of horses. It aimed at being a factory now, did a farm, and would end up by being one. Then there would be little to be learned, little to hold interest.

Harry laughed at the vehemence of his pessimism. Just as he frequently laughed when John told him some of the facts of his own first years as a hired man. And seeing that perhaps only with humour could such unknown experiences be transmitted to one who could never really know, John had often found himself telling his own story as a comedy. Surprising Harry by some incident from it and himself catching the smile immediately. A comedy. It was a word which had crept into his head in the early days of talking with the boy – and it stayed there. Rubbing itself carefully over the past like a lucky charm. So it had been that. A comedy.

He knocked out his pipe and stood up. The farmyard was half-shadow, half-sun – hay scattered on the ground, the men propping themselves against the wall, a few hens parading warily at a distance. The open door of the farm-house letting out the chatter from a television set. His thigh-joints ached as he stood up. It was as well that things had become easier on farms. He was slowing down. In a past time he would have been left way behind. Now he could keep up: at this pace, he assured himself, he could keep up until he dropped dead.

Sheila and Harry walked out from behind the stables, she leading, himself most carelessly following. John nodded to the others and set off for home, relying on Harry to catch him up, which he did.

As they walked together through the village, Harry glowed in his grandfather's company. They came to the cottage and he stayed for a while to watch his grandmother patting the butter she had made. The wet slap was like a sweet metronome in his mind, counting the heart-beats.

He freewheeled down the hill and lifted his hands from the handlebars. The bike swung under him as he swayed from side to side. He would see her in two hours and then walk her home in the dark. The air whipped into his face and he shouted, senselessly, back into it; his shouts became a song to the sky.

The table, which he had once called his desk, was placed in front of the window. He could see over the roof-tops of the short-boundaried town, beyond the two chimneys – of the gas-works and the swimming baths – out on to fields drenched green or yellow and the hills under the sun. Neatly on the table were the books he had been gutting but now abandoned: *Roman Britain* by R. G. Collingwood and *Anglo-Saxon England* by Stenton. Two of the books on his reading list for Oxford. He would be going 'up' in a few months. The books were stacked on top of three files, each of the files marked by a small white label which described their contents. This was a fortress on the table, moated by pens and pencils, a severe imitation of the life he had let himself in for.

Now he was scribbling with a biro in an old notebook, curling his left arm around the top of it as if to hide it from the scrutiny of those serious works. His arm was a barricade, and behind it, the pen dashed and paused on the page, crossing out words, changing their order, until the verse he was attempting appeared as a cluster of blue stringy letters. This table was too low for him and the front of his thighs pressed against its edge: the steady pressure, which had once been used by him as a pretended trap to keep him there working, was now become a necessary physical pleasure. As the images lit up his mind and he waited for the word which would describe them, the weight of the wood on his legs was now a body against his own, now a tree, a rock, a hand: at that point the words were sounded. Outside the fresh, warm summer afternoon: it made no call on him.

In these notebooks there were many attempts at verse, and a few pages of prose. He had made an agreement with his father to work for him a certain number of hours each day – in the pub and the cellars – in return for two pounds a week, which was as much as he needed; and spent as much time as he could on the reading list sent him by his college and in attempting to write something of his own as now with these lines. He had just written 'Contemporary Dilemma (1)':

> What to do and why to do and who to do it with.
> Where to live and how to live.
> Whether this or this.
> The true fakir relaxes on his bed of nails.
> He knows what's good for him.

The last line impressed him greatly: such poetic cynicism had scarcely been known before now, he thought.

Somewhere in the notebook he had made a distinction between poetry and verse, deciding there was only verse and prose – and poetry wherever it occurred: an early and elementary distinction but one which pleased him constantly, became like a favourite toy. A knowledge of metre at school had seemed like a magic key. Then he had read Cummings and Pound and Eliot and now his lines sprawled or were contracted at whim or will, he was never sure which.

While he worked at the verse, he would use the pauses to write imperative notes to himself. 'Must read all Shakespeare this summer.' 'Must get Baudelaire *in the original*.' 'All art is *unceasing* practice – Blake.' 'Comfort is next to stillness and so death. Accept chaos.' 'The Marchioness went out at 5 o'clock –

Remember that!' 'Before writing, sit perfectly still for ten minutes.' 'Bodily grace and strength are allied to mental and spiritual power. N. B. Tolstoy rode horses, did work-outs, ploughed fields, fenced, chopped trees.' Commands which he would strive to obey, forever charging into the arms of failure. Choppy sentences which appeared embarrassing on the following day but crucially important at their moment of inscription.

He was aware of a necessity for secrecy. Everybody he knew in the town would think such urgency directed to such an end as writing as proof of conceit or senselessness. Many times he felt himself merely self-indulgent, and when he went up the small streets and stopped to chat with people about marriages and injuries, births and alliances, local crimes, deaths, football and trade, the gossip seemed so substantial that its solidity had a moral force and seemed good while his own scribbling by comparison appeared unnecessary, a waste of effort and so no 'good'. Yet somehow there was the hope and sometimes the certainty that the shadows in his mind would take on substance.

There were other times when he feared himself a stranger to all, to everything. A stranger to the way the fly knocked itself against the window pane, how that slip of wind cuffed the empty packet of crisps, stranger before a hand trembling between caress and blow, to the turn of a face in the dark, the stone of the pavement was strange to him, that it should be hard, grey, yet closer, ash-surfaced, old sugar. And in strange dreams at night came the air-raids from the endless past; sirens blew in his ears, bombs of guilt dropped on to his mind, the ack-ack of the present fled whitely to the skies in defence, ambulances carried excuses through the tunnels of consciousness, and all around lay wounded hopes and dead ambitions. All clear! – he sat up in bed, wondering at the silence in the house, that the noises he had heard had not blasted the whole town awake, but there was only a lorry changing gear at the bottom of the hill. Then, most strange, the eye of his mind would slither from his head and regard what remained: like an eye in a painting by Picasso, it would be detached, now like a marble, now a fish, now the beam of a lighthouse swivelling around with its one cyclops' shaft to illuminate the blackness, all forms shadows –

and it would sit there, in the corner of the room, mesmerizing him to unheard cries, unsounded, rending only himself who had no matter.

Being Saturday, Harry would be back for tea at five and his father would open the pub at five-thirty. No peace then.

He left off the verses, could never concentrate on them for very long and picked up another notebook in which for some time he had been outlining, most tentatively, a novel. Not a page was yet written but he regarded it as much more possible than the verses. It was to span three generations and concern a family much like his own. The more he read, the more he thought that his sort of people appeared in books as clowns, criminals or 'characters' and it offended him. Everywhere, it seemed to him then, on the wireless, on television, in films and magazines, ordinary people were credited with no range of feeling, no delicacy of manner, no niceties of judgement: and women like his mother laughed at as 'chars', their opinions and attitudes thought to be trite because their expression was, often, commonplace. One reason for writing the book would be to set that right.

He looked through some of the notes already made. 'A family history which concerns a family who do not consider themselves a family (unlike The Buddenbrooks or The Brangwens) and have always been strangers to history, even their own.' Notes beside that: 'e.g. my father tells me absolutely nothing of his life – considers it lived, but not worth telling.' His grandfather, also, did not talk about his past: at least, not to Douglas; from what Harry had said, it was obvious that the old man did talk there – and Douglas was jealous of that. 'People such as my family are the numbers to the alphabet of history: the words, sentences and Proper Names are outside their scope/hope.'

Another tack: 'Epic – pre-grandfather: Heroic – Grandfather: Silver – father: Decadent – self.' Afterwards a note – 'too facile'. Again 'Grandfather was entirely bound by circumstances and to a great extent controlled by them once initial choice, very limited, made: in short, *moulded*, something *inevitable*: father – the mould breaking but petrified by the flow of lava: self –

attempting to break it deliberately, start anew and yet keep the old – What?' More. '1st generation – the forging of the weapons: 2nd – attempt to use them: 3rd – attempt to do without them – unwanted.' 'Who from the working-class – really from it, no school-teacher-mother-literary-uncle in the background, has spoken accurately and lastingly? Good mad John Clare. If only Lawrence's mother had not been so classy.' He had tried more particular themes: '*Love* – Grandfather had never once mentioned the word love. The most he says: "I think a lot on her." Could not mention the word to him. Father – affectionate to mam, but mention of Love makes him nervous. Completely paralyses mother. Self – uncomfortably use the word "sex" and am either intolerably prudish or unrestrainedly licentious.' Or: 'Grandfather's life "closed" at eighteen: father's at about twenty-two – in both cases with marriage: marriage being like the reverse effect of dynamite, as if a rock had been blown open and then the film were run slowly backwards – and all the fragments came to home in it.' And 'How far can you make the history of one family that of a country?' (Later – 'not worth trying'.) Another: 'Could have a line going through the book about WORK: as important as Love.' Note in margin: 'More clichés': Note under the note: 'Clichés are the midwives to new discoveries.' (Later, next to that 'Christ!')

He had tried to write something down, but the instant that someone known in real life came to mind he felt that it would be intrusive to write on such a basis. What he knew deflected him and yet without it he was without everything. Then he would feel desperate – as desperate (though it would appear to pass soon) as the time he had been told that Harry was not his 'real' brother. For what seemed totally secure would become completely estranged: as all the 'brothers' and 'sisters' of his mother had done when he found out about them, as his father's 'mother' was not 'real' and so yet more 'uncles' and 'aunts' and 'cousins' changed. If only he had the wit and confidence to make a comedy of it all!

And it was embarrassing to write of people who might recognize themselves: what right had he to do that?

So he would decide to tell it all metaphorically, inside the head of a man who was dying. Or he would write out such as he considered 'the facts' and finding that two pages was enough, leave it at that for a few months. Sometimes he thought that the writer of such fiction was a dinosaur : but this was a pose, adopted from intellectual essays in which most things he wanted to do were described as decaying, disintegrating or dead : he had to ignore that or forget the whole thing. He had too much confidence and too little sophistication to do that. And while he waited for the words to start, he filled in the time by filling out his notions on the book.

Was it about social man, my friends, or political man? Who had ever distinguished them? There was the question of 'Rise and Fall' : his grandfather considered (obliquely was this stated) that Douglas had 'done well' : therefore – risen? One look at that old man convinced Douglas who had fallen. Rise and Fall was useless. Perhaps the nearest he came to satisfying himself was when he wrote – 'It should be a series of pictures. Flat where little is known. Dense where more is known. Icarus is the attempt : Narcissus the enemy.' But that seemed pretentious, like everything done at this damned table turned desk turned table – five pieces of wood arranged in one horizontal plane three foot by thirty inches supported at each corner by four vertical columns, three feet high – One generation, two, three : one-two-three : 1-2-3, 'play the ukelele' : 1-2-3, 1-2-3, as old as a waltz, that point equidistant between manners and desire.

That was the trouble, whenever he made these notes. He would start off with a feeling or an image which was solid in his mind and in the act of writing it would catch words which came from a foreign territory. And there was the choice : the town versus the school, parents against teachers, friends against books, movement versus stillness, ease and strain, living and writing and the one somehow betrayed the other or fought against it. But what did it matter, this writing, what could it matter to anyone he liked or even knew?

Unless, perhaps, he could draw them in by Naming them. Using real names, real places. He would find a Cumbrian name for his family and have a fictive self both appear in the book and write it and so he could both know 'everything' – as the old novelists did – and have a partial view as would be necessary. If he *did* write it, he would use these notebooks – but tidy them up – he always enjoyed making better sense of what he had once done.

These matters were clearer in his head than in the notebooks, for when the page was down – then ... then he could scarcely describe how a smile passed from mind to lips across to other lips which returned the smile within a world of transitory privacy. And he let himself sink to the silence which would give him the written words.

How was it that his mother, who was afraid of leaving Thurston for more than a few days at a stretch was yet ever willing to dash off and see a sight, a parade, a show, a shop, a display? Would take to irregular country buses and the lonely terminals of urban pleasures with constant enjoyment while his father who could have settled anywhere and had wanted to settle anywhere but Thurston had to be prised from his seat for any expedition not to his own selfish satisfaction? This afternoon, for example, Joseph had whipped off to a Hound Trail, leaving Douglas and his mother to clear up. To explain and describe that: to make fiction of it and use that truthful disguise accurately ...

He hated to watch his mother working, though she moved with unforced rapidity and was far from complaining, he hated the idea of it. The idea possessed the reality and he hated to see her working.

There was a debt to pay there. He would have to see that his parents did not suffer for the help given him. Money would be important: the pub job did not carry a pension and his father was rightly determined that such slender surplus as there was should be given to his wife or spent on the boys. Sometimes Douglas saw his father as the man in those sketches put out by an insurance company at that time: four portraits of the same man, at 25, 35, 45 and 55 – driven grey and anguished by the knowledge that he had not taken out an insurance policy. Nevertheless Douglas would not take on a regular job while waiting to go to University: nor would he ever, he decided, in his later vacations. A hand had been offered and no tip required.

If his hand could later be offered in return – so much the better: if not, then at least he would have given these books their proper chance.

He got up from his chair – not to pace around, for in two strides he would have been out of his bedroom door – but to stand merely, to stretch. The bedroom was his record. Time-tables, that bamboo cross made when he was confirmed, walls plastered with the history of music, literature, religions, maps, a wind-up gramophone with a cardboard box of 78's, command-ments to himself pinned onto the flowered wallpaper, in the chest of drawers his clothes neatly laid out, everything in its place. He opened the door of his wardrobe to look once again at the brand-new three-piece clerical-grey suit.

His mother had taken him to Carlisle for it. He had not in-sisted on going alone, his inevitable embarrassment – even suffering – weighing lightly in the scales against her anticipa-tion of his pleasure. Together on the upper deck of the bus. The conductor knew his mother, of course, as he used the pub, and let them travel without buying a ticket – which threw her into a terrible flutter. She would not insist because that would offend against the (borrowed) grandeur of the conductor's ges-ture; but to travel without a ticket was cheating. Douglas had teased her – advising her to tuck the money in the seat, throw it out of the window, give it to the poor – but she had quickly found a way out by deciding to buy a return ticket on the way back, and throw it away after the single journey. Then justice would be done by the Cumberland Bus Company.

To the best Men's Outfitters in Carlisle. The Very Best. Gloomy depths of lustreless cloth. Douglas had always been a dandy – within such financial limits as made the purchase of white socks and black jeans a most extravagant raid into the world of fashion – and this dark chamber of finespun was a disappointment. He tried to keep the detachment offered by that disappointment firmly in his mind as the ceremony got under way. The man who served them was (of course) despotically obsequious and Douglas rocked on his heels counting to ten, then to a hundred and ten, to prevent an incipient assault. Suit after suit had to be tried for the best to be seen in the long mirrors to be the best.

A solicitor from Thurston came in, who knew them slightly. Had read of Douglas' scholarship to Oxford. Used the acquaintanceship for heaviest patronage. These are 'friends' of mine, he conceded, to the supposedly unbelieving shop-assistants old and young. I know these people, see that they have the best of everything. An intimate whisper in his mother's ear – they'll serve you well now, they know me here. Coquettish confidence which made her blush for his vulgarity. Douglas glared. O, Mr Carstairs let us meet when we are naked or alone. And Good-bye – good-bye – the best here, only the best, the sheep are fed on rhubarb leaves.

Savagely through the suits. One, a tweedy model with a lime waistcoat to set it off. Very smart. He fancied himself in that. Forgot the assistant whose nails were bitten and eyes poached grey, ascended to pity him for this lime green waistcoat was very smart indeed. A glass of sherry? Certainly. His idea of Oxford, though tempered by wisps of information from the front, was still founded in *Tom Brown at Oxford* – and men would say 'the port is with you'. 'Be careful not to spill it on my lime green waistcoat bought at Dunnings and Callow, Carlisle. Port stains.' But in the glass he saw his mother, who, though she nodded at how smart he looked, nevertheless communicated her fear of its being too showy for the sobriety of upper-class scholarship. Her eyes were on the clerical grey. Hand-stitching like the vicar's. Quiet. *Three*-piece, not, like Douglas' grandfather, because it was the old-fashioned habit but because it was the way of the world Douglas was about to enter. And grey had never been flashy. Never.

Nineteen pounds ten. More, he knew, much more than she had got married on. Paid over-hurriedly, a bundle of notes in an elastic band. She had brought twenty-five, to be on the safe side.

Mother. Thank you.

Harry's bike rattled over the grating and he battered at the closed pub's door. Douglas heard his mother's slippers flap on the tiles down the passage as she went to open to him. Why did she wear such battered slippers?

He laid aside his pen and put his notebooks in a big tin box that locked. The key was hidden in a sock in the drawer.

Chapter Fifteen

Joseph arrived back from the Hound Trails at twenty-five past five. He had missed the Old Dogs' trail to be in time for opening. Saturday night: must be there on the dot. Time to pant upstairs, having kicked off his wellingtons and thrown down the old mac (Betty would pick it up).

'Did you win?' Harry bellowed.

'Broke even,' Joseph replied as he took the stairs two at a time.

Twenty cigarettes a day. Too many. Impossible to cut down – impossible to stop. Why should he? Enjoyed it. Good-bye sweet breath and clean lungs. Amen.

Stripped to the waist. Farewell to control of the flesh. White arms thick – though some muscle from the work in the cellar – no shape. The rapid second shave of the day. A trail of trousers, shirt and socks from bathroom to bedroom. Kicking into his suit. He would not make it.

'Betty! Open the front door, eh?'

'I'm untidy.'

'Well get Douglas to do it.' An irritating vision of the three of them sitting there around the tea-pot, exclusive, content. 'He's old enough.' Softest sarcasm. There would be no tea for him – yes, now he was sorry for himself, totally forgetting that he had taken his afternoon's sport at their expense.

'It's half-past five!' he shouted.

He heard Douglas move along the passage with a deliberately lazy step.

'It won't kill them to wait,' Douglas said and the volume was loud enough for the sentence to carry upstairs.

'That's not the bloody point,' Joseph muttered to himself, strangling a clean white collar with a wine tie which would not, never would, settle properly but must always have the thin end longer than the fat end which hung like a flipper on his chest. Too late he noticed that the shirt which had been laid out for him needed cuff-links. 'Betty! Give us a hand with these cuff-links!' What the hell she wanted to buy him shirts which needed – then he remembered: *he* had bought them, at an auction, six for a pound, unworn by Mr Edmonson (farmer: deceased).

Again he visualized the scene. Betty and Harry would be giggling together as the noise of his dressing reached them. She would mime his shouts of 'Betty!' and even, perhaps, do so on cue. Douglas would laugh but reluctantly, half-wishing to shout back at his father. And Betty would most defiantly take another sip of tea. 'Betty!' No laughing matter. A cry of misery. The world would falter a little on its axis if he was not down to meet the first customer on a Saturday night. She ought to understand that. Yet it was also ridiculous.

'Let him wait,' said Douglas, lightly, to pretend it was a joke.

Immediately his mother frowned and got up from the table. Went nimbly across to the stairs, the slippers which had flapped most dolefully now almost rattled on the lino.

'You're not his servant!' Douglas bellowed as she had left the room.

Harry looked at Douglas; decided against it and poured himself another cup of tea. Ate in silence.

Douglas sprawled on the sofa which, two hours later, would be occupied by three stout ladies from Dalston who came every week to 'The Thrush' because they liked the landlord's smile and the sing-song coming from the other room. At this time, it was his, and he desecrated it, shoes heeled into one arm, by his fidgeting ruffling and crumpling all the covers, a cup of tea balanced on the edge of the seat, his face buried in a book. On some days, reading was a fever, and print from sauce bottles, newspapers, books, advertisements, anywhere, would fly to his eyes, never appeasing them.

Harry turned on the television.

Douglas groaned.

Harry turned it up.

'Turn it down.' Douglas.

Harry whistled and watched.

'Look,' said Douglas, in imitation of patience, 'you can *see* a cricket match. You don't have to *listen* as well.'

'*I* have to listen.'

'Moron.'

Harry waited – and then, hearing his father on the stairs, quickly reached out and knocked it off. He, too, was part of the protection for their mother. He knew that if Joseph saw the cricket then he would be so annoyed not to be free to watch it that he would call on Betty to hurry to get changed, hurry to come down, hurry, hurry, so that he might pop in and see it.

'What was the score?' he asked, having first taken a look in the bar to confirm that it was empty. As nobody had popped in off the Carlisle bus, nobody would come until about ten to six. But he had to be *there*. The others did not understand that. Neither did he.

'183 for seven.'

'Pathetic!' Joseph replied, angrily. Then he glanced around, parodying a burglar to excuse his truancy, 'Switch it back on,' he urged, 'I'll get an over in.' He went to the door, glanced again into the bar, then came back, laughing to himself as if in a happy conspiracy with the boys who did not look at him.

But Harry understood the peculiar grip of the disease his father suffered from. At times to himself, also, it was most important, naggingly essential, to know the result of a match or a race, a fight, a game. So he was obedient, turned it on, and Joseph poured himself a cup of tea, another accusation.

The picture came on and he saw the white-flannelled sportsmen and stood perfectly still, concentration wholly given over. The state of the wicket, the form of each of the players, the gossip in the newspapers, his own hunches and favourites – above all, the marvel of the game itself, so slow and gentle-seeming and yet full of cruelties, a ball keeping low – unplayable – and the batsman whose drives and cuts had begun to orchestrate his innings into a great movement was out.

Yet even so Joseph listened for a customer coming up the steps, heard Betty upstairs and regretted the untidiness which caused her back to bend and bend again, felt the bitterly strong rather cold tea on his tongue, softly made comments to Harry and received the answers understandingly. With Harry and Douglas he could be happy watching sport – with no one else could he be really at ease. He demanded not only words – those, least of all, but the right tone, the same assumptions, similar stores of information, and an appreciation of silence.

'He caught that on the bottom of the bat,' said Douglas who had soon been drawn into the others' spell.

Joseph nodded, put down the cup and fiddled in his pocket for his cigarettes. The players changed positions as another over was prepared. The three of them waited as the new bowler and the captain re-set the field.

'*Right* round the wicket,' Joseph murmured.

'Look at that,' Harry answered, though after a pause. 'A suicide point.'

'One good belt,' said Douglas.

'And he'll lose his head,' Harry concluded for him. Unnecessarily, but to show, to touch.

Clearly, as clearly as the picture before him, Joseph remembered the time he had taken the two boys to Headingley, Leeds, for the Test Match between England and Australia in 1948. Betty had gone also but each morning been left with the wife of Arnold, the friend they were staying with : Arnold and Joseph had met in the R.A.F. and written the two Christmases since. At 6.00 in the morning on this holiday, the family had got up – the women to make the breakfast and the sandwiches, the men to chivvy the boys ready and string together the stools which would take the weight off while waiting for the gate to open.

Joseph remembered the taste of the air as they walked to the ground. Men moving out of silent streets, likewise taking their week's holiday for the Test, the easy, unstrained march towards the ground until, even at that early hour, it was a mass of them moving as to a factory – but what a difference! The shoes and boots could have been striking a song from those pavements.

Outside the ground, a queue already – and souvenir programmes for sale, score-cards, rosettes, autographed photos, miniature cricket bats, lemonade and crisps, hot tea and sandwiches, prices very reasonable, the stuff provided decent; everything reasonable and decent that day. So into place with Harry scouting back to see how many were behind them and Douglas counting how many were in front. The boys looked shiny and tidy: white shirts and green V-necked pullovers, short grey pants, grey socks and brown sandals. The two men smoked and chatted about the war: that is they followed up incidents and people through whom they could strengthen the sympathy between themselves: both knew that the friendship of war would die very quickly but each felt more free in it than with those they saw more regularly. Indeed, had not Joseph sensed that there was impermanence he might never have come: not even for the Test. He jibbed at close friendships.

But he was here and the weather was so good that only the very old or the very cantankerous could remember a better summer for cricket than 1948. The crowd would be enormous and on that day, as on every one of the five days, he betted, the gates would close before the game began, all of it adding to the treat.

Then the queue had shuffled through the high gates. Play began. The giants out there – Bradman and Miller and Lindwall: Hutton and Washbrook and Compton. Two of the best teams that ever faced each other in a Test. (And England should have won – Joseph maintained – but for Yardley, their captain: an amateur: at that time England had to be captained by an amateur.) The boys were alternatively riveted or caught up in the peripheral excitements. Now craning forward all but touching Denis Compton fielding on the boundary: now slipping up to the lemonade booth while a particularly intense period of defensive batting filled the strip of green with apparent inactivity. For *five* days they went.

Game over, the slow-jostling-happy crowd through the gates released to the streets: home to read about the day's play in the paper and listen to a discussion of it on the wireless. Perfection was that week: the solid core of his sentimentality and a touchstone for many things since.

'Do you remember that Test I took you both to at Leeds?' he dared.

'Yes.' They replied simultaneously, but did not let that disturb his mood. Both of them now knew that they had been thinking of that holiday while watching this match on the television.

'Neil Harvey made a century. His first Test,' said Douglas.

'I thought *you* might have been useful at cricket,' Joseph answered, half-turning towards him. Douglas shook his head, his eyes still on the screen.

'Well!' said Joseph, suddenly snapped alert. 'This won't do. This won't do.' He patted his pockets; straightened his tie and fussed towards the door: he *was* becoming fussy, Douglas thought, despisingly, despairingly. Douglas tried to repress his reaction but looked at Joseph. The contempt in the glance was venomous. So when Joseph braced back his shoulder blades it was not simply to loosen the stiffness he often felt there: Douglas's darts could stab him.

Harry did not see his 'father' go out, nor did he allow himself to become entangled in the bindings of intuition and assessment in which Douglas often seemed to truss up the whole family. He stared at the television, willing time to go so that he could get out and see Sheila.

At ten to six, Dido came in. With his entrance, the evening began and Joseph's mind turned to his business. Without a word, Dido received his pint of mild and bitter – sucked half of it away in one draw, paused for a few seconds to look at the damage, and then finished it off.

'Now I'll have a drink,' Joseph muttered to himself. 'Now I'll have a drink,' said Dido.

Joseph took the glass and bent his head over the pump to hide the smile.

'She's sittin' well, Joe, sittin' well to-neet,' Joseph murmured.

'She's sittin' well, Joe,' said Dido, patting his beer-barrel belly, 'Sittin' well to-neet.'

He sipped delicately at this second glass.

'We'll be wanting to crack a fiver.'

'We'll be wantin' to crack a fiver,' said Dido.

Joseph brought him the change and gave up the game. You could go mad like that.

Dido would drink steadily from now until ten-thirty by which time he would have taken in about fifteen or sixteen pints of mild and bitter. There were many men who drank seven or eight pints every night of the week : some drank more : all drank more on Saturdays. Dido would take at least a dozen every night he came in which was most nights in winter and summer, fewer in spring and autumn.

He was in love with Betty – though the nearest he came to a declaration of it was at Christmas when he claimed a kiss under the mistletoe and gave her a two pound box of Black Magic.

On account of her he drank only in The Thrush and had made himself its unofficial protector. Joseph had had little trouble over the last four or five years – touch wood – but once or twice he had seen Dido in action on his behalf. And appreciated it. 'This pub,' said Dido, 'looks better than many a house. She has it better than many a sittin' room, Joe. This *bar's* better than many a parlour, Joe. Some of them let their bars go – who can blame them, Joe? *She* keeps hers up though, man, by heck she does. Better than many a sittin' room, Joe : I-tell-you.'

He placed himself in the corner of the settle so that he would glimpse Betty the moment she appeared through the bar door – and looked at the large gallery of photographs – of famous Hound Dogs – which covered two walls of the small bar.

Joseph pulled himself a half of bitter, as much to make sure of its quality as to enjoy the drink. He drank so little nowadays. Yet, strangely, though he had been so much among beer – he still thought there was still in it something grand. Drunks, he had noticed, except stupid drunks who piddled out their feelings like bladderless pups, drunks were treated with respect even when they lost all control. And those who drank deeply – like Dido – and held it, they had a position which they were conscious to maintain.

Lester came in for his one drink of the day. A half of shandy of which he drank two-thirds at the very most, being in training. He would have preferred not to drink at all, just stand and feel at ease with his Uncle Joe (the reason for his coming) but that, he thought, would have been unfair on his Uncle Joe (he liked to repeat the two words in his mind, often) who had a living to make after all : though he knew that his Uncle Joe would not take offence, indeed had hinted to him that he need not drink at all; but 'fair was fair' and a half-shandy was evidence of that fair. He could have drunk orange of course, but that would have emphasized that he was in training rather more flamboyantly than he wished; he was not quite fast enough to drink orange.

Lester specialized in the mile but would have a go at anything. He ran as a professional at the many meetings held throughout the Border districts in season, for comparatively low prize money but real opportunities of gain through the betting. The system was well-controlled and (except for the fell-races) organized on the basis of handicapping. Lester had not been conspicuous this season because of his success the previous year, his handicap had been too great for him to have more than an outside chance of winning and so he had concentrated on seeming to try hard at important meetings, taking great care never to be among the prize money and never to have his name in the lists which were sent off to the handicappers. It was a dull and dicey business but it was his only way of preparing for 'the big killing' which he was determined to make the next season. If they would reduce his handicap, it would be certain.

He trained five nights a week by running to Carlisle and back. Twenty-two miles. He would do occasional sprints and time trials between the milestones along the way. On his head, just planted there it seemed, was a crew cut : the short hairs stood at attention, emphasizing the slim face, smallish skull : less resistance to the wind, and a feeling of sharpness, readiness; a spiky crest.

He radiated cleanliness : as a woman can radiate charm, so Lester radiated hygiene. It seemed he had sculpted himself out of soap and let the resulting form bone-dry in a cleansing wind. It was the cleanliness of The Thrush which impressed itself most strongly on him, next to the character of his Uncle Joe, whom he wished had been his own father.

It was Joe who had encouraged him to run, taken him to meetings (there were always Hound Trails as well as races), bought him his first pair of spikes, advised him to invest in a track suit, supported him in those first two seasons when nothing had gone right. Joe always put a bet on him even when both of them knew he was running to lose. Always had. Always would. This 'always' raised his uncle from goodness to greatness.

It was Joe who had always understood his mother. For Helen's frequent departures, her affairs with other men, her occasional drunkenness and the fights she had started or, more miserably, failed to start – this could have isolated her completely in the small town, Lester thought : but due, he was sure, to Joseph's straightening this out, seeing to that, squaring the other, talking to this man, braving another – she had escaped much of the effect of her own life. Now she was changing : the death of her father, Seth, had sent her on a bender as violent and determined as that of any man : but she had come out of it mildly, lamb-like even, shorn. Now she rarely drank, stayed close to her husband, was no warmer in contact with them all than she had ever been, but seemed abandoned by that demon which would forever be throwing them off. And Joe, many a time, had appeared in Lester's mind to check him as he prepared to slaughter his step-father. George existed now with no bones broken thanks to Joseph alone.

Joseph knew of the affection, even the passion, that the young man had for him and somehow he managed to avoid exploiting it. Perhaps he did not know the extent of it – that even the crew-cut was for him. That Lester was not this lean-boned young man. That he badly wanted flesh to cover him; but this he had made himself, for in this limited certainty he would be sure of finding himself satisfactory enough to present to Joseph. Both of them knew the layers which had been rubbed off in the last two years : where Douglas had become a 'local legend' with the girls through activity which had never broken the skin of virginity, Lester had been a layer, cutting down the women within reach until they lay across every path he took, like sheaves on the side of a road. Where Douglas had 'knocked around with a gang', Lester had really hunted for trouble – three fines for fighting, one stretch of twelve months on 'good conduct' – another offence in that period and it would have been Borstal. The Army will sort you out, the magistrates had announced with relish: but the army had rejected him for flat feet. A blank insult, filled in by those who wished to taunt him for whatever amount they dared to draw. There was the wheeling and dealing also: driving a lemonade van wasn't much and he wanted money – poached salmon, helped Joseph in the cellar while Douglas was away, traded with the farmers, looked everywhere for extra: drainpipes then and a long jacket, velvet-collared, bootlace tie, Elvis Presley hairstyle – deep sideboards and a duck's tail at the back – Teddy Boy: smart.

It was when he had begun to win a few races that he had changed. There could be real money there if he could only get his hands on it, maybe a few hundred, buy a lorry, push off somewhere: just to have it in his hands. And as he homed to the sport for the prospects it seemed to offer, the urgency of his attempt was directed by those long bus rides with Joseph when they chatted about this and that and worked out the tactics for a race.

Joseph recognized his family, his father, his uncles and his own brothers, much more easily in Lester than he did in Douglas. For though Lester was shrewd, he could not hide his intentions and looked what he was: with Douglas there were the distances imposed by the space he demanded for himself – and in that distance it was difficult to tell.

Lester came close to the bar now to take his glass – and winked most heavily when Joseph asked him where he was going. 'You'll get caught one of these times,' said Joseph, uncertain before this fact – as always, and again he could do no wrong for Lester thought that his uncertainty came from a most delicate regard for his privacy, rarely encountered in affairs like this – the fact, well enough known, that Lester went through to the village of Kirkby every Saturday night to sleep with a woman who had three children and an avaricious husband who did night-shift at the week-end for the double-pay.

'Nivver,' said Lester, calmly.

And Joseph hoped not – for the other man's sake. How could he tell Lester he thought badly of this? When only part of him did feel so.

'It's all above board,' said Lester, certainly following Joseph's hesitation – though attributing it to different motives. 'I telt her to tell *him* and she telt him, I'm sure o' that, Uncle Joe.' He paused. It was not quite enough. 'An' I always see she puts them kids to bed – fust, thou knows.' That clinched it. He could afford to spread a little now. 'Grand kids they are an' all, Uncle Joe. There's nowt I wouldn't do for them kids.'

Joseph saw the husband about the town, cheerful enough. It wasn't the first time this had happened to him. Nor was it the first time Lester had set up with a married woman – 'they never miss a slice off a cut loaf,' he said.

Once a week only. Would not have it interfere with his training. This was yet another sacrifice which would have to be paid for, Lester thought to himself most grimly: one way or another.

'I've been thinking,' said Joseph, 'maybe you *should* run at Ambleside next week.'

'*I* thowt that meself!' exclaimed Lester, delightedly.

'In the *half*-mile,' said Joseph.

'Oh.' Lester considered. He could find no solution and so he waited.

'You need to go flat out for once,' said Joseph. 'I don't like to see you messin' yourself about. You can give the half-mile everything you've got and still do no damage.'

He waited. It was their only point of disagreement – the way in which Lester was nursing himself this season. Joseph saw every reason for it – the handicapping was haywire and Lester had been unfairly clobbered the season before; moreover, given the system as it was, there was absolutely nothing else to do if you wanted to continue among the winners and not just have the one good season: and he would excuse Lester a great deal – not merely because he liked him a great deal but because he understood – clearly – the lust the young man had to get some money together and launch himself. Yet it went very hard against Joseph's principles: he liked to see good running and would follow Lester anywhere – but really he preferred the amateurs because they did it for nothing. When people exerted or stretched themselves 'for nothing' or 'just for the love of it' he was entranced.

'I might git a ticket,' said Lester, half-cautious, half-proud.

'It might start to look suspicious if you didn't pick up at least *one* this season,' Joseph replied.

'Ay, there's that.' He paused. 'I was thinkin' of t'mile. They'll all be there. If I was well back in *that* field, an' it looked good – well – there's a chance.'

'Them fellas'll be too canny not to notice, Lester. There'll be Michael Glenn there. He knows when somebody's loiterin'.'

'I can mek it look good.'

'They'll smell it out.'

'Think?'

'Yes. Have a good go at that half-mile. Give yourself a treat.' Lester drained off his shandy.

'Reet, Uncle Joe: that's settled. Half-mile she is.'

He nodded, happily, nodded at Dido – and left.

Joseph knew that he had leaned on this nephew and regretted having had to. He would have liked to be able to talk to him openly about anything – try to go through all the points about this running business, the woman, the search for money, the contempt Lester expressed for George – liked, in fact, to have known him as 'a friend'. But it had not happened like that – and the way in which they met allowed no great liberties on either side, however intimately they might appear to talk and act. If he was afraid for Lester, he could do no more than place signposts before the areas he considered to be dangerous: he could not follow him in.

In a few moments the other two buses would arrive back from the Trails and the pub would be full to begin the Saturday night. He walked out of the bar and stood at the bottom of the stairs. 'Betty!' He shouted. 'Are you ready yet?'

* * *

It was the interval. They had seen 'Look at Life', a cartoon of 'Tom and Jerry' and the trailer for the next film. Now was the time for ice-cream.

Harry got up uncertainly, much surprised that his legs would carry him, and went down to Mrs Charters who sold the refreshments. Thurston cinema was small. Capacity downstairs – 120: upstairs – 48. Upstairs they were of course: two shillings each. He wished it had cost more. Lucky. Not a back seat but only two rows from the back and on one of those truncated rows – of three seats – the third seat empty. Only half-full. Harry knew them all and all, it seemed this night, from the greetings and winks, wanted to be known to Harry. Sheila was a country girl, a stranger, and her preliminary blushes had helped to keep her anonymity. They had sat most correctly through 'Look at Life' and he had taken her hand only at the end of it. In 'Tom and Jerry' he had squeezed and nearly left his seat at the force of the squeeze returned to him. His knee had shot out to jam against hers and both had slid forward a little way so that they sat ankle to ankle, calf to calf, knee to knee and half her thigh to one third of his. During the trailer she had taken off her cardigan and casually he had slung his right arm around her shoulder. Then the interval and the arm had jerked back as if on a piece of string, bumping her head.

Too soon the two tubs of Strawberry Favourite were bought and he had to turn and walk up the red-carpeted steps towards her where she sat so calmly. He was overwhelmed with admiration at her self-control, sitting there, managing to look even a little bored, now turning quite at her ease to examine the lucky couples hunched in the back row with the flagrantly unnecessary raincoats draped over their knees – even raising her white arms to her hair to put a slide in place, so calm while his legs tottered up the few steps, his stomach lurching to an imaginary ship's roll. What a girl! Just sitting there as if nothing had happened!

This bit would be difficult for he knew that despite the ice-cream and the small wooden spoons which most thankfully employed the tongue – conversation had to be made. Otherwise he would feel a fool. He pushed back the waxy circle of cardboard, laid bare his frozen pat of pink and scraped the small spoon rather disconsolately across the surface. Douglas would have chuntered away with no trouble: made her laugh – without telling jokes – just made her laugh.

He decided to tell her something important.

He had got a job on the *Cumberland News* as a cub-reporter. Three pounds seven and six. She nodded and dug into her ice. Of course there would be his National Service to do in a year or so but that was why he had taken the job – when he came out it would be too late. He looked for applause at this cunning and brilliantly calculated stroke of prescience: to himself it appeared even Machiavellian so rarely, he thought, could anyone so excellently have organized their future. She licked the waxy circle of cardboard and laughed at his stare: then thrust her arm through his – locking it, he wondered, or encouraging him? Which? Which? Then, most determinedly, she asked him about Douglas: about Douglas and his present girl, about Douglas and the other girls he had been with. Harry answered her willingly: rather proudly. As the light dimmed and a certificate came on the screen to declare that *Singing in the Rain* was fit to be seen by everyone, Sheila sighed and said 'He's so smashing looking,' squirming as she said it. Harry was shocked: as if his brother had been insulted.

The film began and her head slid on to his shoulder. He felt her hair thick on his neck and let out his breath so carefully – she must not be disturbed – that he almost choked and did, in fact, splutter, had to turn away. But the action had released his arm; he could not have done better had he done it on purpose. No hesitation this time. His arm went around her shoulders with an experienced swing, a swagger in the elbow. She sighed once more and this one, he knew, was for him. He bowed to peck at her brow and was met by her lips, reaching ravenously up to his own: they clamped against his mouth and her tongue rushed between his teeth rapid as a terrier, searching furiously. He responded by thrusting his own tongue into her mouth – though never before had he employed this sort of kissing – 'French kissing' they called it, and they foraged away while

Gene Kelly went liquidly through a routine. Parted, gasping – and immediately set to once more. Below, from a lake of longing, Harry felt a rise, like Excalibur. To balance this his hand slid down from her shoulder to clutch her under the arm. The fingers touched the bottom of her breast, pouched in cotton. They lay there lightly, numb. She leaned herself down on to his hand and made a cup of it. His feet pushed against the ground and the breath went out of him.

The pub was at high-tide. In the singing-room, Jack played the accordion and Ronnie Graham whistled *In a Monastery Garden*. A woman squeezed her thighs together against the emotion engendered by the stinging tone of his whistle and against the bladder about to weep in sympathy : not wanting to run the gauntlet down the man-blocked passage to the Ladies in the backyard : a change from lager to a little drop of port would do for the moment. Many thanks. Such good sing songs. 'If I were a Blackbird' (with imitations) would be his encore.

The Hard Men in the darts-room played on despite the crowd, and the arrows thudded into the board. Shanghai they were playing and a bull to finish on. One man was trying for it : thud, thud, thud, the arrows streaked towards that central black, feathers brushed back along the shaft. Douglas was serving there.

In the corner of the bar sat Dido – like an immense turtle overturned on the sand. Mild and bitter *if* you don't mind. Mild and bitter. Crowded here as everywhere and a stranger making a bit of a nuisance of himself in the corner, Joseph keeping a steady eye on him.

John was in the kitchen in his corner seat drinking brown ale. Grand when your son was a landlord. And Joseph always saw him all right. The three ladies from Dalston sat, wadded in satin with deep décolletée, plump as Christmas geese, breast to breast on the sofa with gins and the little red cherry on a stick, listening to Ronnie in the singing-room, murmuring the word of the songs to themselves : swaying together.

There were almost a hundred people in those four small rooms. The waiters called as regularly as porters 'Mind your backs, please,' 'Mind your backs, please,' and the trays of drinks were held on high passing through the crowd, the ark of the covenant.

Betty and Joseph managed behind the tiny bar, serving the waiters, serving the bar. They worked together like a music-hall team, even an act, so expertly did they swing the bottles and pull the pumps: a family act – at once moving and intriguing. Rapidly, rapidly the orders came and it was now that Betty abandoned all attempts to add up the cost of long orders and Joseph did all the calculations while yet he served as quickly as she did. They seemed perfectly matched but Joseph felt her resentment beneath the cheerfulness like a cold current under warm waves. The pub bored her and she defended herself by working harder and tiring herself. And she had no liking for him, Joseph thought, was lost in a concern for the boys which she could not share, even with them. But it was this double-act which upset him: to the customers cheerful, to himself bitter – moods following each other as rapidly as pictures in a reel; Douglas could be like that too.

'Mind your backs, please. Mind your backs; your bellies won't save you.'

Lester watched her get out of bed. He saw her pull on the dressing gown and blush a little when she felt his look on her, yet he had clambered all over her body minutes before. She put her fingers to her lips and went out. He kicked off the bed-clothes and looked down at himself. Muscles thin, relaxed; white body with deep brown neck and forearms, like the marks of chains. In his thoughts, Lester struggled between the decency he wanted to have and a stronger force which, now bitterly, now with satisfaction, he recognized as being nearer to himself. She was a good old thing. She made no complaints – just as well. She put up with a great deal on his account: that was her business. She demanded nothing: had no bloody right to. She took risks for him: her own look-out.

He waited for her. Straight to bed he had come on arrival and would leave it to go straight home. The kids had been asleep. He raised his knees and prodded the calf muscles with his fingers. Yes, they were supple: mustn't stiffen up. One more season – and then this life, these people, this god-forsaken spot wouldn't see him for dust.

Along luxurious lanes pitch-black and rustling with known sounds, Harry cycled very slowly. Sheila had biked into Thurston alone but he had insisted on setting her back, and that gallantry was the bow on the new parcel of feelings which had just been delivered to him. They had kissed and held each other for an hour outside the gate of her farm and he went very carefully now, as if carrying a bowl of water brim-full, afraid to spill a drop.

The day behind him appeared so large that it was only by a miracle that there was room for other days to exist. The haytiming, how she had looked then, the stolen kisses behind the stables, the long wait for the pictures – and then, as if all his life had been but a trickle of powder leading to this keg, the silent explosion of every nerve end, blown to the wind, collected there and swept back on him.

He got off the bike and pushed it, to take more time, to let it have all the time he could.

It was at night that John felt most odd. Then the darkness shrouded him and made him no more than a ghost to the present. And about him, in lanes and away to the hills and the coast, he could sense the free run of the young on this Saturday night: money in their pockets, not tired by work nor afraid to lose it, heirs all to the titles of choice, leisure and liberty: sons of his sons yet, it seemed, hardly of his breed at all. If only he and his brothers could have delayed their birth!

The men who had given him a lift home had dropped him off just before the village and he walked up the hill very slowly, pulling his collar around his throat though it was not cold, clenching and unclenching his fingers in his pockets for they were stiffening with arthritis and he had to keep them moving: long since had his concertina been wrapped up in the bottom of the wardrobe. His knees, too, were painful as he pushed up that slight rise – and he remembered when he could have skipped up there like a buck – and after a full day's work.

They could not understand. Sometimes he told Harry about what it had been like; but it was always the same. It sounded either comic or tragic, and himself a clown or a slave : he could never get it right, show that it had to be in those times, that there had been real pleasure in loaded toil which mingled with the pain and drudgery of it. No. Harry believed him, of course, but could not understand.

Nor could he : sometimes, looking back on himself, he would see the man he had been, see that man loading a cart or in the pits and shake his head as his eyes passed him by – uncompre-hending.

Joseph knew. Joseph could understand. But then Joseph had begun in farm-work himself : and had always been a toiler. But these others ... they were all doing well ... nor was it a cause for wonder ... Things had changed, things, things, which daily deluged him from television and papers ... and men must change with them.

Now on the flat, his shoes the only sound in the village, he walked even more slowly, for this night it was of Emily his first wife and love that he thought. They did not understand : she was there in his mind as young and fresh as ever and he in that mind reached out and took her with ease : only the bodies ruined it all, cold or caged. He was still the same. Still felt the same anger – still felt the same pleasures, more, more in the ease of his eye these days, wanted the same, same lusts and even, strangest of all, the same hopes : yet, being old, he could admit them to no one, would be called a fool and deservedly thought one – and, being old, he had to see each impulse shrivel at the wrinkled exits of his skin – no longer could they be released and fling themselves on the world – forever must they be imprisoned now, and he the jail to his own freedom.

God, God, the feet pushed on : he who had at least never hesitated before his own body, never spared it, never hoarded it, used it as his weapon for life and with it battered down doors of need and desire, stumbled maybe and seen little but

felt enough for any man – now to be slowly stiffened, and not
to go mad, refuse even to show.

Look at the sky – a hard young moon. And the garden,
flushed with blooms. And the door of his house with the key
under a stone.

Douglas counted the midnight strokes and when they had
stopped counted once more, trying to keep both tone and
rhythm of the strokes in his head. On that church-tower he had
stood, many a time, shivering for fear the caretaker should come
up and catch him, intoxicated by the battlements and at the
same time shadowed by the feeling that to jump, to float down
to the gravestones, arms outstretched like a bird, a hawk he
would be, to do that would be possible if only he dared.

He was sitting on the wall of a garden on the Syke Road
above the town and eased himself off it, suddenly aware of the
preciousness of his solitude, not wanting an accidental sound
to disrupt it. Yet he would have welcomed such an accident. He
was going to walk the three miles around the Skye Road : there
was a clear half-moon and so it was cheating slightly; for this
walk was a test of his capacity to bear the solitude he dreamed
to inhabit but which, met, threatened him with disintegration.
But he was calm now, felt strong, could take the test and thus
appease the slavering chops of self-detraction for some more
time.

Still he stood, near the lightless house and lit a cigarette. Few
sounds below in this town he hated to leave. There the faces
he knew, the people he loved – and would never leave, he told
himself, would never abandon – he protested too much did he?
an incision would be made and the limbs would be sawn off unless he went on his knees to stitch every gash. He would do that.

He tried to think of something written on paper, to give
himself a hold on both words and an object, to uncoil a lifeline
which would draw him safely through that moon-shadowed
walk. He saw the scribblings he had made about the novel he
wanted to write, and in the stillness they seemed yet more
unreal. But the thought of writing was at least something : the
only thing to counter this terrible, inexplicable and desperate

emptiness. He remembered that he had read somewhere that only a blank page, an empty canvas or a silent instrument could be a valid response to these times: and here he understood it, for he was overwhelmed by the variety and multiplicity and fear in his mind and felt the madness of skull-bound yet ever expanding desperation; but that way led to Nothing. Better to attempt a 'just representation of general nature': for though the mirror might be tarnished it should never be broken. Should it?

He thought of his parents, set in the town, he thought, like a vein of ore. Was it because of them alone that he was what he was? If he could be good, as he saw his mother good, then he would be glad. How easy it seemed for some to do good actions – for Harry, who never lied, was not underhand, was not led to spill over his faults into harmful effects: but you could not side-step it like that. Even if it were not possible for him to be as good a man as he would like to be, it was certain he could avoid being as bad as he could be. The words 'good' and 'bad' – they came to his mind like places once loved as a child. Yet he could not forget them: sometimes felt himself crippled because he could not forget them. Good and Bad. They appeared 'irrelevant': and he had laughed at them with others: but irrelevant to what? Not to behaviour, nor to purpose, neither to manners nor to thought. Irrelevant, perhaps, to clarity, to will and to ambition: yet perhaps these were an empty count if there was no moral reckoning.

His mother would be sitting on that low stool beside the fire nursing her tea. Her feet half-in those old slippers, too tender even for those old slippers, sore, aching feet. Now, at this distance, he wished he had once had the courage to bathe them.

'Bed?' asked Joseph.

'Hm?'

He knew that she had heard. The distances now between them were so vast: only work united them: yet how long could they rely on that?

'What about bed?'

'You go if you want.'

'We could both go, eh? Eh?' The tone tried to have the colour of light.

'I'll just finish this tea.'

'Come on. Let's go together.'

'Don't keep on, Joseph. Leave me in peace.'

It was often like this now. And as he looked at her, the waste blacked out his mind. They *had* loved each other; now their affection scarcely touched, could hardly co-mingle in the boys who led their lives for them, only met now and then in a person of this town which was all he might ever know until his death, this town which was locking him in, this town which was calling up his last effort, which would be directed to escape.

All he thought of now was getting out: the grass was indeed greener on the other side of this fenced town. As they sat there in the dead hour around midnight, when all but a few in that place were tucked up and those active were at work on the machines at the factory, then he would weigh his chances, prod here, dig there, shake some rubble, make a mark, prepare for when he'd have the confidence to attack. The timing was easy: Douglas's going.

Why was it, though, he wondered, in pain at the thought but unable to repress it, why was it this woman, this love, this Betty, now appeared ugly before him, unlovely and even hateful?

Chapter Sixteen

At the trail his dog failed to come in and he had to wait for it. He had watched all the other dogs come in. Every one. Then the bus driver had sent word it was time to go as the others were getting impatient. The bookies packed up and left. The Crossbridge Committee took down the tent and piled it onto a trailer with the stakes and the ropes: a tractor came to pull it away. Somebody who had offered Joseph a lift in a car and stood with him only after a short while grew nervous; once Joseph noticed this he persuaded him to leave and was annoyed when he did so.

In less than half an hour he was alone in that field: dusk coming on: no sign of the dog. He blew the whistle and waited. There was nothing else he could do. It would be worse than useless to go out into the fells and look for it. If a farmer found it caught in barbed wire or otherwise trapped, he would release it and either send it back on the trail or bring it back to the field. In an hour it would be completely dark and he did not know his way among the hills well enough for that.

He turned up the collar of his raincoat and moved around to keep his feet warm. Now that there was no alternative he almost enjoyed it. Betty would be told and understand there was nothing else he could do. There was something restful about a situation in which there was no choice. And the pressure building up in him to make such a choice about his own life was becoming difficult to bear. He had had enough of 'The Thrush': it had served its purpose. But what else could he possibly do?

From time to time he blew the whistle.

May had thought he might come to the trail and put in an

apple cake for him; put on a clean pinny, ordered her two youngest to be back and scrubbed on time – and tidied up the cottage. When the children had returned to tell her that their Uncle Joseph *was* at the trail and had given them each ten shillings (May took it from them for their post-office books) – she was as excited as she could still always be at the prospect of seeing a relative: especially Joseph. She wished her husband had not gone across into Ennerdale with their eldest son to help with a late harvest: it would have been better had all of them been there for Joseph to see.

And when the trails finished and she heard the cars roar away from the village she put the kettle on. The children had come back before the end of the trail to be clean and tidy as she had demanded – and so they didn't know the reason for Joseph's non-arrival. May wanted to send them out to look for him but she was afraid they might get dirty or run away and play: besides, she did not want to seem to beg.

Eventually she let the children change back into their ordinary clothes and go out: gave each one a fancy cake – the apple cake was unsliced.

So when he did come, she had been alone in front of the fire, nursing her chin in both hands and the cheeks which he kissed were lightly scorched.

'I'll take it some bread, May. I've tied it up against that bit of railing. We don't want it howling its throat out.'

'Here. Give it some of this.' She cut a large segment of the apple cake. 'They starve those poor things – not you I mean – everybody else. Go on then!' Happily, she shooed him out of the door he had just entered. 'I would make them owners run around fell tops on a cold afternoon if it was left to me: and let the dogs sit cosy in motor cars.'

'When's there a bus?' he asked as he re-entered – his first question, May noted: then she reproved herself for being so eager to find fault. 'There's a one at seven to Whitehaven and you can get one to Thurston from there.'

'I won't be back 'til about half-past-eight then – maybe later.' Joseph took off his coat. 'I'll have some tea then. It's too late to bother.' With May he could pretend to this fine carelessness;

convincing both of them that he was capable of forgetting the rush there would be in the pub.

'Aye. You just settle yourself, lad. You must be cold.'

'I kept movin'. And then it just trots up to me as if we'd been out on a little walk. Come up behind me. Next thing I know, its nose is in my coat pocket looking for its bait tin.'

'Well!' May reacted as if she had been given a description of something rare and wonderful. She poured fresh water into the tea-pot and waited on her brother at the table.

'You always could bake, May,' Joseph said, later. 'Haven't eaten apple cake like this for years.'

'Betty can bake.' May would not be counted before his wife.

'Not in the same class. Not – in – the – same – class.'

'Oh – don't say that, Joseph. Last time I came to see you there was some beautiful sponge cake. Don't say that. Another cup?'

'You're very comfortable here,' said Joseph, in rather a lordly manner.

'Why shouldn't we be?'

'No reason, May.'

'I've lived long enough to be comfortable, haven't I? My Christ, I've still got to make do with all sorts of job lots and pass-ons.'

'Now don't get like that, May.'

'Like what?'

'Oh dear. And I've had such a grand tea.' He paused, then smiled at her – 'D'you remember when you used to bring us apple-cake at the Sewells?'

May's expression – which had been perturbed – cleared instantly and she replied.

'We had some good times then, didn't we, Joseph?'

'Sometimes I think that, May : then again I think they were bad times.'

'Now I agree with you, they were. Bad times.' Her brow puckered, indecisively – 'But like – I enjoyed some of them.'

'So did I.'

'They should have been shot for sackin' you,' she declared, warmly.

'Best thing that ever happened.'

'Was it?' She shook her head. 'Bein' *sacked*?'

'Well, if I'd stayed on, I'd have just stayed in service.'

'You would, you would. You were tip-top at it. That's a tongue-twister, Joseph! Like in a Christmas cracker. TIP TOP AT IT.'

'If you say it fast, it's rude,' said Joseph and groaned to himself the moment the observation passed his throat – May would – there it was – blush for him. 'But what I mean to say,' he rushed on, 'is that I'd've looked daft as a butler nowadays.'

'O, you've done very well.' May was on a theme which gave her no doubt. 'Everybody says you've a lovely house – they do, and it's not just because they know you're my brother because most of them don't. And Betty keeps things beautifully – as soon as I set eyes on her I knew She'd Be The One. I knew it. Oh – you've done very well, Joseph. And so have Douglas; and Harry,' she added, carefully, justly. 'Him an' all. All of you.' She hesitated and then, lowering her voice, said, 'Douglas wrote a letter to me from Oxford, you know. He did. Told me all about it.' She waited, not wanting to presume, but Joseph's attention reassured her. 'You wonder where he got his brains from, don't you? I mean – you were clever, you were now, you were: maybe he got them from you. But Betty's clever as well, isn't she?'

'How's David and John and Emily doing then?' Joseph asked, abruptly.

She told him about her own children, defensively, relaxing to praise only when she had weighed his interest and found it sufficient. But to give herself every protection, she cleared the table while speaking.

'Just think, eh, May? – not being able to eat it all up.'

'Aye.' She smiled sweetly. 'Our dad would have knocked our heads off if we hadn't finished everything in front of us.'

'And *he* wouldn't have seen that much food in a week of Sundays.'

'We must be getting old, talking like this,' said May.

'We are,' Joseph replied. He leaned back on his chair and patted his belly. '*That* wasn't just delivered this morning. Took time.'

'You *are* a bit fat. But it suits you. It does! You were a bit thin.'

'I started to put it on in the Forces you know. All that beer.' May shook her head.

'Aye. No good for you. Oh: I mean – having a pub's all right, but drinking isn't – it makes you fat. Mind – I'm fat and teetotal so what the hell!'

Joseph laughed at her confusions; she ran in and out of them like a rabbit playing round a thicket.

'A pal of mine just now retired from the R.A.F.,' said Joseph. 'Went all through with him. He came out a Squadron-Leader.'

'Goodness me!'

'A tidy lump sum and a nice pension for life. And I was in charge of him when we were in together,' he said and could not prevent the lurch of envy in his voice. 'That's the funny part.'

'I don't think it's funny. You could have been a sq – squaw – what was it?'

'Squadron-Leader. No – I couldn't. Not in Stores. He was *fit*, see. A marvellous footballer.'

'Aren't you fit then?'

'Fit? Fit enough, May.'

'Sit on an easy chair – not that hard-backed thing.'

'You don't half take things literally, May.'

'Lit – what?'

'To heart.'

'Aye well. It's as good as any other spot.'

Later, she insisted on walking him to the bus stop. This puzzled him until she took a short cut which led near the churchyard and he understood; their 'real' mother had been buried there, brought to lie beside the first of her sons, who had died soon after his birth. On her stone was mention of another boy, Harry, who had been killed at the end of the First War. May wanted him to see the grave.

They stood there in the cold, the two of them bulky with clothing on heavy bodies. Tinker sniffed at the close-cropped grass and his breathing sounded too loud. Joseph was moved by his sister's sentiment and knew, as he put an arm around her shoulders, that she was having a quiet cry. He, too, would have liked to cry but could not; was beginning to worry about Betty and the pub, beginning to see the customers file in, the faces in the public bar went singly through his mind.

In the bus on the way to Whitehaven, he joggled impatiently on the leather seat. Would Betty remember that the mild had just been changed? Would she have collected the two pounds' worth of coppers from the bus station? Would she tell Michael Carr that his brother wanted to see him and of course she would forget to check the bulb in the back cellar.

Blank outside, past slag heaps and terraced houses, the bus seemed jubilantly lit. He could not get back fast enough. Tinker was under the seat. He knew the conductor and the man had tried to persuade him to sit downstairs so that they could talk: had said, over-loudly, that he would 'forget' the rule about Dogs Going on the Top Deck. But Joseph had insisted on going upstairs. He wanted to be alone for a while: to look at his reflection in the black windows and beyond them to the land-scape he had known all his life. But how he wanted to leave it! His skull would crush his mind if he could not get out.

They moved south soon after Douglas left University; in the summer, when Thurston was most hopeful. And Joseph became tenant-landlord of a large working-class pub which once again needed 'improving'; the work concealed the wound for a few years.

Part Four

Arriving

Chapter Seventeen

As if in preparation for his father's arrival in the morning, Douglas checked through what he had just written of the town he had called Thurston. Deliberately using real names, deliberately allowing his own sentimental feeling about the place to find expression, it was, he thought, a message to his parents.

An evening at the end of summer.

'In the park the braver children have the swings to themselves and dare each other to hang by the legs. In the Showfields the keener rugby players turn up for pre-match training. Harry down there – a useful centre – travelling back from Newcastle to play; and Peasa and his four brothers, the two Bells and the two Pearsons – Taffy surprising everybody with his play at stand-off – Eric Hetherington with his style and mimetic confidence in all things, Keith Warwick the untouchable fullback and Apple the uncrushable trier – there in the green and white hoops they train beside the beck, white shorts against hedges as the twilight comes and Hammy races up and down beside them, urging them on against non-existent opponents, brandishing the net to fish the loose balls out of the river. Across the road there's the shuffle and click of bowls on the pampered green and grave men are thoughtful about their attack on the jack. Beside the green, a few loyalists show face in the Tennis Courts – the Mann girls, Wilson Bragg and Dr Dolan – "to keep the club alive"; the doctor in long trousers because of his bad leg, still hopping shrewdly through a good game. Nearby on the putting green Mickie Saunderson practises the golf shots he's seen on T.V. and does about three an hour – the rest of the time spent looking for the ball. While from the park and the Showfields couples drift along tenderly or tensely, making or breaking the dreams of past and future which whisper most insistently in this still and leisured hour.

'The people *I* know mingle with those my parents knew – for Joey Mitchinson walking along the Wiza, square-shouldered and meticulous, a hard, working man with ginger in his hair and in his character, he who started Infants' school with my mother (when it was behind Market Hill where a garage is now) – in his face I see Margaret his daughter who was at school with me – her wide, magnificent smile – and the same teachers for both, Miss Ivinson, Miss Moffat and Miss Steele – with George Scott the headmaster, in his late-eighties now and still reading the lesson at church, developing his own photographs (and hand-tinting them – nothing was too good for the town he had taught in since the previous century) making lemon cheese and remembering the name of every pupil, every single pupil, not one ever forgot – grandfather, father and son. Stern he had been, quick-tempered – but it soon passed – and believed in Courage, Honesty and Loyalty.

'Of course there was snobbery, bullying, meanness, hypocrisy and despair in Thurston : that is to be expected in any civilized community. What was moving was the warmth of feeling the place evoked. It was in some measure by talking of the town that they talked to each other – and warmth, especially, was transmitted through this knowledge of the people in the place.

'Further up the Wiza, Vince Wiggins would be trailing along watching for trout – and when seen he would stand in the beck and wait for them, "tickle" them, throwing them out onto the bank – something once seen never forgotten.

'Through the gate of the last Show-fields onto Longthwaite Road where Willie Reay would be going for a training run – scarlet satin shorts, the successor to Lester who'd now shot away from the town to a life in Liverpool, rumours coming back half-enviable, half-sinister. But Will Reay pounding away now and through his head the names of famous athletes rolled on a never-ending scroll, their ages and times and weighty remarks – and Geoff Byers just in front of him on a black racing bike, timing him with an ancient inherited stop-watch and using coaching terms with great aplomb.

'On the Syke Road they would be walking the Hound Dogs – Freeman Robinson and Joe McGuggie, Andrew Savage and Old Age – friends of Joseph all and the lean dogs yelping at the end of the broad leashes, the men leaning back as the dogs strained forward, the town they were half-circling, silent below.

'Everywhere small farms in a fold of ground: buildings cuddling the rise of earth, pegged to the landscape.

'Lowmoor Road where they had began to build new houses and the Baths with the boom and shrill of voices coming through the open windows. The Nelson School silent and empty; in the school-house Mr Stowe re-checking the new term's new timetables for the last time and occasionally dreaming of France. Hope's auction as empty as the school, pens and classrooms bare, hall and auction ring, cloakroom and byre. The church, too, all the churches empty, all but the Catholic where the nuns – Sister Frances, Sister Philomena and Sister Pat, the three that Joseph knew best, the three who most employed themselves about the town – where these smiling brides of Christ in antique dress filled the house which was theirs with flowers and chanting. Empty the banks and the shops at this time – Oglonbys, Middlehams, Toppins, Bells, Johnstones, Thomlinsons, the Co-op and the Co-op extension, Studholme's, McMechans, Jimmy Blair and Jimmy Miller, groceries and fish, Lunds with their light bread rolls and Norrie Glaister for pies, Willie Dodd, Radio and T.V. and the Pioneer Stores destined for a brief life against the Co-op, Graham's, Pearson's, Sharpe's, Christies, Morgan Allens, and Miss Turner's. Francis' sweet-shop and Noel Carrick's, the only one still open if you didn't count Joe Stoddart's in Water Street which would open any time you knocked on his back door. Empty the three tea-rooms and the big new car-park they'd destroyed an interesting street for, people out in the fields, in the pubs, in their gardens and allotments, the younger ones at Cusack's café down Meeting House Lane with the giant juke box penetrating the cinema next door which now was a Bingo Hall. And deserted even those mysterious warehouses which stood about the middle of the town. Silent the slaughterhouse, and the Market Hall.

'Dried blood now in the gutters of the slaughterhouse where

many a time Douglas and Harry watched the still or squealing beasts shot and seen them slump and shiver before being hooked by the throat and slit open – always the steam and the lardy skin, like white frozen jelly, which should have been bloodied but stayed white and gleaming – and then the man would plunge his arms into its belly and bring out the pouches, stomach and intestines and the slaughterhouse reeked, the waiting cows moaned and the small boys were dumb at the sight of it all. While nearby, around the corner in that town where everything was around the corner – the covered market stood idle, no mid-week dance, no social, no amateur theatricals, no speeches, just the stalls pushed back and that lovely, deep rather rotten tang in the fish-market.

'There, in the main hall, on Tuesday afternoons would come the slick operators from Newcastle and rhyme off such a gobful of patter that drummed up a crowd just to listen to them. One black-haired fellow selling sheets who never stopped and insulted them all in ways they did not understand – "I could sell more outside a synagogue on a Saturday," he'd say, and bursting with alliterative delight, add "sell more outside a soddin' synagogue on a stupid Saturday, I could; sell more outside a stupid soddin' synagogue on a soddin' stupid Saturday – really, ladies, please!" (But only one in twenty of his audience would ever be *really* certain what a synagogue was. And the Saturday part of it left them all completely cold.) "*I* won't ask you 80s., *I* won't ask you 70s., *I* won't ask you 60s., *I* won't ask you 50s., feel the flannel, madam, who needs a husband with my sheets? *I* won't ask you 45s. and I won't ask you 40s. – now go to Carlisle, go to Carlisle! Go to Binns and go to where else is there in Carlisle? Go where you want and get me a pair of first-class-quality-guaranteed-flannel-sheets-unmarked-and-unspoilt for 40s. – do that madam and I'll give you 60 for them – you cannot buy what I am giving you – and I'll tell you what I'll do I'll tell you what I'll do – one towel, one face-cloth and one sponge – there, free, gratis and for nothing – rob me ladies while I am weak – there – Not 40, not 39, 38, 37, 36, 35, 34, 33, 32, 31 – 30 bob the lot! 30 bob the lot! 30 bob! 30 bob! Thank you, thank you, ladies. Thank you all!"'

He would try to finish it in the morning. He had always wanted to use the real names of the people there. But would they object?

He got up at four-thirty to be sure to finish the work in time. Though he had snapped down the alarm button just a few seconds after it had begun to ring, Betty too had woken up. He could feel her awake there: the breathing shallower.

But she let him go down on his own. They had agreed that she should sleep on until six, and she did not want to change that plan now, knowing it would upset him. Listening, breath-held, she smiled in the dark as she heard him clatter through his breakfast. She had laid it out for him before coming to bed, of course. Less than four hours previously.

She dozed, as pleased as Joseph himself that this day should be so.

He liked to work alone in the silence. Then he had the measure of everything and nothing was rushed though he went quickly. As always, when going away, he ordered matters on two assumptions; one that every possible disaster might occur, the other that Betty would not be able to cope with any of them. It entailed an elaborate system of stacking and securing and always reminded him of those Western films where the people inside the fort prepare to meet the onslaught of the Indians.

He was going to the World Cup Final. Wembley – Yes! With England playing and Douglas taking him – and which of these two facts gave him most pleasure he did not know. He *had* to be up at 4.30 to spend the hours alone, to weigh and balance his excitement.

England In The Final Of The World Cup At Wembley Playing Germany And Himself Being Taken By His Son.

Maybe they would go out on the town after the match: maybe have that long talk he longed for, he'd dreamed of in sentimental moments, when father and son would emerge from the chrysalis of blood and memory and be friends. Now he was certain of one thing. Douglas liked him. Certain. He'd asked him to come and spend the day and given him that one free ticket he had. Joseph fully appreciated how much the young man would have preferred going with one of his own pals – maybe one of those people he made films with or was on television with – but he'd offered it to him.

Pile up the bottles of light ale by the hatch; open all the barrels; fill the drawers with cigarettes, load the shelves with whisky. If England should win . . . !

He put down the typescript and drank some more coffee. The draft of the novel was scattered all over his table. It read so awkwardly that he was embarrassed to put his eyes to it – and he groaned to think how many times it might have to be re-written.

He had published two novels which had been 'quite well received'. The one he was working on now – *The Throstle's Nest* – was an attempt to bring his past directly into fiction in an effort to connect it with his present. Perhaps the only way was not to write it as fiction at all but to make a confession and perhaps the best way to do that was in a screenplay for tele-vision or film where the nature of the medium would inevitably colour what he was saying in the tones of his present mind. The act of writing a novel seemed to put on him a habit from the past which aided but contained him : yet only in fiction had he felt that he was recreating that density which sought release; taking the load off his mind. At present he wanted to lay dynamite around his inheritance, stand back, look around; and then plunge in the handle – like himself plunging into a woman, like his feelings plunging into his past, like his mind plunging into words – to plunge and blow himself into the instant that is Now.

And so *The Throstle's Nest* – so tentative and reticent as to be foolish compared with his expectation. But you could only go at the pace that was yours. He finished the chapter.

'The pig market empty, the old Armoury and the Primitive Methodist church, and Redmayne's factory closed for the night.

'Only the Rayophane still going. There, where Joseph had once been exploited as many a man in Thurston had, unexpected changes had brought expansion and wealth to the place. Royal Dutch Shell had taken it over and decided to invest heavily in it – and to their surprise in a way, those working there were told that they were more efficient, considerably more efficient than, say, their chief rival in St Helens – which was full of "graduate types". None of these at Thurston, only local men who had joined from school and as well as doing a full day's work, had flogged themselves through night school year after year and were now running the place, young men, George Stephenson, Jimmy Jennings and Billy Lowther. It was becoming a centre of great and justifiable pride now, this factory, and they built the chimney higher and higher to take away the poisonous stink of chemicals.

'So down there in the factory fields there was new building and men moving between the "shops" – running through it still the river Wiza, technicoloured by the discharge, oily and fascinating – changing the feeling of the town this extended factory now sweeping across the bottom of Union Street where further up Dickie Thornton had also cut a swathe to extend his colony of pumps and garages.

'The British Legion would be filling up at this time – they were modernizing that, bringing in the old Drill Hall – it would take a lot of trade from the pubs.

'As the pigeons wheeled above Bird-cage Walk and flew out over the Stampery, the double-decker took the new bloods to Carlisle for the disco-dance (Tues., Wed. and Thurs. 3s. 6d.) in the Casino Ballroom. Into the town came the farm labourers on their heavy old bikes, needing the pint they had measured out their money for; and out of it went Ronald Graham, the hairdresser, the man with the most infectious laugh in Thurston, full of news and tattle, who'd made a "turn" of an illness which would have depressed most people for life – there he goes, carbound, nosing his way to the latest village pub of his delight where he'll stand at the corner of the bar and market the day. And out of it too, George Johnston, thoughtful and preoccupied, exercising his basset hounds and in his mind assembling the book he has to write on them, dreaming of the small dogs at the courts of the French Kings, finding perfection in a paw.

Into Thurston came the boyos, the Hard Men from the villages and estates, to lounge in the corners and take an occasional drink – the darts players loosened up in the rooms as yet empty of all but them. And out of it went Mr James for a walk, maintaining a fast pace, concentrating on Collingwood's Idea of History, breaking it down and re-assembling it, preparing to introduce it to the upper sixth in autumn.

'Most of all in the town there are these men like you, Father,' Douglas wrote, 'because Thurston is full of men like you. Who've been hauled into work and have recoiled into play. Who've been drummed out of childhood and dragooned into a society which had dug itself into them like the man at the slaughterhouse and pulled out your entrails for its own use. Who've come not to expect though they've not stopped demanding, not really to hope though desire can't be killed – "ordinary decent people", the phrase writes you off too glibly and yet you would take it as a compliment. But you saw what might be in the war and in your sons all of you, and pushed for it, and won a little. So now we see each other in sentimental stereotype half the time – but that's all right; it's the dry men who flinch at sentimentality and the timid men who are afraid of stereotypes, not understanding that you can be type and individual, both unit and man without contradiction or surrender.

'The centre of the town is very calm : you could walk up the middle of the road without too much worry. Keeping to the pavement, is William Ismay, having closed the shop and arranged the next day. And in him, for me,' wrote Douglas, 'both of you, the town and myself meet. Approximately the best man I ever met – *well* met in Will, we are . . .'

He read through what he had written and wondered about the embarrassment but decided he had not lied nor romanticized, only omitted and there was still time.

His father would soon be at Paddington and he'd promised to meet him at the station. Why did he need so much looking-after when he came to London. Already, annoyance was assault-his intended placidity and even though prepared for it, time was needed to drive it away.

He made his bed and cleared up the breakfast stuff in case an accident brought his father back there.

He lived in the bottom half of a four-storied Victorian terraced house in a street which had been decaying badly for over thirty years; he had got the down-payment from a film script and his formerly regular television job helped him secure the mortgage. His parents could not understand why he had not gone straight to a suburban semi-detached and sometimes when he came down the steps as now, and stepped into a half-eaten wad of chips, shuddered at the lorry which churned past the new flats being built around the corner, saw the cracked fronts of the houses, the long-peeled paintwork, the broken steps and damp walls – sometimes he agreed with them.

But not as he turned at the top of the street and walked down towards the underground, towards the centre of London. Then this part of town seemed ideal – a place he *had* to live in if he was to keep alive in the present. Otherwise there was nothing but retreat to Cumberland which could no longer be merely a memory – must be the past or a living place.

He walked down this hill of North London and saw the spread of city before him, the place for 9 million people. To the south and south-west, the parks and commons of Wimbledon, Richmond and Ham and the deep domestic luxuries of Surrey; to the south-east, docks and Dickens, Greenwich and the Tower Blocks covering the cinders of the blitz; and slung between them the bricked undergrowth of London, from Wandsworth to Barnes. And on the North side of the Thames – the City – even of wealth still, sucking sterling gluttonously, fattening those who commanded the centre of the town and lived in Westminster, Belgravia, Knightsbridge, Kensington and Chelsea. Then the dreaded Inner London Area of which his was part, where Victorian property threatened disaster to those who colonized it as they themselves had once been colonized – Jamaicans, Pakistanis, Nigerians, Barbadians, Irishmen and Indians – joined by those, like the Duke of York, who were 'neither up nor down'; the continental exiles and the provincial adventurers, all faces, all colours, all hell or heaven depending, a place becoming as dense to his adult mind, he sometimes thought, as Cumberland had been when a child.

And more, more. Because as he walked towards his father and tried to think of the Final, the Cup, the Excitement he forgot it all and saw only the face of Mary whom he could meet this night; her blue-grey eyes soft and serious, her smile as sweet as any happiness, her hair in his fingers, draping his wrist.

Lester had travelled all night. He had scented the gang's intention before they themselves had really tasted it – left the club instantly and snatched the few clothes he kept at Moira's place. He'd caught a bus to the edge of the city. His own car was being repaired and he had only a few pounds cash.

Besides – who would think of looking for Lester Tallentire on a 32 bus or making for the A6 to thumb a lift south? He'd made more of himself than that! And they'd never have dared turn on him if he hadn't had such bad luck lately. Succeed and they'll jump in a lake for you; fail and they find an excuse to turn. Best thing to do was this, best thing was to go south, let things quieten down, get something together and then come back. Or maybe stay south; he'd often wanted to – put it off – no need – now there was no choice and that always helped.

The lorries wouldn't stop – the lights seemed to make straight for him, examine him and then pass on rejecting him. He would not hold out his hand and waggle his thumb like some sodding hitch-hiker! They must know why he was standing there at this time of night with a suitcase between his feet and his hands jammed in his trouser pockets. He wouldn't beg! He had no coat – couldn't endure them – but it was a warm night and he was in no hurry.

It took him over an hour to get a lift and he was lucky even then to be picked up by a fat little prattling Welshman who always looked out for company about this spot on his twice-weekly run of 350 miles south. 'Company keeps you con-cen-traat-ed,' he sang – and the alliterated refrain, invariably employed, it seemed, was meant to be the slyly jocular seal on this transitory acquaintanceship. He could have been excused for passing by, for Lester presented no sympathetic sight: in a well-cut dark suit, white shirt and dark tie, with black hair, dark skin, good looks, he seemed the last man to need help; while his aggressive manner – apparent even when standing at the road-side – was too much of a risk. But the Welshman had his rules and stuck to them : nobody in the cabin for the first 100 miles, then the first one you saw – never been let down yet; many a grand crack. He might have broken the rule had he known about the knuckle-duster in Lester's inside pocket; highly polished and wrapped in a clean handkerchief. But Lester fell asleep and even at the transport café said little; ate his bacon sandwich and looked around, so obviously bored by the Welshman that even the prattle faded.

It was not until he had walked about a mile through the town which was the lorry's destination that he firmly decided to call on his Uncle Joseph. He had heard of their move south and been only mildly surprised : his aunty Betty would resent it, he knew that, but in the end she would have to follow Joseph and his uncle had often said he would like to get out of Cumberland where he was too well known to be himself.

He went to the railway station to have some breakfast in the buffet and clean himself up. It was too early to call on them yet. While Lester was in the Gents impatiently waiting for the hot water to prove itself, Joseph passed by outside, unseen and unseeing, on his way to the London train.

When he saw the sign he stopped to gaze at it.

JOSEPH TALLENTIRE Prop :
LICENSED TO SELL ALES, WINES, SPIRITS
AND TOBACCO.

He remembered how in Thurston he used to stand outside 'The Throstle's Nest', transfixed at the sight of his own name up there. And how, the time he'd been had up for that robbery he'd cut the report out of the paper to look and look again at his name in print.

He stood and felt himself checked. There had always been so much to look forward to in going into his uncle's previous pub that he had deliberately delayed doing so to enjoy the anticipation. Something else, though, as well. Despite the un-changing warmth of the welcome he had always been afraid that he might be imposing, 'putting on' Betty's generosity and Joseph's interest: occasionally he'd turned away so as not to presume too much. These feelings were from a past which seemed so distant — for his last years had been such a chasm after the plateau of his earlier life — that he wondered at his own memories; they were so unexpected, like a rope bridge which hangs across a ravine. What he had been and what he now was! If they knew all he had done they would not even let him in.

And that last thought pleased him! For so often had he come there doubting himself good enough to enter: almost rubbing off his soles on the door-mat so as not to dirty aunty Betty's scrubbed floors: all but introducing himself to his uncle Joseph as if convinced the older man could so easily forget him; always feeling that he had to be on his best behaviour and burdened with a sentimental gratitude towards them for their understanding of his times in 'trouble'; a passionate feeling of thankfulness which he thought would never die but had died. He was glad to be going in carrying the last few years secretly, to be received as a prodigal when on the run from a beating-up because of a botched job. Oh — they knew he'd been in trouble while a teenager, but nothing could be held against him in Thurston since he'd left: he'd been acquitted of the robbery charge; not enough evidence. Witnesses were hard to find.

So he went in with a swagger and pretended to be unmoved by Betty's delighted surprise: agreed to stay the day so that he might see Joseph on his return from the match and looked around appreciatively. They were doing very well, these two. A few bob had been spent on the place — you could see there'd been money spent, not big but some. And the till clanged busily.

What more can be said of that day of glory when England won the World Cup?

The drink they had before the match was excellent — Douglas took him to a quiet, rather exclusive little pub in St John's Wood where they had home-made steak and kidney pie (and

Joseph regretted that Betty would never go in for catering – 'doesn't like the idea of Staff, see, Douglas? Puts her right off, telling people what to do'); where they had a couple of pints of bitter to which Joseph conceded some points; where of course he introduced himself to the landlord and itched to get into details about the nature of the trade and the size of the takings, always letting it be understood that if the place was attractive enough he might keep his eye on it and watch out for future developments; where there was the silence when they realized they were to be alone together and the glancing at each other tentatively, to prise the face of the stranger from the presence of the son and father.

Then outside the ground itself – that twin-domed yet most ordinary place which had supported so many fantasies of so many ordinary Englishmen as teams had come up for the Cup and gone down fighting : the touts there shouting £5 for a 15s. ticket (soon to be sold at 'fair price' – they overestimated the public's willingness to risk missing the match which was to be certainly seen on television by 500 millions was it? Some un-imaginable number of intent eyes and 100,000 people actually there) and the Refreshment Tents – as at Agricultural Shows, said Joseph, programmes, balloons, team photos, colours, and everywhere that chant which had become England's Cheer as the series had progressed.

Inside the ground, among a crowd of miners from Barnsley. There were about 30 of them and they worked together at a pit in a village near Barnsley. They'd made 'a reet do out o' this World Cup'. Somehow – Joseph never asked them if the pit had been forced to close down – somehow they had taken two weeks off work together, as a gang. Hired a coach for a fort-night : booked themselves into boarding houses in Liverpool and London, organized tickets for the most impressive number of games and sailed up and down England in a trance of football. Joseph watched Douglas talking to one of them in particular – a wiry little man who kept referring to The Party and was soon launched on a description of Oswald Mosley's meeting in Barnsley Town Hall in 1936 and how the Party lads had tried to break it up. Phrases came over to Joseph – 'those Blackshirts wore knuckledusters, you know, under their gauntlets' – 'we plastered Barnsley wi posters' – 'the People was being fooled – they were – they didn't know what a Fascist was'; and he saw Douglas relax in that old man's company as he did in John's; and was jealous in a way, puzzled in another because these fellows who followed one path undeviatingly were *not* the strong men they appeared, Joseph thought: it was easier in many ways to hold than to let go, to stick than to change, to keep than to give. He wanted to tell him that.

But he was away with one of the miners who'd spent some time in the West Cumberland coalfield and worked with people he knew. And from the swapping of Cumbrian names, they went on to the names of those in the World Cup – now become as well-known as neighbours: the brilliant, delicate Brazilian Pele; Eusebio the oak-thighed star of Portugal and Yashin the Russian goalkeeper, black and gloomy. They laughed about the 'little North Koreans' who had surprised everybody, and agreed about the bad luck of Argentina. If only the Americans really played Association Football, Joseph thought! And suddenly he remembered Mr Lenty, the cobbler, and that time they'd chanted the sheep-count and the old man, dead now, had sworn that the American Indians counted in the same way.

It was strange the two of them sitting there in the back-kitchen watching the game on television, their dinners on their knees. Lester had helped in the pub and carried up the cases from the cellars with such efficiency that the man hired for the job had been rather put out until Betty had mollified him by emphasizing the word 'nephew'; family gave privileges. But 'nephew' was far away from the feeling between them now, the blue plates heavy with fried food humidly pressing onto their knees as they sat in armchairs side by side and watched the game, the one because he was an enthusiast for football, the other because she loved an Event.

For Lester had already made up his mind what he would do and in some flicker of his feeling Betty had guessed it. The grit rubbed between them, as yet infinitesimally small but already it was growing. Yet Lester had been all smiles; charmed the ladies, impressed the men. He had lost his sharp-boned rawness and become 'really handsome!' as Betty thought to herself with pleased surprise. And there was something very 'manly' about him – in the bar there whether playing darts, talking or just having a drink, there was a confident, certain-footed, easy command about him. He knew what his life was worth.

What was it then? He could not have been more attentive. Got up to help her with the tray. Made sure she wanted to see the game. Brought her a cushion 'for her back' (unnecessary – but both of them enjoyed the charade in the same way, she thought) and explained things to her about football, quietly, simply, not shouting like Joseph or making a complicated fuss like Douglas. Yet ...

As if facing up to a puzzle-picture in a newspaper, Betty leaned back in the chair and closed her eyes and tried to think of every single thing that had happened involving Lester since his arrival. Something there was which she not only disliked but feared, she realized. A real though slight shiver went across her body. She *was* afraid of him and half-opened her eyes to make sure he was still where he ought to be. His plate by his feet, the knife and fork neatly crossed, sitting back, legs crossed, with a cigarette, an ash-tray held thoughtfully in his free hand, absorbed in the match.

She closed her eyes again and nestled her head into the arm of the chair, imitating sleep to stop thinking about it. Time and again she was plagued by such feelings: such strong reactions to what first appeared as nothing at all; the invisible end of an invisible thread which she picked at and picked at and sometimes *did* unravel.

Perhaps Lester reminded her too strongly of Thurston. Somewhere inside her there was a sob – as heard in her mind as if it had been declared out loud. In the end Joseph's arguments had exploited her own frustrations about matters in general – and she had come to think their cause was the town, its abandonment the cure. But now she felt more isolated than ever in her entire life. She did not know how strong the net of acquaintanceship was until it was no longer under her; nothing now to break her falls. And though she loved people from

Thurston to drop in on their way to London or to Cornwall for holidays – loved it and would celebrate their arrival with a release of gaiety otherwise now preserved in measured form for the self-satisfaction of a job done well or coincidences chiming – yet she feared these reminders too. They were too harsh. As she plundered the visitor's gossip her mind's eye swept up and down the main street, patrolled the alleys and courtyards, inspected shop and market and church – then rushed back to the box made so strongly for it by the old imperatives of duty and loyalty : but really bound by necessity. There her love for the past would be locked up until, again provoked by such direct contact, it would escape once more and bruise itself in taking pleasure.

So she appeased herself, that is for the few painful minutes during which she willed her memory to be dead. That passed, however, she found her doubts unresolved and was worried yet again. Because what had the lad done wrong? Why did she take against him so? For it was no less than that now; she could feel herself turning against him, all the positive, welcoming expressions of her body and emotions were being blocked by this silt of doubt.

A loud roar from the crowd brought back her attention to the match. Lester turned and grinned at her – widely baring his teeth. 'We've scored,' he said, 'we're in the lead,' and she pretended to be only half awake so as to disguise her shiver as a yawn.

'When it was fully realized that the Fête was to be on such an important day, such a day of days for some of the menfolk – I refer of course to the Final of the World Football Cup Competition – then it was too late to change. Mr Wolfers had lent his garden, Mr Russell had allocated the small marquee (free of charge, as ever, our thanks to Mr R.) the Women's Institute had issued rules for cake contests of, let me say, all shapes and sizes, and pleas had sped forth from the Mother's Union for Jumble; the A.Y.P.A. – our brave Young People – had begun the sixpenny raffle with the greatest enthusiasm and one heard stories of strangers importuned on top of Knockmirton Fell itself with the request to buy a pink ticket for Mr Wheldon's kindly donated *Pair* of Chickens – in short, our annual fête was under way and, after a fashion, I'm proud, yes – that hoary old sin crept quietly in – proud, I repeat, to say that not even a World Cup Final can stop our parochial activities. Mr Whitehead at the gate tells me that we are only a score down on last year when, you might remember, there was a freak thunderstorm the night *before* which worried some of the mothers.

'Of course we all want England To Win. And here's where we *score*, as it were. For not only can you enjoy the fête – and I earnestly beg you to spend all the money you can rightly afford; believe me the church tower will benefit enormously and everlastingly – remember, only £9,625 to go in our grand slam for the £10,000 – but not only can you contribute to the mile of pennies – the white line kindly painted by Mr D. Jones to whom our grateful thanks – or catch the piglet (loaned by Mr Duncan, one of 9, I'm told, all doing well) or guess the weight of the lamb (our thanks to Mr Copping – a pet lamb this belonging to his daughter Joan), not only, say I – to use the tricks of that man on television who introduces all the old music hall stars, I forget his name – thank you, Mr Odges, I'll make a note of it – not only can you do this – and don't forget the treasure hunt behind the garden shed – a shilling a peg and a pound for the crock of gold – (Mr McGahern's annual donation) not only (I mustn't forget Mrs Bomford, must I?) not only can you guess the number of raisins in her four pound fruit cake – who else is there? – ah! Mr Hamilton has brought his Hoop-la once more, genuine Victorian Hoop-la – and Mr Farrer's presiding over the Dub-Tub and the sisters three (forgive me ladies but fitting it all in makes me a little light-hearted, not to say headed, we *all* appreciate your endless devotion to St Jude's) the Misses Powell are there once more with the exquisite embroidery on handkerchief and – head-band is it? That other thing? – Art from a long lost past preserved for us only by the devotion of those sisters and quite reasonably priced. Yes, as usual, tea will be served by Mrs Strawson and Mrs Bloomfield boiled the water – sandwiches by the W.I. and cakes by sundry : *so* – not only do we have all this – but in Mrs Wolfers' conservatory – that is behind the house – there is a specially in-stalled television set (thank you, Mr Mapplebeck) on which our more sporting brethren can watch the efforts of their fellow-countrymen in their fight against the German.

'I now declare the 1966 St Jude Garden Fête and Fund Raising Afternoon to be officially open.'

The Rev. Duncan, a young man but centuries-fat with a happy complacency which had begun as a good-natured banter-ing of 'the natives' and resolved itself into this unctuous face-tiousness redeemed however by his undoubted generosity and constant hard work – in clerical grey now padded across the deep green lawn and came to Harry with a copy of his speech.

'You'll find all the names mentioned there, Mr Tallentire. All you'll need are the prizewinners : I could give you those now if it would help you for your dead-line.'

'I think we'll manage, thank you. And I *have* to stay. They want a colour piece on it this time.'

'Ha-ha! "English Life goes on while England fights Again for Victory".'

'Well – I suppose so. They do one a year, you know – for all the ads you fête-people put in. This year it was you.'

'You're a football fan, Mr Tallentire, I can tell that. Slip round to the conservatory – I'll give you plenty of colour. It's my trade, you know.'

'No, I want to do it for myself – no offence.'

'None taken, my boy! Please – say whatever you like about us! We can take it.'

Thus do heroes bare themselves to the elements and the Rev. Duncan felt no less courageous as he paced towards Mr Hamil-ton's Hoop-La, having dared the *Cumberland News* to do its worst.

Harry had been unhappy about the job for several reasons. There was the match, of course – but now he'd be able to see some of it at least. No – it was this complicated business of the assistant editor who liked him and was always trying to help him and Harry wished he wouldn't. He did not really want to be helped. He was very happy. Very happy to collect names at rugby matches, football matches, socials, prize-givings, fires, anniversaries, meetings – wherever there were names to be collected he was more than happy to copy them down and worry that they were correctly spelt in the final edition. And like all good provincial newspapers, the *Cumberland News* was well aware that every name was a guaranteed sale – and they had the special provincial pupil-distorting small-print to meet that situation. *More* than happy. He loved to motor around Cumberland in his second-hand Mini – going to villages he'd never visited before, finding out more and more about this dense and endlessly interesting county, its names in his notebook ready for the press. He was known as 'the reporter' in villages and sometimes addressed as such by vicars or small children. That suited him fine. He wanted no more. And when he married he wanted to live right here and do exactly the same thing for the rest of his life. The job paid as much as most – less than a foreman at the factory – but pleasanter work altogether. And the *pleasure* in knowing everybody, having all those names in his head. If a slight pride was there it was just in this authority and when arguments developed in the pub about who it was and name of what? – Harry would pursue the matter like a hound until he'd tracked down the correct name and then feel great relief and a sense of accomplishment.

But this assistant editor thought he was made for Better Things; kept tormenting him with encouragement to do full match reports for Carlisle United Reserves or interview Mr Simon who bred racehorses or this sort of thing – a 'colour piece'. And gamely, Harry took on these jobs, not wanting to disappoint the man's expectation of him and thinking himself somewhat greedy, perhaps, in keeping the easy work (though everyone else in the office regarded it as the slogging bit) and feeling, hopelessly, that a 'reporter' ought to be able to turn his hand to a 'colour piece' or a full-length report just as easily as a Scout Rally (how he loved to copy down the names and numbers of all the troops – Wigton St Mary's 2nd Troop – Bothel 1st, St Mungo's 4th, Aspatria – and get the patrol-leaders and seconds and scoutmasters just *so*).

He was no good at this other. And it took him hours.

Now, feeling his stomach clenched in dismay at the prospect

of interspersing the names with 'descriptive passages', he wandered across to the wall – nodding to the many he knew as he passed them by – and looked across the fields towards Knockmirton Fell, its cone-shape clear on this bright afternoon. He loved this part of Cumberland – just where the plain went up to the fells which ringed the lakes: those bare hills, boulder, bracken and scree, figured by sheep or now the occasional hiker. It moved him more than he would ever be able to say. As did this fête, in its way; people making do, enjoying themselves, coming together for company, yes, but for a decent purpose outside themselves as well. He could not understand how anyone born and bred in this place could ever willingly leave it.

Perhaps his affection for the place was due to his grandfather, John, with whom he now lodged. In that meticulous, old-fashioned household there was peace and certainty; restlessness was dismissed as weakness, alternatives to present settlement – mere fripperies.

There was a shout from the conservatory! England must have scored. Briskly he walked back across the lawn – he would labour at the piece through the night. Perhaps they would soon realize he wasn't good enough – that was his hope – and leave him in peace.

The game. Of those at Wembley and others all over England watching television many linked football inextricably with working-class conditions of life, where prize dribblers were nurtured in narrow back-alleys; in the Depression when 'it kept you going' and the War when 'there was nothing else to do'. And the team which stepped out for England was somehow of those times. This was 1966 and there had been Beatles, Swinging London, Trendiness and self-conscious Pop Culture – but this England Team were short-back-and-sides, hair with a parting, soberly dressed, modestly spoken, rather serious – a few beers and a quiet life, cautious, a good job done and no excuses Englishmen. They had come out of the bad times, this team – typified by the stern-faced Charlton Brothers from a mining village in an area so hard hit it was a wonder it had not revolted – but there was no revolution, just perhaps a more open belief in the notion of the dignity of ordinary men. Intimations of such thoughts passed through Douglas's mind and as far as he could tell, similar feelings and others yet more insistent were present in the minds of those around him.

The final brought the Prime Minister flying back from Washington – to his credit.

The actual game was not as good a game of football as the semi-final when England had beaten Portugal; there was good fortune in playing in your own country and at your own stadium; but the chief aim in a cup competition is to win it – which England did; well. Nor did the fact that the victory was gained over Germany detract from the sweetness of the triumph. London rang that night with car-horns and drunken singing and twelve names were ceaselessly invoked: Banks, Cohen, Wilson, Moore, Charlton (J.), Stiles, Peters, Hurst, Hunt, Charlton (R.), Ball and Alf Ramsey, the Manager, soon to be knighted; no less.

They travelled back into London in the Barnsley coach and by closing time Douglas needed a rest. He had taken them all to a big, friendly pub near his house where he knew there was room to move, entertainment later on in the evening. (Piano, drums and occasional double-bass.) The amount of beer sunk in the first few hours was awful to think about. When he got back home – his father insisted on coming with him – Douglas had time only to make a swift postponing call to Mary (he was in no state to see her anyway; and perhaps, for once, he would connect with his father – only that). He asked Joseph to wake him up in two hours, hit the settee and was out. Joseph, by no means empty himself but steady enough still, regarded his prostrate son most tenderly: it was the first time they had got drunk together. Betty had half-expected him to stay the night and he had every intention of waking Douglas up just after midnight and going on to one of those drinking clubs he'd told the Barnsley crowd about. He phoned her and was pleased Lester was there to look after her – had always liked Lester: liked everybody tonight: the whole world.

He saw the words 'The Throstle's Nest' and was glad to think that Douglas was writing about the old town : then he read bits of the novel – it was not very long, that first draft : took him about two hours – fitted in well with Douglas's sleep.

Later, in the drinking club (which Joseph did not think much of) he found himself sitting in a quiet corner with his son and told him he'd read the book.

'Did you like it?'

'That's hardly the point, is it?'

'I suppose not, no.' Douglas hesitated. 'I'm glad you read it. I'd never have shown it to you.'

'I read your other two. I would have read this when it came out.'

'Yes. But maybe I would have thought I ought to have shown it to you *before* it came out. So that you could object if you wanted to. I mean, if you think there's anything to object to. I'm a bit drunk.'

'No. I follow you all right,' said Joseph. 'And you *sound* sober enough to me.'

O Christ, another silence! Another of those empty spaces which had pocked his life with those he ought to have loved.

'Well?' Douglas asked.

'Well. I quite enjoyed it, Douglas. You think you've got me weighed up – and you're wrong though you're entitled to your opinion; and you can't talk straight about your mother – but then you never could. There's a lot left out of course – I appreciate that.'

'What d'you mean "appreciate"?'

'Now then, Douglas.'

'No. What do you mean? Are you thanking me for it?'

'Should I?'

'You know, dad, I know less about your private life than I do about Bobby Moore's.'

'That's not unusual, is it? I mean – your mother and me aren't famous, are we?'

'No. O God, this is getting nowhere! Have another.'

They drank off and Douglas unnecessarily went to the bar himself for the drinks. Joseph anaesthetized his son's irritation with sentimentality. 'You don't seem to realize,' said Joseph, smiling as Douglas sat down, 'that I'm still a bit sideways – it isn't everybody has a book written about him. Not a bad book either ... you got your mother in that part with the eggs. Straight as straight she is. And although *I* can see things in it – I doubt if others will. Cheers.'

'What do you mean?'

'You've been very careful, Douglas. A bit like a detective, I thought – you've covered up where it mattered most. *That's* what I mean by "appreciate". You haven't got me, though.'

'No. I had to invent *you*. I don't know you well enough to describe you.'

'Now what does that mean?'

'It means I don't *really* know what you feel about anything: say about what you've read. A little, a lot; mild, or murderous; flattered, or furious; a bit proud or a bit disgusted – I do not know.'

'No, Douglas. And you'll never get to know, either! And I'll tell you another thing – you haven't said the half of it about yourself, either. Not the half!'

'Dad. Let me tell you this which will, might, just surprise you. Do you know that because of your dreams of Perfection – all those lies about Perfect Love and Perfect Heroes and Perfect Marriage and Perfect Honesty and Perfect bloody Worlds – because of that I've been slithering about with a view of the world which is about as useful as a wooden leg to a sprinter? And the violence between you! And what you would not say and would not *let* be said! And –'

'Hold on, lad, hold on. We all have problems. But they're our own private business, Douglas. *Private*. Now you rang Mary was it? Mary, yes – tonight. Well two and two makes four, even to those that never went to Oxford, son, and you know that I am curious – but it's *your business*. Right? And I want to tell you something – I want to tell you this.

'You've got a chance. No. Don't shake your head like that. You have a real chance.

'Now what I'm telling you is this. Let her rip, lad! Bugger everybody! You just put down whatever in God's name you think's right! Don't ask, don't worry, if you're all right in yourself and you're not after hurting somebody – you can't go wrong. Just get it down – that's what you've picked to do. Get it down!'

Betty had let the woman go home who'd been so carefully commissioned by Joseph to spend the night with her should he not return on the last train. Lester would be staying, she thought, and though her unease had developed into suspicion as the evening had gone on and he'd charmed his way boisterously through the customers – yet almost as an act of penance, she had dismissed the unspoken and unproven charges. Moreover, and giving her strength, the more worried she became the more convinced she grew that Joseph would return : he had not phoned which he would have done had he been staying. And Douglas would have enough to do in the evening without trailing around with his father. They'd never spent an evening together yet. Once, such a hunch would have been tied to a feeling like instinct, but perhaps more prosaic; that mixture of observation and experience based on intimacy and affection which can come to seem like instinct : frightened now, she relied once more on it – but the tie had been broken and the hunch was wishful only.

When, just after 11 o'clock, Joseph *did* ring up – rather drunkenly, she thought, which coloured her reaction, and said that he was staying on, she could have shouted to him to come back – but Lester was no more than a yard from the telephone, and she dare not, pulled a face at Lester, as if to say 'aren't husbands terrible!' and pleasantly informed Joseph that his 'nephew' was here, emphasized the word gaily as Lester had once liked it – but who *was* this confident, sprawling man spread out in the best armchair? – yes stay, of course stay, no Anne had gone home but Lester would look after her – looking well, yes, he was looking *very* well.

She put down the telephone briskly to overcome the trembling and walked to the back-kitchen to 'wash-up and tidy up and then upstairs' humming a sentimental pop song under her breath and listening to Lester turn the pages of the evening paper as a scared child might listen to thunder.

In bed, light off, she bunched up her knees to her breasts and clenched her eyes tight shut hoping to press sleep on herself; hearing every creak and breath of the house. A large house this, the biggest they'd had, and the pub itself huge, too vast for them really, but a good living. Tried to think of Thurston which was what sometimes helped her to go to sleep. She'd start at Burnfoot and go up the street, looking out for people to stop and chat with, say hello to: and how she missed that in this new town! To spend an entire afternoon at the shops and meet not one soul you knew! Godless. In Thurston, when she'd gone to Carlisle for the shopping trip, her first gossip on returning had been, always, to tell them all who in Carlisle she'd met from Thurston. But they couldn't go back – could they? Once you'd left you never *could* go back – could you? It would be to admit that once they had thought Thurston second-best. And having *chosen* to leave (though she'd fought it; silently in the end but so obstinately that the withered roots of their love had been wrung utterly and were dead forever) but having seemed to have chosen to leave – that irrevocably altered your relationship with the town, made you above it, lost it to you. Deep in these unhappy but easing reflections she relaxed and was not startled when she heard Lester come up the stairs.

But he did not close the door of his bedroom.

Now, tensely awake, between panic and tears, she waited. After two o'clock he moved most carefully and in stockinged feet crept down the carpeted corridor and into the upstairs sitting room, over to the sideboard (he'd measured the distance and removed the obstacles in the afternoon) and there were his uncle Joseph's takings where they'd always been in the black tin with a gold canary on a silver tree worked on the lid in some sort of wire. He ran his thumb over it as he'd often done when putting away the money his uncle had been pleased to trust him with to show where *he* stood after Lester's early troubles. There was a little satisfaction in this reversal but more of disquiet and he was most careful to put the note face up.

Dear Uncle Joseph, [it read]

I know this will make you a bit mad but I'm in trouble and I'll pay you back. You know I keep my word when I say. I'll pay you back no two ways about it. But I've got to keep moving and anyway this is a bit much to ask you for to your face. Sorry.

Best regards,
Lester.

There were the takings since Monday, including Friday and Saturday – well over £350.

Strangely, as Lester went down the stairs he *knew* that his aunt Betty had heard him and yet was forced to pretend she had not for fear of the complications which would arise from the admission of the knowledge. Similarly, Betty understood that he had divined her attention – the catch of a footstep was as loud as a street greeting – but she willed him to ignore it and felt happier with him than she had done all day when he did that and let himself out – almost noisily, the forms having lapsed and strode across the gravel outside their back door to clamber over the wall (thoughtful that, too, knowing that while she might dare leave her bedroom to re-bolt the downstairs door, she would never find the courage to go outside and lock the backyard door after him) and then away.

The shoulder of relief became a trembling and that helped the fear to the surface of her mind where it leapt in monstrous shapes, seizing on her imagination with horrible force and terrifying her.

Alone, alone, she hated to be alone. The walls would come in, the door would blow open, the ceiling press down, her mind abandon her body, her body dismember and dissolve, alone, alone and yet with this grit of embarrassment which would prevent her from going out to find a friend, going out to seek help, going out to admit the terrible fear into which all her thoughts and feelings now trembled and fell, were sucked down and drowned until faintness and exhaustion left her to sleep.

It was mid-morning when Joseph got off the train and he decided to walk to the pub though it was about a couple of miles from the station. Along the Kennet Canal he walked, slowly, re-living the match and thinking about Douglas, looking at the swans oil-spattered from the pleasure boats.

Down the canal to where it joined the Thames – at the gas-works – and he smiled to himself at the cartoon nature of this pub-besides-the-gasworks-with-customers-who-still-took-snuff, smoked Park Drive, drank Mild, insisted on a Ladies Bar and organized all their own teams and the Outing to Brighton in Summer. What a game it had been! And the way England had come back at them in extra time – marvellous.

Lovely morning. And in these tiny gardens – what flowers people grew! The roses that bloomed here in six feet square of soil! He stopped to pull one to him, a large yellow rose with some dew still on it, still now at this time.

At the pub he looked above the door, as always: JOSEPH TALLENTIRE Prop: LICENSED TO SELL ALES, WINES, SPIRITS AND TOBACCO. What *name* would Douglas use in his book?

Before he went into the pub he dreamed: that he would save enough money to buy a house for himself and Betty – just an ordinary little place, but really his. That they would live there and he would do the garden, she dust the rooms, grandchildren arrive, a swing on the lawn, drinks with his sons, chats in the sitting-room, discussions in the 'local'. With all his might he tried to think that this would work for Betty and himself.

But it ignored the facts. Inside that place before him was a life which had to begin again if it was to be lived at all. He could serve and wait: no more: which called for love or need and the one seemed as far away as the other this bland morning.

Without any premonition, he went to the door and stopped before opening it, under the sign of his name, took out a cigar-ette as if arming himself with it. Over thirty a day now; have to cut down. He spent more in a week on cigarettes than his father had earned as a living wage at his age – much more; yet Douglas would spend the same amount blithely on an evening's pleasure.

He inhaled deeply and went in.

JOSH LAWTON

MELVYN BRAGG

"A portrait of innocence, and set in a rough, lovely Cumbrian village it has the lilt and inevitability of an old ballad"

THE TIMES

"Mr. Bragg is – or seems – an effortless writer. He never strains for effect, simply achieves it. The pleasure to be had from this book is that of feeling, without having been exposed to any lies or romantic evasions, that the world is perhaps a better place than one had thought"

THE SUNDAY TIMES

"The book is exciting, not just when it is dealing with blood and adultery, but also in the gentler passages . . . a pleasure to be remembered"

THE FINANCIAL TIMES

"With this novel, Melvyn Bragg has established his place in English letters to the extent that his Cumbria is as potent a literary region as Hardy's Wessex, Lawrence's Midlands and Houseman's Shropshire"

NEW STATESMAN

CORONET BOOKS

STRANGERS AND JOURNEYS

MAURICE SHADBOLT

There was Bill Freeman, orator and revolutionary.

There was Ned Livingstone, the rock-like and taciturn pioneer.

And there were their sons, moving self-consciously into a new world where the devils of the South Pacific were gradually exorcised.

Compared to Patrick White, Maurice Shadbolt has written in *Strangers and Journeys* a novel about the New World of the southern hemisphere that is raw and brutal, gentle and tender.

"The novel New Zealand has been waiting for ... Shadbolt succeeds in telling a credible story about credible people while offering a strong stark vision of our species, its heredity and environment"
THE SUNDAY TIMES

CORONET BOOKS

THEIRS WAS THE KINGDOM

R. F. DELDERFIELD

R. F. Delderfield's mighty Victorian family chronicle –
storytelling at its most masterly

Theirs Was The Kingdom is about Adam Swann's
numerous family and his ever-expanding network of
transport depots, first established in *God Is An Englishman*. Now they probe as far north as the Scottish High-
lands and as far west as the Dublin Pale.

Alex, his eldest son, is a professional soldier. Another
son, George, is a pioneer of motor transport. An adopted
daughter, Deborah, works with the famous journalist-
crusader, W. T. Stead, uncovering the terrible injustices
among working-class girls who could be bought and
sold like chattels.

Caught in this kaleidoscope are the fads and feuds, the
loves and hates of an age when the complacent mould
of mid-Victorian England was beginning to crack.

CORONET BOOKS

RACE OF THE TIGER

ALEXANDER CORDELL

He left the grinding poverty of the Old World for the jungle-law life of the New

Born to the riveting penury of Nineteenth Century Ireland, Jess O'Hara and his high-spirited sister, Karen, flee their wretched homeland for a new life in America.

Exhausted after a nine-week crossing in an overcrowded, disease-ridden "coffin ship", they arrive in Pittsburgh – the thrusting, turbulent steel capital of the United States. Surrounded by smoke and fire-belching chimneys, deafened by the beat of giant hammers, they struggle to adapt to this alien world.

At first resisting the tug of easy wealth, Jess forsakes his fellow immigrants and bulldozes his way to fame and fortune, exploiting the love of two women to become a financial tiger in a city where mere jungle-law prevails.

CORONET BOOKS

ALSO AVAILABLE IN CORONET BOOKS

MELVYN BRAGG

☐ 19852 4   Josh Lawton   40p

MAURICE SHADBOLT

☐ 19854 0   Strangers and Journeys   95p

R. F. DELDERFIELD

☐ 16225 2   Theirs Was The Kingdom   60p
☐ 15092 0   The Dreaming Suburb   50p
☐ 15093 9   The Avenue Goes To War   50p
☐ 15623 6   God Is An Englishman   60p

ALEXANDER CORDELL

☐ 15383 0   Race Of The Tiger   45p
☐ 19484 7   If You Believe The Soldiers   40p
☐ 17403 X   The Fire People   40p

All these books are available at your bookshop or newsagent, or can be ordered direct from the publisher. Just tick the titles you want and fill in the form below.

....

CORONET BOOKS, P.O. Box 11, Falmouth, Cornwall.

Please send cheque or postal order. No currency, and allow the following for postage and packing:

1 book – 10p, 2 books – 15p, 3 books – 20p, 4–5 books – 25p, 6–9 books – 4p per copy, 10–15 books – 2½p per copy, 16–30 books – 2p per copy, over 30 books free within the U.K.

Overseas – please allow 10p for the first book and 5p per copy for each additional book.

....

....

....